Praise fo

"Miner has done a masterful job in transporting the reader on the ride of a lifetime —an exceedingly long and rich lifetime…readers will devour this tale until its unexpected end."

Military Writers Society of America - 2020 medal winner

"The story is very original, being set in the future but reflecting upon the past…the plot is also well crafted—it draws the reader in and develops tension and a little excitement while remaining plausible…"

Indie BRAG - 2020 Medallion winner

"The author's account is vividly conveyed and meticulously researched…a gripping tale of military adventure…a moving tribute to the remarkable sacrifices made during wartime."

Kirkus Reviews

Ron Miner has done an absolutely fabulous job with this well written, well paced story. Let me recommend it to everyone, because it's a story for all of us.

Tom Burkhalter
*author of **A Snowball's Chance***
and five other novels of the Pacific War.

"A fantastic read, I cannot recommend it enough."

Energy Rae Reviews

The Last Word

by Ron Miner

RIVERDALE PRESS

The Last Word
By Ron Miner

Copyright © 2020 Ron Miner
Registered Library of Congress
ISBN: 978-0-578-67537-4

All Rights Reserved.
Riverdale Press

This is a work of fiction. Names, characters, places, brands, media, and incidents are either the product of the author's imagination or are used fictitiously. The author acknowledges the trademarked status and trademark owners of various products referenced in this work of fiction, which may have been used without permission. The publication/use of these trademarks is not authorized, associated with, or sponsored by the trademark owners.
This book may not be reproduced or otherwise transmitted without the expressed written consent of the author except in the case of brief quotations in critical articles and reviews.

Sketches and graphics by Ron Miner

Cover photo from the Howard Miner collection
Background photo image of *Man Wearing Black* courtesy
of Ozan Safak, a photographer from Istanbul, Turkey

You can write to the author at BlackCatWWII@gmail.com

Find out more at sketchesofablackcat.com

*There is nothing like sitting in a welcoming space
and listening to stories about things
that we've never experienced.
To all those who have made this possible…*

Author's Note and Acknowledgements

Early in 2014, I had the privilege of filming and interviewing the first in a series of World War II veterans about their participation in the Black Cat Squadron. I was surprised to learn that Alex was also a friend of my father and that they had served together for a time in the Pacific Theater in 1944-45. Over the course of the next several years, another nine veterans would be kind enough to allow me into their homes with a camera, and I found each of them welcoming and their stories compelling. These gentlemen became more than interviewees to me. They became friends. I soon learned it was a kinship that comes with a price—friends who were already in their nineties or more when I met them. Many have now passed since filming. Some have not.

To date, ten first-hand accounts of this squadron's activities—night missions, rescues, and just plain monkey business—resulted in a cache of wonderful but, as yet, unpublished material, sometimes dramatic, often humorous, and forever historically significant. A part of it supplemented my father's own, hand-written accounts and led to a second edition of my first book, *Sketches of a Black Cat,* in 2016. But some of the information came afterwards, and several of the interviews concerned another part of the squadron operating near New Guinea, in an area geographically distinct from VP-54, my father's unit. I felt these were stories not to be missed.

The Last Word is a novel that uses portions of real accounts as they were described to me by members of the Navy's Black Cat Squadron and a Privateer (Liberator - B-24) squadron of the Pacific Theater. The episodes are woven into an approximate timeline, as it occurred, but as with any historical fiction, the history is blended with imagination to create twists and turns that enliven the storyline. Many of the experiences are expanded and vivid—a reenactment, in a sense, of first person experiences to introduce readers to an important group of veterans who did their part to make our world safer.

The key point in all this is that we feel a sense of urgency concerning World War II's participants. Yes, we will be able to hear from them through written, recorded, and filmed material, but we will no longer be able to ask them questions, listen to their answers, probe for more insight. The give and take with remarkable people from the most significant war in human history is priceless. Their memories and emotions ache to be freed from the confines of my notebooks and film recordings. I hope, in *The Last Word*, I've managed to properly celebrate them and their exceptional place in the unfolding of history.

It has been my honor to sit down with and talk to the real cast of characters who detailed their World War II involvement. I would like to thank Walter Genuit (VP-101), Jim Shields (VP-33), Lou Conter (VP-11 and a USS *Arizona* survivor), Karl "Doc" Livingstone (VP-52), Elliot Schreider (VP-54, VP-116), Harold Koenig (VPB-54), Alex Catlow (VPB-54), Bob Pinckney (VP-54), Del Fager (VP-54), Win Stites (VP-91), and their families who have spread the word about the squadron. Thanks also to Bill Anderson on behalf of his father, "Flip" Anderson (VP-33, VPB-33), for adding his father's eloquent words and interview material to my library, and to Mike Goodwin, author of *Shobun: A Forgotten War Crime in the Pacific*. Mike's father (VP-33, 101, 29) was part of an ill-fated Black Cat crew, captured and killed in 1944. And, of course, I'm so grateful to Al Bell (VP-48) for his many contributions and support of the project.

They are all heroes in my estimation.

Additionally, I would like to thank my inaugural readers—Bill, Barb, Ginger, and my wife Heidi—for their thoughtful feedback, suggestions, and perspectives. Heidi, especially, has tolerated my long periods of isolation in the "bunker" this winter, keeping a fire going in the stove and giving me a valuable opinion whenever I needed it. And special thanks to Anneli Anderson, who for the third time has been so instrumental in developing the book's format and cover.

Foreword

Each century produces a milestone or two in the grand arc of history. Except the 20th century. It witnessed an avalanche. The history books will still talk about—or at least, mention them—a thousand years from now. Flight. Computing. The human genome. The atomic age. The first space travel. The internet. We could each add our own candidates to that list.

We would all add World War II. The global upheaval it entailed was without precedent. It generated an immense volume of commentary, analysis, probing, and reflection. Books will be written about it long after the last echoes of that cataclysm fade (for example, the Civil War ended one hundred and fifty five years ago and the Library of Congress archives indicate over seventy thousand books about it). In the shadow of such events, there are endless stories without which the record is incomplete.

Yet, a truly authentic historic source remains open only as long as the people who actually lived it are able to share their experiences. Beyond that, all is interpretation.

That window of opportunity is rapidly closing.

Since we have so many stories already, why do a few more matter? Because a human experience of this scope deserves all the insights we can glean from it. That occurs most powerfully when interviews bring forth memories that would otherwise remain obscured by the distant fog of war and dimmed in minds crowded with many decades of living.

The youngest documented World War II enlistee was fourteen. The oldest living man recently died at one hundred and twelve. A man born in 1927 who enlisted at fifteen could plausibly live into the late 2030s. If he remains mentally alert, the last World War II story told in person could occur less than twenty years from now.

Survivors of war carry memories impossible to grasp by those of us who did not share in them. That is especially true for beneficiaries of their sacrifices who come along generations later. The original context has long since disappeared. So how can a novelist refract defining experiences and make their essence comprehensible to us? The answer: by consolidating them into a main character who speaks to us on behalf of all the others. A simple dialogue then enables us to relate, like sharing memories with an old friend.

Author Ron Miner gives us Owen Trimbel, a personality he assembled from a series of actual interviews conducted over eight years. He found the interview process thoroughly rewarding, with compelling stories that augmented his father's own experiences as a pilot with the Navy's Black Cats. I found myself profoundly affected by his first book, *Sketches of a Black Cat*, so much so that I wrote to him. Over a year has passed and we continue to connect through correspondence and even in person despite living thirteen hundred miles apart! We share a deep respect for the special Americans he writes about.

Ron's interviews continued after his book was published, crystallizing into a collection of impressive narratives—but direct interviews were becoming increasingly hard to come by. *How long*, he wondered, *before there are no voices left to record?*

The richness that comes from talking with and listening to men who lived and survived experiences like his father's became one of Ron's central motivations for writing this book, something he observed in his *Author's Note*:

> *Their memories and emotions ache to be freed from the confines of my notebooks and film recordings. I hope, in* **The Last Word**, *I've managed to properly celebrate them and their exceptional place in the unfolding of history.*

The dedicated men and women who have served America, or anyone who cherishes those patriots, will find Owen's path through the treacherous waters and improvised landing strips of the vast Pacific a rewarding journey, indeed. Moreover, Owen's exploits shed light on the midpoint of a unique chapter of American flying history.

Operating American military flying boats from the water began with Glenn Curtis's 1912 Model E and ended with the last flight of a Martin P5M-2 Marlin, exiled to the Smithsonian in 1967. As a former P5M pilot, I was privileged to experience that mysterious space where ocean and air currents battle for domination. Negotiating that space is a unique experience for both pilots and crew. Ask Owen Trimbel.

Through diligent craftsmanship by someone who cares deeply, we connect with what is relentlessly inaccessible. That is also how we honor and pay homage to those in the past who have given so much to help create our present.

The Last Word does exactly that as it speaks with sincere authenticity to all Americans.

Al Bell
LTJG USNR Retired
Peoria, Arizona

Chapter 1

"Alert! Braking!"

Dan reflexively grabbed the steering wheel as the car pitched forward, his eyes jolting up from the iPhone's dashboard screen. The wispy image of a deer's haunches vanished into the late night shadows of forest foliage as the *Chevy Amp* self-corrected.

"Sorry about that, Dan," oozed Samantha's not too sexy voice over the car's surround sound system, as she tried to soothe the flush of adrenaline that had his hair standing on end.

"Scared the bejeezus out of me, Sam! Can't you come up with something better than that? You've got more cameras on this wagon than the paparazzi! Didn't you see the freakin' thing?"

"I suppose you're right, Dan. I can suggest another superlative, or feel free to recommend one. My reaction time was .13 seconds, about the same as the blink of a human eye and well within objective guidelines. Can I make it up to you? I see there is a Quick-Charge/UBank station four miles ahead that serves espresso. How about some coffee?"

"Sure. I guess we could use a break, huh. Sorry I snapped at you."

"All's forgiven. Remember, when it comes to bruised feelings I'm not supposed to have any. We'll be arriving in five and a half minutes."

Self driving had come a long way in the last fifteen years and certainly, there were advantages. But there were also times when Dan would have preferred just hopping into his old Subaru and bushwhacking his way through the Minnesota backcountry like he did when he was in journalism school at UMN-Twin Cities. He and his buddies thrived on midnight riding then. They squeezed in with just enough room for a six-pack and headed over to the river—King's and Queen's Bluffs were both favorites. Wandering along the rocky ledges overlooking the Mississippi in the darkness, it was a wonder one of them didn't fall in—*How long ago was that? OK, I graduated in 2002. That makes it...hell, thirty-six years I've been at this now? Still with the same paper.*

He shuddered to think of it. A long time, long enough to still call it a paper, even though the *Winona Bulletin* hadn't really *printed* anything for nearly ten of those years. His byline appeared twice a week and as a "veteran" newsman, he found more than his share of plum assignments these days. Better than the dreary nights covering the city council meetings or the sports beat. Still, not a heck of a lot happened in a modest town like Winona, and Dan had considered moving on to a larger market with more complexity. Better opportunities. Then he met Jenna. She liked the small town way of life, and he loved his wife.

"We're approaching our destination, Dan. How about I call in your order? Sixteen-ounce vanilla mocha, no whipped cream?" Samantha expertly guided the vehicle across the pavement toward the charging station as Dan scrolled through his mobile wallet. "No thanks, Sam. I need to stretch my legs. Keep the home fires burning. Be right back."

"Searching for home fire. I'm not finding any results in our area, Dan. Is there anything else?"

Personal assistants, of course, came with choices, and when Dan first browsed through personality attributes for Samantha, he went with "spirited." But not only was Samantha a little quirky, she could be awfully literal sometimes. Dan wondered what she would have done if he had said he needed to take a pee. *There is a market that has fresh pod peas eleven miles ahead on the left. Would you like that one?*

He snapped the charging head into the car's side port and went into the near blinding fluorescence of the shop's interior.

"Help you?" asked the young woman behind the counter as she adjusted her hair. She had the modern spray tan look that was

CHAPTER 1

all the rage these days, and apparently, northern Minnesota was no exception.

"Hi, uh, just a five-minute quick charge and a vanilla mocha. Sixteen, no...no whipped cream. *Is that Sam laughing out there?* Restroom open?"

The woman nodded and pointed with her eyes at the key attached to a serving spoon, hanging just to her left. She then pulled a sixteen-ounce cup from the stack and started the grinder, her wrist bell bracelet loud and jangly, clinking in time with her movements.

Coffee in hand, Dan walked back toward the car. He found the commercial paint job embarrassing, an off-white background veneering the sleek automobile's body, with images of vintage newspaper clippings and pages covering every square inch of it, like decoupage. Local advertisers paid for the strategically placed, oversized electronic display ads that added color to the fictional edition. Each month, the ads rotated, and some of them could be real stinkers. Like the erection products.

At least they supplied him with a car for the trip, and there was no gas to buy.

Even with Samantha driving, Dan was ready to call it a night. He'd left work a little early to pack, but it had been a real stretch getting everything together on such short notice. "Hey Sam."

"Uh-huh?"

"Is there a decent hotel out here anywhere?"

"Sure. Three, about twenty minutes from our location. A Best Western, a Quality Inn, and a Radisson Hotel all show occupancy. Do you have a preference?"

"Which one has a bar?"

"Oooh, I think you better choose the Radisson, Dan. Serving until 1:30 a.m."

That decided, Dan settled back and looked at his messages. Jenna was still concerned about the kitten. The little guy hadn't been feeling well, running a high temperature, and the vet was at a loss. He wasn't even a year old yet and seemed to be getting worse by the day. She had gently protested when Dan announced the paper's sudden assignment, one involving a trip halfway across Minnesota that would keep him overnight. Jenna was a person who was heavily invested in her family, and that included animals that found their doorstep or had digital portraits featured in Saturday's homeless pets section. He could feel the anxiety when she asked him why he needed to take this trip up there right now, while things seemed to be hanging in the balance.

But he had no choice really. This was not the kind of story that could wait, he'd explained. What could he do? He still wasn't even sure why he'd been singled out for this, or for that matter, why his paper was contacted instead of the *Star-Tribune* or one of the other big Minneapolis dailies. Pulitzers had been handed out to some of the hotshots up there. The *Winona Bulletin*? Little league trophies. Yet here he was, three hundred miles north and at the approximate segue, the point from which some suggest the state is covered by nearly as much water as soil. The land of ten thousand lakes.

The Radisson did have a bar, and after Dan had secured a first floor room and dropped off his belongings, he headed straight for it. At this hour he hadn't expected to see much going on, but the place was surprisingly peppy. He pulled a stool away from the handsome bar rail and sat down.

"What can I get you?" asked a rugged, silver-haired bartender dressed all in black.

"Bourbon and seven, if you would."

"Coming right up. My name is Ted. All we have is a snack menu after 10, but we can still rustle up a sandwich. Like anything?"

"Sounds great."

Ted expertly slid Dan's drink and a short menu toward him. "Business in the area?" he inquired, wiping down glasses as Dan surveyed the choices.

"Actually, yeah. I'm up here on a story. More of an interview, I guess. There's an old gentleman that lives west of here that, if you can believe it, fought in World War II."

CHAPTER 1

The bartender broke into a wide smile. "Hell, you mean old Owen Trimbel? I haven't seen him in years. Navy guy. Glad to hear he's still chugging along. Damn, he's got to be, let's see..."

"A hundred and twelve."

"Geez, is that right?" Ted let out an impressive whistle. "You know, he used to come into Bunyan's Bar and Grill every so often when I worked up there, sip a Schmidt Beer for an hour and talk with his buddies." He continued with a chuckle, "But he outlived 'em all, even the ones way younger than he was. After that, I'd hear something about him now and then, a Veterans Day article in the local rag here a time or two, but it's been quite a while. How's he doing?"

"I've never met him. In fact, never even spoke to him." Dan took another sip of his drink. "I'm heading over there tomorrow. He and his daughter must share a place. Hell, even she's nearly twenty years older than I am."

"Well, I'll be. You're going to interview Owen Trimbel. I hope he's holding up okay. A hundred and twelve! Damn!" A message from a waitress with a drink order blinked on Ted's console and he quickly grabbed four glasses and headed toward the mixers.

Dan tossed back the last of his bourbon and slid a ten across the bar. Vending machine would do for tonight. He needed to turn in. As he stood, he found himself softly repeating Ted's final refrain. "I hope he's doing okay, too," he whispered under his breath. "Hundred-and-twelve-year-old Owen Trimbel. The last surviving World War II veteran in the world."

THE LAST WORD

Chapter 2

Jenna's on-screen expression said it all, and her voice wobbled as she continued. "He's getting much worse, Dan. Poor Charlie, he's so sick. I have an appointment at the vet today, and she's going to give him more fluids and do some blood work. I don't know what to do. I love that little guy." Her voice cracked as it trailed off and she briefly looked away from the monitor.

"I know, honey. I wish I could give you a hug. He'll be alright. Charlie's pretty tough. And he's in good hands with both of you on it." He sensed from the look on her face that it was time to change the subject. "Did you get that package from your mom yet?"

"Not yet. Something came for you though. I had to sign for it. It's from an aunt somebody-or-other. A big envelope."

"Huh. I haven't heard from Aunt Somebody in years. Wonder how she's doing?"

"Quit," she admonished. "Are you meeting with them today? The World War II guy?"

"Yeah, I need to call out there in a few minutes and see what we do next. I don't know if he sleeps all the time or feels strong enough to go through with this. The daughter isn't much of a talker. I don't think she's really onboard with the whole thing."

"Once they meet you, things will be different," Jenna reassured him. "You have that magic, you know."

"Yeah, right. Magic. I just hope I don't somehow upset him and kill the guy. Wouldn't that be magical?

'Oct., 18, 2038 — Reporter responsible for end of an era. Chooses self-aggrandizement over the greater good.'"

"Oh, now stop! You'll do great. Good luck today, sweetie. I miss you!"

"I miss you too. Maybe today we'll get Charlie back in the pink. I'll be thinking of you both."

They said their final goodbyes, and Dan sat a bit longer on the edge of the bed with her voice and image still swirling around in his head. She was such a caring and sensitive soul, and he felt crummy about being away from her, even though his intellect told him that his reasons were sound and that she probably understood. Probably.

Jenna was a native Minnesotan, raised on a farm well west of where they now lived in Winona. She and her sister had attended a small elementary school and each graduated with only a handful of classmates, about ten percent of the school's total enrollment of seventy-five. The two of them spent much of the summer working in barns and stables around the farm milking and feeding the animals, collecting eggs, and picking beans. Afternoons were often devoted to their beloved Appaloosas. Jenna had named her horse Luna. She was the oldest, and had been a rider nearly as long as she had been walking.

Early on, the girls were active in 4H and occasionally loaded up the horses and headed toward St. Cloud and beyond for competitions. For a time, the two of them continued their love affair with everything equestrian, and after high school, Jenna occasionally searched for a competitive event to work with Luna during summer breaks from college.

Dan, just out of college himself, was killing some time in Stillwater after interviewing for a position with the *Gazette*, the town's small local newspaper. He wandered past the County Fairgrounds where it appeared some kind of rodeo was taking place and decided to take a look and get something to eat. There was a buzz of activity in the equestrian area. He glanced in and his eyes fixed on a young woman, who appeared to be talking with her horse. Once they seemed to have an agreement, she smartly tucked a boot into the stirrup and bounded up, swinging her leg over and settling into the saddle.

CHAPTER 2

It was a striking scene—this tiny woman perched on nearly a half ton of horseflesh, yet so perfectly in control and entirely captivating in jeans and a madras shirt rolled up to the elbow. Her auburn hair was drawn back into a pony tail that swayed in time with the Appaloosa's counterpart. What he noticed most was her smile. It radiated throughout the arena, the kind of smile that began inside and quickly took over her entire face. Infectious. Whatever it was, Dan had caught it and he quickly made his way into the grandstand. Twelve months later, they were married on a small bridge spanning the creek on her uncle's ranch near Stillwater.

Dan shook his head. He needed a brain reshuffle. He was supposed to call mid-morning sometime. It was 9:30 a.m. *Is that mid-morning? Why didn't I clarify things with the daughter, nail down an actual time? Better wait till 10.*

He decided to rehearse. There was nothing like the awkwardness one felt while fumbling around when something went wrong and an audience was glued to your every move. Lighting problems, a weak battery, a mic that wouldn't pair.

Dan pulled his iPhone Pro-150 loose from his wrist, separated and stretched it into the two camera sections he would use to video, and then slid each into its respective telescopic camera-mount tripod. He liked to position them about ten feet apart, creating a view from both sides that gave options when editing. He had learned the hard way that a runny nose or inadvertent pet in the background could ruin an otherwise powerful or poignant moment, and he would kick himself for days afterward.

"Sam, please give me LED, and let's start with *maximum warm*." Lighting was sometimes tricky, and Dan suspected Owen was pale as a ghost, so the warmer the better.

"Dan, I've made the adjustments to all light and sound settings. The cameras are synched. Would you like to begin auto-check?"

"I would, Sam. Say, where are my glasses?"

"Found them." She displayed the location, on the desk underneath an open book, on screen.

After running a sound check and watching a few seconds of playback, his mental checklist was nearly complete. Surely the Trimbels would have some kind of basic wireless charging capabilities, but just in case, Dan was comfortable that the six hours of reserve battery life should be plenty. Why did he nearly laugh out loud at that thought? *A hundred and twelve years and six hours. Yep, that should be enough.*

He felt ready to film. Funny how he still thought of it as a filming, when there hadn't been any film involved for years. Just little pulses of energy flying around out there somewhere and ending up in an editing room computer back at the office. His home office. In college, it was just about the writing and reporting. Now everything was so consolidated—a journalist was a multitasker. But a nose for a story was still paramount, and Dan was known to have an exceptional snout.

Maybe it wasn't the life he had planned for himself. There had been temptations, attempts to lure him away from his small town occupation and slide him into a high profile gig with the *Tribune* or even the *Chicago Sun-Times*. His resume included honors at UMN-Twin Cities and a fellowship writing for *Atlantic Monthly/Atlantic Media* in Washington, D.C., for a year. He had published his first book in 2015. It was a non-fiction work that followed Charles Lindbergh's ascent from an early childhood in Little Falls along the banks of the Mississippi River to a legendary pioneer in aviation, but he had written it from the perspective of Lindberg's opposition to war.

No, he hadn't anticipated any of this, but it was a life he cherished. Jenna had changed him. His early ambition to live smothered in urban intensity, grappling with a world of deadlines and frantic readjustments vanished a week after he had met her.

Yet, while Dan had enjoyed some measure of success with his byline, blog, and position with the *Bulletin*, something still puzzled him. Here he was in the middle of lake country and about to meet the final member of a very historic fraternity for a concluding interview, and he couldn't for the life of him figure out why.

CHAPTER 2

Why me? Prominent historians and university professors from far and wide would do backflips for this opportunity, yet somehow, he had been culled out of the pack and was now headed to Shevlin, Minnesota. What was there in his track record that would justify it? Could it be one of the several stories on war veterans he'd compiled over the years had impressed someone? Or Owen, himself?

There was one in particular that still resonated in his mind. A number of years back, he and Jenna had been traveling, a vacation in the Southwest taking in the glorious canyons and parks of Utah and Arizona. They spent two nights in Sedona at a lovely bed and breakfast, and the innkeeper had suggested her favorite restaurant in town—*The Secret Garden*. It was busy when they arrived, a forty minute wait, so they lingered at the bar with cocktails and took in the atmosphere. Sitting next to them, an older couple nursed their drinks and the gentleman, probably in his early nineties but in great shape, smiled and asked politely, "Where are you folks from?"

This began a thirty-minute conversation and eventually, they joined Red and his wife at their table for dinner. It was a perfect evening and the new friends decided on a bottle of wine with dinner to toast their good fortune. It was at this point that the ladies excused themselves. "We're going to powder our noses!" Jenna exclaimed with a mischievous smile.

"So you're a writer?" Red asked.

"That's what they tell me," Dan smiled. "Reporter and features mostly. Some magazine work. How about you? You said something about flying. Airlines?"

"I spent a number of years in the Navy. Went to Japan in the 1950s, then stateside after that for a while."

He told Dan he flew PBM Mariners, large seaplanes that the Navy used for patrols during the Korean War. They were a relic from World War II and by the end of the Korean conflict, they were practically obsolete. He moved up to P5Ms afterward.

As the wine began to talk, Red quite unexpectedly launched into a tale about a foggy morning in San Diego. It was an early spring day in 1959—the Cold War was in full swing.

"I was the Officer of the Day for Patrol Squadron 37. It was a quiet day and, partly because of foggy conditions, we decided the duty crew would depart San Diego and fly to the Salton Sea for the rest of their twenty-four-hour alert duty. There's seldom any fog out that way. A little after noon, we intercepted a mayday from a plane piloted by two friends of mine, Jake Collins and Mack Dawson."

Red hesitated and took a sip of his wine. As he swallowed, he closed his eyes, allowing his head to tip back ever so slightly. He told Dan the mayday call concerned a raging fire in the starboard engine and it was out of control. It had ignited the transmission-like Sundstrand Unit that converted engine revolutions to a constant speed for running the DC generators. The Sundstrand, unwisely, was made of magnesium—a blowtorch metal if exposed to fire. "Jake managed to get his crew out of the plane and they parachuted to safety. Mack, the co-pilot, bailed out next, but had the misfortune of picking the instant they passed over a ridge. His chute never had time to open. Jake, as the 'Captain of the Ship,' set the automatic pilot for level flight and headed for the waist hatch—three steps to the flight deck, six more to the after station, and then stepped to the hatch. He was apparently standing there when the plane rolled on its side and plowed into fields of massive boulders and manzanita near the little town of Julian, throwing his body clear of the plane."

As the communications officer, Red was immediately dispatched to the crash site to retrieve any remaining code books and devices. This was the Cold War and his job demanded it. "What I found were pieces of Jake Collins strewn throughout the manzanita branches over a distance of about a quarter of a mile. No code books survived. Neither, of course, did Jake or Mack."

Dan realized he'd been holding his breath. "Geez, Red. A story like that…I can't imagine how you felt." He paused. "I get the feeling there's more."

Red released his clenched eyebrows, and as his eyes reopened, his gaze was warm and thoughtful. They each took another sip of their drinks, and he turned his head toward Dan.

CHAPTER 2

"Jake was awarded the Distinguished Flying Cross for doing what the Captain of the Ship has been charged with for hundreds, maybe thousands of years. The last to leave. That heritage does not diminish the commitment by a real human—in real time—to do what is appropriate. We are, after all, but human.

"This was the Cold War, but we were not technically at war. Consequently, we all signed waivers, accepting that we would not be eligible for veterans' benefits. I would sign the same agreement again. Still, I've often wondered what their families endured, a burden that their fellow citizens should have helped shoulder. I will never know."

"Would you mind if I recounted this story for my readers, Red? I have a feeling they would really connect with it."

The consummate gentleman, Red simply replied, "Sure, Dan. I hope they do connect with it. Or can. But you know, we can't be the same after living through those experiences. And we can't expect anyone without those same experiences to understand what it feels like. They may get it intellectually, but they can't be expected to feel it in their gut, which is where it lives forever."

The ladies returned, still sporting sheepish grins, having lingered much too long in the nearby gift shop. As it turned out, this was an unexpected gift for the two men.

THE LAST WORD

Chapter 3

"Hi, Sandy? Dan Callahan with the Bulletin...Yes...I'm fine, and how are you this morning? I hope I didn't call too early...Great. So what would be...OK...Yeah, I should be able to make that work. One o'clock it is...Directions? No, I...Hard to find? I should be fine. I...The Smart Car is really a moving map...No, your address should be all I need to find it...Yes, I look forward to it too. See you then."

Sandy had explained that her dad was an early riser, but took frequent naps. He usually did his best right after lunch and the caregiver would be gone until just before dinner.

"Sam, let's go do an interview."

"Nice! All systems engaged and we'll be traveling U.S. Highway 2 toward Shevlin for nineteen minutes, then continue north. Would you prefer 'Blues for the Road' or perhaps 'Intermezzo' for the drive this morning?" echoed Samantha's warm, omnipresent recommendation.

"Something different. How about *Acoustical Crossroads*. A little twang would probably be just what we need."

"Mmm, let me see. OK, I'd like to saddle up an oldie for you by Kacey Musgraves." Kacey's rich tones soon swirled through the Chevy as Dan studied his notes and questionnaire.

Samantha guided them off the Paul Bunyan Expressway, fluidly merging onto Highway 2 between two iCars. Dan recalled a time as a boy when the family had piled into the old family car and come up to the lake. There was a small seaplane base there that he and his dad wanted to check out, but his two sisters had their own priority, namely, Babe the Blue Ox, who was apparently grazing somewhere in Paul Bunyan Park. Dan, being the oldest, wasn't thrilled about the diversion, but compromise was his dad's specialty. Both sisters squealed with delight at the huge and bizarre, squarish statues. Dan could still recall his impression, an oft-repeated slice of family folklore: *"Are you kidding me?"*

As the car left the city limits, Dan rolled down the window to enjoy the cool midday breeze, rich with the scent of overnight rain and fresh mown grass, with a hint of conifer, maybe white pine or spruce. On a distant field, a piece of farm equipment busied itself, its reddish silhouette complementing the lingering yellow hues of aspen and ash beyond it. They reached an intersection and began heading north, deeper into the contradiction common to rural Minnesota—a vast patchwork of country forests, lakes, grazing lands, and intermittent houses sprawled across its gentle terrain, and all this wildness neatly arranged into near perfect, gigantic squares and rectangles. Occasionally, a byway would bisect one of them, and sometimes a river, creek, or an imaginative pioneer road builder seemed to have fiddled with the symmetry of it all, wiggling a waterway or gravel surface in free-for-all fashion, just to confuse things. Dan could see that they were now approaching such an area.

"Your destination is on the right, one hundred feet." Samantha slowed the car and stopped in front of a barbed-wire fence protecting a well-weathered barn.

"Sam, where are we? There's no driveway."

"49129 Bramble Creek Road is on your right."

"Sam, it's a barn. Sandy Atkins doesn't live in a barn. What's that up ahead? That gate."

They crept ahead about fifty feet, where a pair of gravel tracks wound around and past the barn, vanishing into the trees. As Samantha squared up on the primitive lane, Dan could see the taillights of a vehicle in the clearing ahead. "Let's try it, Sam. It's muddy. Don't get us stuck, OK?"

"Stuck? My traction sensing indicates the roadway is adequate." She paused. "Well, shall we proceed?" she asked, her tone sounding slightly annoyed. Dan wondered, *Can she do that?*

CHAPTER 3

The tires alternately crackled on cinders and splashed freshly muddied puddles against the car's sidewalls as Samantha eased down the lane toward a ripe-apple red, early model SUV. Two men were leaning against it, faces glued to a phone screen. "Stop here, Sam. I'll walk in."

Dan had a hard time believing Owen lived here, but he grabbed his bag for looks, just in case. He had been told he had a nose for news, and this time, he thought he smelled another reporter.

One of the men, in his plumpish forties and wound a little too tight, looked up. "Thank God! We are totally lost! Are you from around here?" he asked.

"Uh, not exactly," Dan replied cautiously. He took in the fellow's features, a comical mish-mash of clothing choices with a much too small ball cap perched atop an oddly bovine head.

The other fellow—gaunt and bony-shouldered with a flat brimmed ball cap spun to the back and, perhaps, wound even a little tighter—complained, "This place is like a black hole, man. Everything is wacky on this map. It shows us in a river right now. We're trying to find this Bramble Creek Road, but there's no signs and no signal strength. We must have the number wrong, too. Missing a digit or something. "

"Who or what are you looking for?" Dan asked.

"What's that name again, Hank? Trombone or something?" He hoisted up his belt. "I think it's Trembles. Yeah, Trembles."

I knew it! Bandits! Dan reached for his bag and pulled out a couple of menus from the hotel restaurant and looked over at his two rivals. "Well, I've been all around the neighborhood sharing our message, but I haven't seen anyone by that name. I seem to remember a Bramble Creek over in Waconda. About ten miles."

"Maybe we should try that, Hank. Thanks, guy."

Dan dialed up his best, over-the-top affected smile. "Sure. And it is truly a pleasure meeting both of you. Before you go, please allow me to share these booklets, each filled with the word of Jehovah, our Lord. He has an important message for all of us." Dan held out the two menus and, scarcely taking a breath, continued. "If I could have a few minutes of your time, I'd like to tell you more about him and perhaps quote some scripture…"

The two strangers cowered back and politely tried to disconnect from Dan. He smiled again, thanked them, and with a pretense of disappointment, returned to the car at a brisk walk, hoping they wouldn't see the signage that covered it.

"Sam, disengage self-driving. I've got it. I'm backing out."

"Automatic driving now disengaged, Dan."

Dan bounced and splashed his way back to the main road, and as he swung the automobile's rear into the roadway, he could see that Hank and his friend were still huddled around the phone screen. After an unintentional tire spin, he had the car safely around the bend.

Now that they were out of sight, Dan returned control of the car to Samantha.

Dan was getting flustered. *Crap, I'll just call her.* "Call Sandy Atkins, Sam."

"Dan, you made a call to Sandy Atkins at 10:04 a.m. Her phone location is five hundred feet north of us. Would you like me to take you there?"

"North? It's a forest. We're taking roads, right?"

"Yes, I prefer roads, *Dan*." There was no mistaking her tenor this time. "It requires an access from the north side of the creek. The destination is a six minute drive. Would you like me to take you there?"

"*Or not!*" is probably what she wanted to say, Dan thought to himself. *Is it possible for Sam to be developing an attitude?*

"Absolutely," he said, sinking down into the seat and letting out a deep breath. Things were starting to get interesting.

During the five minutes and fifty seconds it took Samantha to weave her way around the woodlands, fallow fields, and over a sizable creek, Dan wondered how to avoid a rude interruption at some point during his interview with Owen. Samantha turned down a forlorn looking gravel road, and after about a hundred yards, announced the destination. Indeed, a driveway was where

CHAPTER 3

you might expect it, alongside a sagging and dented mailbox with faded, illegible hand lettering, except for the final numeral– *"9."*

"This must be it," Dan muttered, feeling a simultaneous tingle of anxiety. *Why am I nervous? I've done this dozens of times.*

He had Samantha stash the car behind an old pick-up where it was largely concealed, and gathered his things. *Guess I'm ready. Damn, am I shaking?*

The charming old farmhouse had the look of a large cabin, with simple features and a handmade essence. He made his way up a spindly, curving concrete walkway, heavily worn and mossed-over at its edges. The small wooden stoop was overlaid with strips of roofing shingles—for safety he supposed—and creaked under his weight. A short railing with a wide wooden top cap was used to display several potted plants, one a rather stunning miniature pine of some kind in a ceramic dish. It reminded him of something very ancient, perhaps of an eastern culture. *Japanese?* he wondered.

He tried the doorbell, but judged it wasn't working, and after inhaling deeply, gave a gentle knock.

A booming, full-throated bark roared from inside the house. *Crap that sounded big!* In an instant, he could hear an admonishing voice and footsteps approaching. The door swung open, and a smiling, striking woman with fashionably short, cotton-white hair greeted him. "Hi, you must be Dan. I'm Sandy Atkins," she said, her voice cheerful and vibrant.

"A pleasure to finally meet you, Sandy."

"No trouble finding us?" she asked, hoisting up on the doorknob and giving the door a brisk kick to shut it.

"Oh, no real trouble at all." *Except for getting lost.* "You were right about it being a little out in the country." Dan had a hard time believing this woman could be in her early eighties. She had a warmth to her demeanor, her blue eyes were engaged and smile genuine. She wore delicate gold earrings and a sage green sweater, rounded at the neckline and profiled by a petite, cameo pendant necklace. His first impression of her was that she seemed very... athletic. Like a long since retired gymnast or tennis player.

The short foyer opened into a large and dramatic, rustic living space, richly washed in warm browns and autumn colors with windows along its entire length, giving it the feel of a hunting lodge. To the right, another oversized doorway opened into an adjacent hall.

"People get lost all the time around here. Signals aren't very strong or something, ever since all that changing of the phone towers to those satellite thingies. People like to say it's a vortex!" She let slip a giggle. "I kind of like it that way. Well, let me take you in to meet Dad. He likes sitting in here by the wood stove." She continued at a whisper, "And I guess I should warn you that he's probably not quite what you expect."

She led him through the short hallway, illuminated with vintage sconces and adorned with framed photos. *Family*, Dan presumed. One photo was a handsome image of a uniformed serviceman, posing respectfully under the wing of a large plane—a study in black and white. The sound of the clock's sweeping second hand followed them as they turned into another dimly lit room. Dan's eyes immediately zeroed in on the stuffed chair less than fifteen feet in front of them. Curled up in it, but draping over its edges, was a huge, brindle boxer-mix—glaring at him, eyes two steely-brown beads, and adding in faint baritone, the kind of menacing growl that stopped Dan in his tracks.

"Hey! Stop that! Hear me?" Sandy scolded. The dog's face melted into indifference and to Dan's relief, he simply rolled over.

To the right of the dog was the wood stove, glowing and cozy next to a stack of wood and kindling splits. It lent the comforting scent of escaped wood smoke into the air. Adjacent to the stove was a small table with a tiny lamp that cast its subdued light onto the unmistakable gleaming barrel of a Colt .45—lying on its side, but clearly pointing into the room and more or less in Dan's direction.

Seated in the overstuffed, Naugahyde chair was the slightly slumped figure of a modest-sized man in blue jeans, with wide suspenders that rolled up and over his shoulders across a blue and

CHAPTER 3

mauve flannel shirt. His eyes seemed not to notice the two of them entering the room, peering ahead blankly instead, directly in front of him. Random wisps of hair tried unsuccessfully to conceal intermittent dark splotches and a slow-to-heal wound of some kind, still bruised and radiant red.

"Dad," Sandy called to him, loud enough to be heard. "Dad, it's Dan. He's here to see you."

Dan's reporter-self kicked in and he smiled as he walked toward Owen, hand extended. "Good afternoon, sir. This is truly an honor."

Owen moved his ancient head to face Dan, its weight causing it to list from the effort, his stare as empty as a blind man's. His mouth and jaw shuddered as he struggled to lift an arm and then a single finger.

Alzheimer's...dementia? Dan thought. "Is he all right?" he asked Sandy sheepishly.

"Dad!"

"Listen, Sandy, if this is a bad time…"

"Dad, come on." Owen now had his arm upright, and the single finger leveled and quivering in the general direction of the table across the room.

"Dad, knock it off!" Sandy insisted. "He just wants the bottle opener."

As if taking off a mask, Owen's face broke into a wide smile. "Want a beer, son?"

"He loves doing that to people when they first meet," she said, feigning a frown at Owen, and struggling to prevent it from dissolving into laughter. "You told me you'd behave!"

"I try to have a little fun at least once a day...Hope you'll forgive me." Owen reached out his hand and Dan shook it with a grin. "Have a seat."

Where? Dan thought, looking over to the only available chair, thoroughly smothered in boxer.

"Bilge, get off of there! Let the man sit down," Owen chided. Bilge stood, sneezed, and shook until all traces of the sneeze and any dog slobber were well scattered about, then reluctantly hopped off of the chair and curled up again at Owen's feet. Dan hadn't noticed until then that the dog only had three legs.

"Offer of a beer is still on," he continued. His voice had a crackling rasp to it, but was stronger than Dan had expected. "You'll have to open it…I'm hell with bottle openers anymore."

"Thanks for the offer. Are you having one?"

"Of course…It's happy hour in Pensacola, right…Sandy, join us?" He looked over at his daughter with a captivating grin. The man had sparkle. Dan wondered, *Has he had that all his life?*

"Maybe later, Dad. I'll get some snacks. Be right back." Bilge popped up and followed her into the kitchen with barely a detectable hitch in his gate.

"I'm allowed one beer every couple of days or so…One of my few indulgences." He took a slow but experienced swig and followed it with a satisfying swallow. "Mostly, days are cluttered with routines as you get old…Pills, peeing, doctors, peeing."

Dan laughed out loud. *Not what I was expecting? She was right about that!*

"So how long have you and Sandy lived out here?"

"Oh, let's see. Shirley passed back in '23…We were married over seventy years." He tried unsuccessfully to restrain a small, polite belch. "Only ninety-two...and still a fox! But one morning, she just didn't wake up…Heart attack while she slept." He took another sip. "I think about her every day."

Owen spoke slowly, but clearly, Dan noticed. In short phrases, as if pacing himself.

"Two years earlier, a bad winter storm had everything iced up…and Sandy's husband went off a slick bridge into a ravine… Coma. Never came out of it. It was tough on her…losing her husband and mother in such a short time. This was their place, and she decided…no insisted, that I needed to be where she could keep an eye on me. So I moved out of the old family farmhouse and in here."

Sandy walked in with a tray and overheard the tail end of the exchange. "Why are my ears burning?"

CHAPTER 3

"'Course, she didn't count on me hanging around so long," Owen added with a snicker, followed by a throaty cough. Then another.

Sandy passed around the nibbles and the two men nursed along their beers, easing the task of getting acquainted.

"I couldn't help noticing the revolver on the table. That for me?" Dan said.

"Never know…I needed to be sure what you were selling was something we wanted. Mostly, it makes a nice paperweight… Keeps the mail from blowing away when Sandy opens the door."

"Oh, so it's not loaded. That's a relief."

"Of course, it's loaded…Who doesn't load their paperweight?"

"Touché. Maybe I should change the subject. So what did you do for a career, Owen? You didn't stay in the Navy, right?"

"That's right. Well, I was pretty young when I went in… Lied about my age…but everyone told me I looked older than fifteen, and I guess it was true." He licked a little dip off of a finger. "So when I got out in late 1945, I was just turning nineteen. At first, I felt kind of, you know…lost. My life was so structured for four years…responsibilities were simple. Act like navy, take care of your buddies, and when the moment comes, do what the situation requires." He gave Dan a pensive gaze. "Now I was back and on my own…everything seemed so different. When you wore the uniform, folks opened doors for you or bought you coffee. Without it, I was just me."

"Huh," Dan replied, surprised by Owen's remarks. "Did you start looking for work right away?"

"Not right away. I spent a week in Hawaii with my Uncle Phil…It was kind of awkward because of Paul, my cousin…He was mixed up in the mess at Ford Island on December 7…I got sidetracked in California for a couple of days, then I went back home." He paused and set the bottle down next to the revolver. "Thank God for family, you know? It was good to be back on the property…walking through the woods, fishing. I helped out Dad for…I don't remember, maybe a few weeks…or months," he said with a shrug.

"There wasn't much work in Minnesota for a…well, *gunner*. I didn't have much of a skill set. When I was floundering around in California, I discovered redwoods," he said, almost beaming, and glanced up at an imaginary canopy. "Fell in love with the forest. When I heard there were jobs up north of here in the woods… well, I jumped at it. I worked with a timber crew…I think a year or more. It was hard, physical work, and I was in great shape."

Sandy interrupted. "Dad, tell him about the nursery. He grew all kinds of things. Even some varieties of roses that are now named hybrids."

"Owen…you holding out on me?" Dan said with sweeping inflection in his voice.

"Ha! OK, I'll come clean…" He told Dan about his sixty year relationship with the plant world. Hybrid and hardy roses, bonsais, conifers, shade trees, and Minnesota-hardy fruit trees were among his specialties.

"I liked working outside and with the soil…I dunno, maybe after being cooped up in the fuselage of a plane for four years…I didn't want to wind up in a cubicle somewhere."

"Where did this all this happen?"

"After a year, I wasn't right with the tree cutting anymore. About that time, I got word that Dad had passed…rather suddenly. A simple surgery, then *oops*…a mistake. Then a blood transfusion. They got the blood types wrong," the words coming as he shook his head side to side.

"I kept Dad's place going after he died. I had some field stock, a little bare root, some containers. A few greenhouses…Not too much. I didn't have many helpers…We mailed a lot of plant material around, too. I never got rich, but it paid the bills…Kept the fridge stocked with beer. You know, the important stuff," he said with a chuckle.

Dan's mind bounced between the conversation and a stream of internal impressions. He was enchanted by this man. His manner and the ease of his exchanges—a kind of country wisdom with

CHAPTER 3

a slight Minnesota lilt—showcased itself for another half an hour. But there was work to do.

"Well, Owen, I'd like to spend some time this afternoon hearing about your navy duty and war experiences. And if you don't mind, I'd like to have a couple of small cameras running to record it all. Sure beats taking notes."

"Cameras, huh. I don't really have a good side...My mouth may not cooperate either. So don't expect Spencer Tracy."

"No pressure at all, just pitch and catch. I promise you won't even know they're running. Anything that you don't like in it, we will just edit it out of there. Sound OK?" Owen gave an unconvincing nod. "This little pin is a microphone that goes into a button hole and it will send sound back to the cameras, so no bulky stuff."

Dan snapped his phone apart into the two filming modules and pulled the pair of lightweight telescopic tripods from his bag. With the cameras anchored, he positioned the units to get different perspectives, then pulled his chair between them so Owen wouldn't look into either camera while speaking with him. After a quick sound check, they were ready.

"I'd like to begin with some really, stupidly basic questions, Owen. All set? What is your name and how do you spell it?"

Owen gave a short, hearty laugh, replying, "Oh sure, start with a tough one, Dan..." In exaggerated monotone, he revealed his name, a distinct letter at a time, then raised his hands triumphantly. "Tah-Dah."

Dan navigated through the other basic information that was required for the *Library of Congress Veterans History Project*–questions necessary to properly document the interview. Finally, after what seemed like days of buildup and preparation, *finally*, he could begin the fun stuff.

"So, Owen...how'd you decide to join the Navy?"

Owen's gaze remained fixed on Dan, as if he hadn't heard him. He then gently tipped his head back, eyes toward the ceiling, closed them, and took a deep breath.

Recollections of a distant past began to stir, stoking a whirlwind of memories, his mind moving like a time traveler...

THE LAST WORD

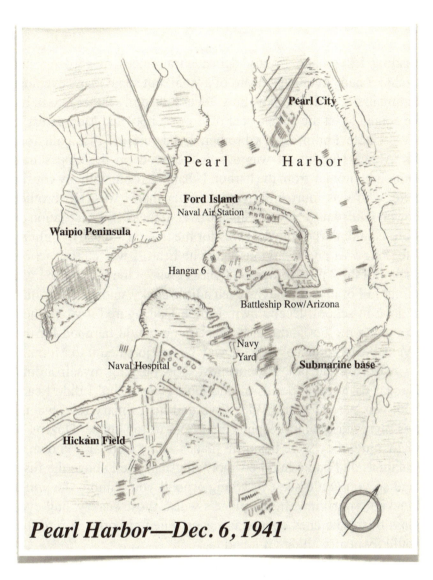

Pearl Harbor—Dec. 6, 1941

--∞-- Chapter 4 --∞--

I loved this place. It was so very different than Minnesota, where everything was flat, and while beautiful, it had a harsh edge to it. And cold as all get out. Here, the breeze was always warm, each day full of white clouds and lush, green tropics. Stiff, rustling leaves and fronds, delicate fragrances of gardenia and orchid. I had never even heard of a lanai, but spent many evenings sitting in one. I don't know how I ever talked my father into it, but he agreed to let me have a year off from school and I jumped at it!

Uncle Philip, Dad's brother, lived just off the main road in ʻĀlewa Heights. It was a neighborhood on the slopes near Honolulu, not far from the harbor. I shared a room with my cousin, Pete, who was fourteen, a year younger than I was. His brother, cousin Paul, was a Navy mechanic over at the Naval Air Station on Ford Island. Part of the deal was for me to gain a sense of military life. Pete was pretty envious when he heard I was cutting school as part of this "jobs" program. I guess I was at the age where I was pretty full of myself, maybe even a little cocky, and wasn't getting it done in school. Deep down, I think Dad figured it would help straighten me out and that the discipline would be good for me. "Valuable experience" was the way he had justified it to Mom.

During the fall, I spent most days busying myself around Hangar 6, doing all kinds of odd jobs. No pay, but I didn't care. Paul was part of Patrol Wing Two and his primary responsibilities revolved around keeping the PBYs in top shape. Dozens of them. God, they were beautiful planes. They were also known as Catalinas and had a hundred-foot wingspan, well above the fuselage so you could see everything around you without the wings blocking your view. In the plane's waist, those snazzy, bug-eyed glass blister hatches opened up, even when airborne. A bird that could fly nearly all day if it had to.

One of my jobs was to go through the cabin after flights and clean up. Some crews were pretty sloppy, and the next group wanted a clean plane. Once onboard, the smell of fuel and exhaust always lingered, mixed with the faint odor of cigarettes, and in a strange way, I found it appealing—like the familiarity of your grandfather's pipes on a rack near his favorite chair, or the smell of fertilizer and animals when you first walked into a barn.

The cockpit was up high, above the nose. Throttle handles hung from the ceiling, the two steering yokes were blunted and surrounded by a honeycomb of gauges and dials. I couldn't

CHAPTER 4

imagine how anyone could know what they were doing up there. I'd crawl under the cockpit and into the nose where a bombardier or nose gunner was stationed. For patrols, it was used mostly as a lookout. As I made my way through the cabin, it felt like being inside of a whale, with massive ribs exposed and wrapped with a dark metallic skin. Above my head was a short ladder reminding me of my treehouse back home. The engineer had a seat up there, in the pylon between the engines, and had his own set of controls.

I'd wipe the radio and tidy up the navigator's desk, then head through a bulkhead door into the galley area. Here, I'd clean off the table and fill the steel canisters with fresh water, then check the bunks and shake out the blankets.

My favorite part was through the next doorway. The oversized blister hatches bulged outward, away from the cabin on both sides, and I suddenly felt like I was in the Nautilus, twenty thousand leagues down.

All the while, Paul scurried around, checking for engine oil leaks and working through his check list. If I was quick enough inside, I could follow him as he moved from task to task and see how it was done.

My biggest thrill was getting a lesson on the .50 caliber machine guns that were tucked in beside each blister. Paul slid the glass hatch to its overhead position and swung one of the guns into place. I'd follow his instructions, sighting and pivoting from side to side, blasting imaginary bogeys. Dumb as it sounds, there was a shortage of live ammunition and it was portioned out very carefully. In fact, gunnery practice in general was a problem since many of the emplacements were on people's private property, and the notion of a bunch of military guys waving gun barrels around didn't appeal to them. So what ammo there was needed to be stored and locked up. Anti-aircraft guns were scarce, too. Paul said that he had heard there was more concern about sabotage at the base than anything else. I'll bet there was as much firepower on those planes as anywhere on Ford Island. Even so, Paul promised me we'd get a chance to squeeze off a few rounds when they headed over to the range some morning soon.

Maybe my dad was right. I seemed to take to the idea of enlisting, being one of the guys and part of a team. I watched as the pilots in sunglasses walked cooly around the aircraft, looking it over before a flight. The crewmen all seemed to have a swagger, pulling themselves aboard as they exchanged friendly insults with the ground crews. I took my share of teasing, but hit it right off with one of the youngest guys, Johnny.

I saw Johnny a lot during the late fall when he had a little down time between flying days and if Paul didn't have me busy working. Sometimes the two of us would take the ferry into town and spend the afternoon exploring and messing around. Back home in Minnesota, there always seemed to be farm chores and the closest town was so far away. My younger sister and I got along fine, but with Johnny, it was a little like having an older brother. One day, we were sitting on a curb sipping Cokes and he was telling me about patrolling in one of the Catalinas. Then right out of the blue, he said, "You know, you're close to six foot and strong as an ox. You look as old as I do. Why don't you go sign up? Those recruiters are competing for guys like crazy around here."

"Aw, I'd get caught, for sure. Maybe next summer, when I'm sixteen, my dad would sign for me. I hope you're still stationed here."

"Hey, it doesn't work that way. You sign up, who knows where you'll go. It's a big Navy." So much for that idea.

It was Saturday, and I was finishing up some chores at the end of the afternoon, when Paul stopped me with an offer.

"Tomorrow morning I'm heading over to pick up my buddy, Will, and heading into town for liberty. The other half of the fleet came in Friday by surprise and all eight battleships are here. I've never seen it happen before. Don't suppose you'd be interested, but another friend of ours, Lou, is a quartermaster on the *Arizona*. We might be able to take a look around."

"Seriously!" I could hardly believe my ears. "What time?"

"Get over there early. I've got roll call and should be at the dock by eight bells. Can you make it?"

"Can I!"

CHAPTER 4

I awoke to the chatter of parrots and was dressed and ready before anyone else was up. Cramming some bread in the toaster, I hastily poured out a large glass of juice as Uncle Phil walked in, heavy-eyed.

"Can't even let a guy sleep in a little on a Sunday?" he asked sarcastically.

"Sorry, Unc, I didn't want to oversleep. I'm meeting Paul at the harbor. He's got a friend onboard one of the battleships. I'm really looking forward to it!"

"Really? And how are you planning to get over there?" He cocked his head slightly as he rummaged for a coffee cup.

"Well, uh, any chance you could run me over to the ferry?"

"Before I have breakfast? This is going to cost you. I think there are some weeds that need pulling in Mother's garden when you get back. Deal?"

"Deal!"

We were at the ferry dock just as it was beginning to load, and I breathed a sigh of relief. A twelve minute ride and I would be able to walk over there comfortably before eight. I didn't want Paul waiting around.

What an impressive sight! Not one or two, but an entire row of battleships docked tightly together in pairs. I don't know how anyone could ever get used to the size and complexity of a battleship, even if you were lucky enough to serve on one. I could only dream. From the shoreline, I could see some of the men on the *Arizona* beginning to assemble, dressed and ready. The nooks and crannies that made up the towers and decks were alive with activity. She was stunning.

I stood adjacent to the big ship, anchored inboard from a smaller vessel that I couldn't make out. Several other curiosity seekers and navy guys were gathered a few feet away. There wasn't any sign of Paul yet, and I wondered if he ran into a snag and we wouldn't be able to get on board. I looked back. It was hard to take my eyes of off *her* and even from where I stood, there was just so much to take in. I could hear a few notes from the band tuning in the rear fantail and the distinct sounds of the crew milling around.

The voices, laughter, and the mechanical whirring and clanking. The soul of the ship on a bright Sunday morning.

I turned and looked back to the north, hoping to get a glimpse of Paul's jeep. By now, I was getting nervous that he was held up for some reason, and our adventure would be a big disappointment. Above the tree line, I could just make out a line of aircraft approaching through the morning's hazy cloud cover, probably returning from a search mission. I expected them to land at Wheeler some distance inland, or over at Hickam Field across the harbor toward Unc's house. It was the strangest thing—several in the formation broke away and lost altitude. At first, I thought they were dropping the sand bags the dive bombers used when practicing, but it was early Sunday morning. Very odd.

An explosion spun me around. It was near the tip of Ford Island and down near the hangar. There it was again! Smoke curled up in the distance and groups of planes seem to converge from all directions. More explosions! Now I could feel them! On the *Arizona*, I saw several officers with binoculars, sweeping the skies, shouting orders down to the crew swarming the deck below. Alarms roared. I crouched, unsure what was happening. To my left, a pair of planes swooped in low across Battleship Row, and I finally realized they were making a run—attacking our ships!

One of the bombs exploded and there was a towering geyser of water alongside the *Oklahoma*. The two planes pulled away as crewmen aboard ship were scrambling to man the anti-aircraft guns and get to battle stations. Directly across the harbor, more attackers. Bombers, heading directly toward the first two battleships. They dropped their torpedoes and my heart sank as both the *Oklahoma* and *West Virginia* were hit. It was chaos, and the group of us huddled on the dock now realized we had to find cover.

I scrunched down behind a tree and one of the navy guys started yelling that we needed something to shoot back with. We were in a grassy, shrubby area near the end of the Row, and the buildings seemed so far away.

The planes just kept coming. Waves of them, with many more at higher altitudes. By now, some of the Arizona's guns were

CHAPTER 4

returning fire. It seemed she had been hit at least once, but was fighting back and crewmen were everywhere. Explosions and machine gun bursts were all around us and became deafening. It was then that a bomb from a plane that no one saw, slammed into the *Arizona* beside the number two turret.

There was a lull, then an explosion that nearly knocked me over blew up the front of the ship, sending it some fifteen or twenty feet into the air before she broke in half. A thunderhead of smoke and fire ballooned into the sky, and with it, a wave of searing heat we could feel on shore. Everything from the mainmast forward was on fire. Furious fire.

I didn't expect to see anything moving on deck as some of the smoke cleared, but slowly, a few crewmen began to stand. As those who could regained their footing, several men came screaming out of the flames. They were forced to the deck so they could be helped and wouldn't jump overboard. The water surrounding the ship was ablaze with burning fuel and oil. The mainmast was now leaning. The smaller ship I couldn't see clearly was shooting lines over to some guys stranded up there. They started across, hand over hand. The lines burned through and I couldn't tell if they made it or fell into water. It was horrible!

Such a feeling of helplessness. And anger. Anger beyond anything I'd ever experienced. I found myself punching the ground with tears freely flowing down my cheeks. The planes were gone for now, and it seemed the entire world was on fire. Those left alive were moving into lifeboats, abandoning ship. There were bodies floating and sailors trying to swim. I'd never seen a dead person before. They were everywhere. Crewmen in the lifeboats struggled to pull survivors out of the water. We rushed over to the water's edge and began dragging more of them ashore, many badly burned. People were rushing from all over to the scene, trying to do something, anything. I felt sure it was the same all over Oahu. Were their troops now on the beaches? Tanks and equipment?

What was next?

THE LAST WORD

Chapter 5

Dan realized he was staring, his mind awash with vivid imagery as Bilge lumbered slowly over to Owen and nuzzled his hand.

Owen's face was flushed, his eyes damp. He took a deep breath and coughed. "Paul's jeep was on the bend when it was strafed…It rolled over on him. He was gone when they found him." Owen again cleared his throat. "I'll always wonder if he was trying to get to me. Make sure I was safe."

Sandy interrupted. "Could anyone use a glass of water? I could use a glass of water."

"Yes! Please," Dan said.

"Thanks, Dear, I'd love some," added Owen.

As Sandy left the room, Dan felt he needed to cut the silence. "Uh, Owen, would you like to take a break, bathroom, anything?"

"Me? No…although it's rare these days for me to pass on a bathroom break." With a gentle smile, he continued, "Naw. Doing OK." Sandy returned with a tray of water glasses. After a few sips, Owen struggled to set down the glass, his hand seeming to have a mind of its own. "Of course, there were more planes, a second wave…Guys in the lifeboats fired rifles into the sky and the ship went under in ten minutes." His face, for an instant, went stony. "The armor piercing bomb that hit next to that gun turret went through the five decks below it."

It had been a potshot, slamming right into the lower handling room where a million pounds of powder in one-hundred-and-five-pound bags detonated. Owen turned to face Sandy and Dan again. "Anti-aircraft guns were firing from all around us by then. Finally…some planes were going down."

Dan grimaced and found himself wanting to ask Owen a question. But he could sense that there was more.

It was then, Owen continued, that the dive bombers spotted the *Nevada* trying to make it out of the harbor and hit it—hard. The helmsman managed to beach the ship to keep it from blocking the channel. "High altitude bombers attacked all the airstrips… so much damage. Finally, it was over." He sighed, then looked Dan right in the eye. "The bravery of those men on the Arizona, the Nevada, everywhere around the harbor. Seeing it, feeling it. I decided right then and there…I had to enlist."

Sandy refilled Owen's glass. "I don't think you've ever told me all of this before, Dad," she said, her voice a little unsteady.

Owen's smile seemed to say, *I know*. "They fought the fires for days. At first, divers went down with torches…tried to cut the steel hoping to get to survivors. Mostly, they found bloated bodies." Owen recalled how everyone was doing something—tending wounds, stacking sandbags. Some helped with manually pumping up and down on air pumps for the shallow divers. Others worked on new gun emplacements. Over at the hangar, there were more fires and destroyed planes littered the area. "They'd been parked wingtip to wingtip…helped protect them from sabotage, they said. Sitting ducks for an air attack. Thirty-three of our PBYs were destroyed or put out of action."

He reached for his water glass and the ice rattled as he went on. "It was a beehive of activity…all around the harbor. There weren't any lights after dark again in Oahu until 1944. Everyone expected to see Jap soldiers *every* night…martial law was declared, and jeeps with .30 caliber machine guns patrolled the streets and were ordered to shoot anyone breaking curfew for…I dunno…for as long as I was there."

Dan adjusted his seat and ran his fingers through his hair. "It sounds as if you were already part of the Navy in everyone's eyes."

Owen nodded. "By the end of the first day, I guess it seemed like I had become one of the guys…I still had my *Dixie Cup* that Paul gave me on my head…sooty and worn. I was taking orders…

CHAPTER 5

running here and lifting there. In time, I heard some other volunteers talking about enlisting. They were older, but because I was more familiar with the Navy than they were…well, no one thought anything of it."

Sandy and Dan looked at each other, then said in unison, "*Dixie Cup*?"

"You know. The cap. Popeye."

"Popeye?" Dan still looked confused.

"Don't tell me you don't…Popeye was before your time?" Owen looked incredulous. "Sandy?"

"Yes, I know who he is and you know I never watched it. And I didn't know he wore a *Dixie Cup*."

"OK, I get it," Dan said, feeling a slight blush streak across his face. "The little white cap on your head. So I'm guessing you enlisted with a group of older boys?"

"We all went down to the recruiters and got in line…It was a mob scene…As I'm slowly moving forward, I heard them tell some guy in the line next to me…'You're too young. You need a parent's signature.' They gave him a form…I decided to exaggerate my age, and told them I was seventeen and a half. He looked at me and I thought I was in…He says, 'You still need a parent's signature.' I told him, 'My dad's in Minnesota, and there isn't any way to get back there.'

"He looked at me…and then hollered over at the sergeant two lines over. 'Hey Phillips! Can you talk to this guy? He's got a problem.'

"So, I waited through another line…when I got to the front, he asks, 'Where's your paperwork?'

'That guy told me to come over here.'

He says, 'How old are you?'

'Sev…Eighteen.'

'What are you doing in this line? Parent signature forms only! Look! Name here, birthdate there, sign it…OK, give it here!' He stamps it. 'Now, take it over there. Next!'

"And…I was in the Navy!"

"Heh! Love it," Dan said, with a pat of his thighs. He stood up and peeked at the camera screens, then satisfied, paused and rubbed the back of his head as if it was a genie lamp full of questions. "Your training. You did that in Hawaii?"

"No. Not right away. It took some time…I was trying to get a telegram back home to let them know I was all right. But I didn't want to tell Dad about any of this…I ended up with a batch of new recruits on a fruit boat headed for San Diego in January."

"OK, then you did your Basic Training *there*?"

"Uh huh."

"What was it like?"

"Yeah…Basic was just that. Basically doin' what they told you. We marched, we cleaned rifles, we did push-ups, we made beds, we cleaned toilets…That's where I first learned you never clean a toilet with your mouth open."

"Dad!"

"No matter how bad they smell…"

"Dad!"

"Wish my mom had taught me that."

"Gads. I'm sorry, he gets this way."

"Don't be sorry," Dan said, shaking his head. "I need to remember that one. Did they teach you anything else?" he said with a chuckle.

"I made it through OK, I guess…was an Aviation Machinist Mate, 3rd class petty officer for a while. They shipped me off to gunnery school because I told 'em I could shoot."

Dan's iPhone band rumbled on his wrist. "Ah…Owen, excuse me a second." He stood and looked at the camera screen again as a message from Samantha scrolled across it. *While you folks are all enjoying a nice snack, I'm wasting away here in need of an update. Password please.*"

"Cripes! Sam, not now. Can't this wait!" he said in a very annoyed whisper.

"If it was me, I wouldn't. And I guess it is me."

"Oh, for Pete's sake. Sam, this is a really bad time. Let's just

CHAPTER 5

get back to the filming, shall we?" He turned and faced the others. "I'm sorry Owen. We were talking about...your training, I think," Dan said, wondering what this spate of flakiness on Samantha's part might be doing to his video.

Feeling a bit off his game, he decided to regroup. *Perhaps a little more early background. Growing up. How many people in the entire world could tell me about life dating back over a century?*

"Owen, you grew up near here, correct?" he began.

"I did. 'Course...I don't remember much about the 1920s... but we had a farm during the early years of the Depression. Probably a good thing for us, too. We didn't feel the effects like they did in other places. Dad raised crops and some animals." He gestured with both hands. "Cows and chickens, mostly. We had a couple of goats, more like pets than anything."

Dan glanced over at Sandy and could see her face light up. She had the look of a little girl, captivated by her father's stories.

"He had a cistern and a pipe up the slope at the top of the property. Real marshy up there...springs that seemed to just run out from nowhere, and it filled that cistern right up. Enough water for the house as well as all the livestock and gardens." Owen took off his glasses and rubbed his eyes, as if to summon the image of the farm's borders. He took a sip from his glass and continued. "Off to the east side, the water trickled into a furrow...made a small creek a couple of feet wide that we played in. So much wildlife in there. The creek ran along the edge of the property...then headed south. You probably know it as the Mississippi."

"Whoa," Dan looked up. "Seriously? The Mississippi starts on your property?"

Owen broke into a wide grin, and chuckled. "That's what Dad said, anyhow...He was a bit of a bullshitter..."

Sandy was caught mid-swallow and her near-choke surprised all three of them. "Sorry, I wasn't expecting that," she said, wiping her smile with a napkin.

Owen paused and stared ahead, reflecting. "But there used to be lakes and springs all around there that...oozed...drained into one another. It was hard to know which one was first. Things have changed a lot since those days. Anyhow, he always said that spring was magic. Good for us."

Dan nodded. "Well, you should definitely bottle some of whatever you were drinking!" he added, reaching for his water glass and making a mock toast. After several swallows, he felt refocused. "Can you tell me a little about what life was like on a small farm in Minnesota in the 1930s?" A second or two passed, and Dan noticed Owen again close his eyes and gently roll his head back without speaking…

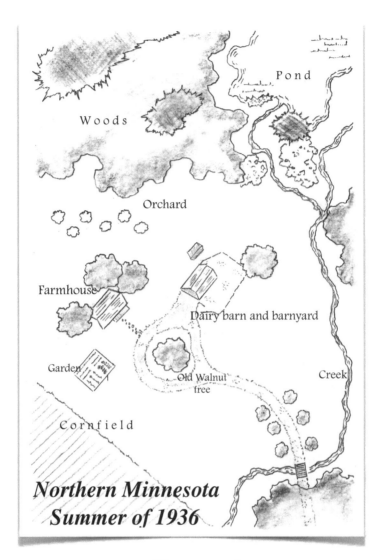

—ᴡ— Chapter 6 —ᴡ—

Dad's place was about a hundred acres and I knew every square inch of it. I loved exploring and galloping through the meadows and marshes with Dangit, our doorstep retriever whose mom must have been a shepherd and whose father was a mix of wolfhound and I don't know what.

We could have just as easily called him "Scrambled Eggs."

Up in one corner of the property, there were springs, gushing and plentiful, that migrated through the soil from the big lakes to the north. They fed a large pond with boggy coves and patches of cattail and pickerel weed. I was never sure if Dad or the neighbor, Mr. Donaldson, threw the catfish in there, but a few were legendary. Some even had names.

Days were filled with chores in summer and school and chores the rest of the time. Dad always used to say, "If you learn to tickle Mother Earth with your hoe, she'll laugh with a harvest." I must have tickled every funny bone in her body. There was milking, although my sister got stuck with that most of the time. Or fixing fences that seemed to magically fail overnight. Collecting and splitting firewood took up many of the days when it was warm enough you didn't need it. Planting and picking often replaced homework in spring and fall.

The Depression played havoc with supplies, but we had it better than most. Farmers were important enough to keep supplied with fuel, but even with allotments, trips to town became rare. There was more than enough to do around the place, so I never had time to fool around in town anyway.

The farmhouse was a clapboard two-story, set up on a knob of land with a view of the creek from the porch, but high enough to stay dry when a wet spring gave us a river down there. Our front porch had rockers and Adirondack chairs to enjoy the cool evening breezes. Evenings—gently rocking with an ice tea or lemonade, the four of us watching as the sunset blushed, our eyes combing the skies in search of a shooting star. The front porch was my favorite part of the house.

My bedroom was upstairs at the end of a pine-floored hallway, just past the "fake squeak" Dad says he installed so Mom would know where I was at night.

One of the best parts of waking up each morning was the smell. Kitchen smells, the fireplace and stove. Mom's bacon, muffins, toast. You needed it all, too. Summer days could be long ones living on a farm.

CHAPTER 6

We had an old mule, Clarence, and Dad hitched the ornery son-of-a-gun up every week to keep him in shape in case the tractor broke down or gas prices went too high. There was an art to plowing with a mule, one that nobody ever explained to Clarence. Dad taught me how to outfit him with a collar and bridle, then stretch out the reins and snag them on the furrow or plow. Two heavy canvas straps ran along his flanks back to a wooden tow bar that had a big grappling-style hook. The hook slipped down into a ring attached to whatever implement we needed that day.

That was the easy part.

Clarence preferred grazing to plowing, and each season he seemed more cantankerous than the last.

But Sundays were for church and fishing. And I much preferred the second part of Sunday. My tackle bag and can of night crawlers were my bible and song sheet. I never felt closer to God than when I was fishing. A pond like ours was like a snapshot of all His work. At attention on the far side was the forest, not yet a victim of the axe, and the pool itself was brimming with life. It was all in there. Reptiles, amphibians, and insects that swam and flew. Deer, raccoons, and an occasional bobcat or black bear came visiting. Even the star-nosed moles paddled about and worked the edges, looking for worms and making mounds. Of course there were fish, and incalculable aquatic plants. Each time I went up there it was a diverse, medley of creatures, from the smallest benign periwinkle to the predatory snapping turtle.

Then there was the thrill of hooking a crappie or occasional largemouth, seeing the pole tip bend and the line slice through the water's surface as a yet unseen leviathan began a furious flight to escape the hook.

Or the sensation of looking back to where your bobber had been, puzzling a while before lifting up on your pole, held fast with an apparent snag. Then the snag slowly begins to move away. A chill went through me at times like that. Could it be "Slick" or "Gus" or the dreaded "Tanglefin!" Catfish that had eluded capture for so long they were measured in feet, not inches. You never needed God more than you did then. So I thought.

My lucky spot was out along a fallen log that extended beyond the cattails and gave access to the deeper water and a hollow on the opposite bank. Dangit and I tightroped the first section until two tree limbs flared, creating a nice sitting area. With enough line and a deep set of the weight, I could drop a bobber in the shadows and then have a seat, bide my time, chew on a little sweetgrass.

I was nearly to that sitting spot, pole and tackle in hand, when Dangit spotted a pair of mallards on the far side of the log and jumped in after them. The log shifted violently and sent me and my pole flying. There was blue sky, a thud, the sound of bubbles…then darkness.

Something was hitting me. There was shouting. "Owen! Owen, come on, listen to me son. Wake up!" I looked up and directly into Mr. Donaldson's face…and threw up.

"OK, son. That's OK. You did good. Let me get you over on your side and pointed away from me," he said with a laugh. "Lucky I came along when I did. That dog of yours was barking up a storm."

My first impulse was to apologize. But I was still woozy and a little disoriented and nothing like words would come out. After a few seconds, I managed a "Thank you, sir."

And then, "Tanglefin…did he get away?"

Chapter 7

Dan was surprised to learn from his parents that he had been as blue as an eggplant when his mother delivered him in the wee hours of a turbulent Minnesota night. It had seemed, for hours on end, as if lightning split the sky each time his mother screamed. There were times when she wondered if she would ever forgive him.

Then the moment arrived and relief was exchanged for concern. The doctor worked feverishly to untangle the tightly wrapped and compressed umbilical cord. Within a few minutes, baby Dan had survived his first ordeal as the newest member of the human race.

It was strange he had picked this instant to reflect on those earliest moments from his life—a time, of course, of which he had absolutely no recollection. Yet, Owen's stories spoke to Dan and had him wondering about the random nature of fate—that delicate strand that sometimes separates life and death. What if things had played out just a smidge differently—his mother's labor had lasted five more minutes while he languished, desperate and strangling—how dissimilar the interview with Owen would be. *What if Dangit, Owen's barking, doorstep retriever, had never shown up on his doorstep at all?*

"Do you think there are still any catfish in that pond today, Dad?" Sandy asked.

"I have no idea," Owen replied, matter-of-factly. "But I wouldn't suggest going swimming in there."

"Good advice," Dan concurred. "Fishing sounds like a favorite pastime of yours."

"It was. And over the years, I tried to squeeze in some trips here and there. I liked to go up to the Boundary Waters with some buddies, but never could stay too long…with the nursery and all."

"Beautiful area."

"It is. Used to trail ski up there when I was younger. You could get lost in the snow plenty easy, too. Yep, some great fishing. Bass, walleye, pike." Owen grinned. "I remember a trip one summer with some friends. We had canoes and all our gear and enough food and beer to last a couple of days, I guess."

"Oh, I think I know where this is going," Sandy smiled.

"Well, we had a good day. Caught some fish, saw a moose and a couple of black bear on the shoreline. Later, feasted on fish and beer. A little too much of one and not enough of the other, as I recall." Owen briefly frowned, more puzzled than scowling. "I usually had a pup tent, but didn't take one for some reason. And I kept thinking about that moose. So when everyone turned in, I volunteered to tend the fire. Didn't want to get stepped on." Owen fed chunks of wood into the fire until he had a nice blaze going, then slipped into his sleeping bag, a bulky primitive affair. "It was dark and moonless. The Milky Way is something up there. I guess I must have passed out. The next thing I know, I'm hearing a loud, crunching sound."

"Oops," Dan said. "Don't tell me…"

"The fire was dead out and it was so dark. The noise sounded like it was just on the other side of the fire ring we'd made with rocks. Cans being crushed, maybe some of our pans or trash. Now I was thinking black bear."

"Uh-huh."

"Quietly as I could, I leaned in toward the fire ring and grabbed ahold of a rock. As I started to withdraw with the stone, I heard a noise and looked up. Right across the fire pit from me—there it was…"

"No. A bear?"

"Worse."

"A moose!"

"Worse. This moose had a white stripe up its back. And it wasn't alone."

CHAPTER 7

"Ugh!"

"I slowly let go of the rock and retreated into my sleeping bag like a frightened turtle. In a couple of minutes, these damn skunks started running around and right over me. Never been so scared."

Sandy and Dan, cheeks aching, were lost in laughter at the same instant.

"Then, I swear that they started dancing. Right on top of me. Little shits."

Sandy snorted, and now her ears even hurt.

"Well, I cowered in that bag for a good while until they finally stopped. I wondered if they'd gone, or if they'd just dance on over to where the others were sleeping. But I didn't dare move or make a sound."

Dan watched, blurry-eyed, as Owen made a skittering motion with his rawboned right hand that looked more like a chicken foot than a skunk.

"Just then, I see a flashlight go on in one of the tents. It flashes up through the fabric…then this way and that. And there's a scream and a sound like feet kicking blankets. Suddenly, the light went out. Now the whole camp smelled like skunk."

"Oh, Dad." Sandy pleaded, exhausted.

"The next morning we had to burn Steve's tent."

Sandy, feeling the need to move around, got up with the water pitcher and refilled everyone's glasses. "I haven't heard that one in a very long time."

"Nope. Didn't see that coming," Dan admitted. He thought to himself, *Sounds a little like a tall tale from the South Pacific.* "I'm almost afraid to ask if you hunted around the area, too."

"Dad had me target shooting at a pretty young age and we'd go out bird hunting. Pheasants or wild turkeys…that sort of thing. Geese used the ponds in fall. I found I had a knack for it. When I went into the Navy that was a question they asked from the get-go." He squirmed in his chair, distracted, and reached a hand underneath him. "What the…" He tossed the dog's chew bone to the floor and continued as if nothing had happened. "Anyhow, before

I knew it, I was on my way to gunnery school. By then, I was done with Basic and had been to aviation machinist school up in Chicago. Once they were convinced I could hit what I was aiming at and knew how to handle everything from pistols to .50 caliber machine guns…well, then I got my first taste of radar equipment in one final school in Virginia. A few weeks later, I was shipping out."

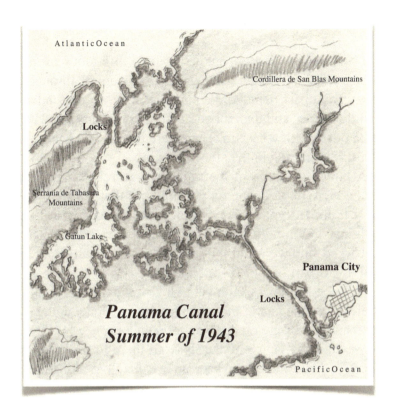

—m— Chapter 8 —m—

My eyes were as big as an owl's. And each time we made it up another step, my smile grew even wider. It took all day to travel across Panama in a troop ship stuffed full of navy guys, and I was enjoying every bit of it.

It didn't start out this way. Christmas Day I boarded a ship in Chesapeake Bay, heading south. It was forty-five feet up to the main deck, and before we'd gotten very far, the waves were coming over it. Everyone was seasick. I couldn't even hold down water and didn't eat for days. The seas finally calmed and temperatures warmed. I lolled around in the sun and what a pleasure it was enjoying a meal without losing it overboard.

I soon hugged the rail again, but for a different reason. This canal was amazing! First it seemed to take you uphill, through huge doorways and past rusted old equipment that had surrendered to the jungle's vines and underbrush. After moving across a lake, we were on our way down again. Then there it was. The Pacific—teal blue and shimmering in the afternoon sun.

A bunch of us spent the night in a warehouse in Panama City, and were up at dawn, only to find out that we were now to board a train. In typical navy fashion, we chugged back across the isthmus, returning to very nearly where we started. There, we disembarked, and we were shuffled, sorted, and dealt—and lo and behold, I was part of a PBY Catalina crew.

And we had an assignment! This was exciting. Finally, all our training would be put into play and we would be doing something to help. We were on our way to Ecuador.

We started flying sub patrols from there to practice for the big show to come and also to keep an eye on things along the coast of South America. Reports of sightings—subs and ships—came in all the time. But you never knew how seriously to take them. After a week, it began to feel more like we were flying around these magnificent islands to make sure that the giant tortoises and blue footed boobies remained safe.

Some of the officers were equally concerned. There was an army base on the same island where we were stationed, and it happens that a one-star general and his aide insisted on coming aboard and giving us a "flight check." He felt his best opinion could be rendered from the copilot's seat, and he settled in there as we lifted off.

Soon, we circled a beautiful island with a crescent shaped lagoon, remnants of an ancient volcano, and schools of manta rays frolicked in its calm waters. It was what he had come to see.

"Do you have any facilities on this aircraft?" he asked after we had been aloft for another half hour or so. It was hard to be sure, but some of us thought he looked a little rocky as he climbed aboard. Maybe a little too much, a little too late the evening before?

CHAPTER 8

His aide escorted him to the rear of the plane where there were, not surprisingly, two options. The usual in-flight option of a cone funnel with an exit tube allowed relief, and with a simple twist of the valve, a person's burden was dispersed into a hundred-knot wind speed.

A second option also existed, and appeared to the untrained eye, to be a makeshift outhouse including a hatch, and hinged seat.

When the wavering general, with the help of his aide, wobbled through the bulkhead doorways and narrow passages in search of "le toilet," we all assumed this to be nothing more than simple draining of the oil. A few minutes later, the aide appeared in the front of the plane again, unescorted, and with an anxious look on his face, asked, "Do you have some water?" It seems the good general had chosen to use the "sit down" facility while airborne, and a good seventy-five knots of that wind blew everything he was doing right up his back. The aide had the face of a first time father as he carried an assortment of rags and one of our stainless steel drums of water to the rear of the PBY. Even with our airspeed, they stunk up the whole plane.

THE LAST WORD

Chapter 9

This yarn about crisscrossing an entire country and flying brass on sightseeing missions did nothing, Dan thought to himself, to dispel the waggish notion that there were times when it seemed the military just couldn't get out of its own way. He looked over at Sandy for her reaction.

"I thought it was funny," she tittered.

"Kind of an inauspicious introduction to the war, I'd say," Dan muttered, as he sifted through his notepad for a new direction. "So where was this exactly? I'm a little confused by the location."

Owen appeared unsurprised. "After Pearl, none of the coasts felt safe. Even in South America. In hindsight…maybe none of this was necessary. But German U-Boats made their way near enough to our eastern ports to sink a lot of ships headed for Europe. The Japanese had subs too…even used fire balloons later on in the war. Like a baby hot air balloon with flammable explosives. They launched thousands of them hoping for random hits on populated areas. Or a lucky forest fire in Oregon or Washington."

"It does seem justified then."

"I think so. Our Navy Catalinas were in the middle of the struggle over the only U.S. soil captured by the Japanese. Up in the Aleutians off Alaska." Owen's face took on a more sassy expression. "Cold up there though. I've lived in Minnesota all my life…but I've always been glad they didn't send me up north. I have enough trouble with my socks as it is."

"Socks?" Dan asked.

"Yeah," he said. "Where do they go? I'm rummaging around for some warm socks and I have a dozen that don't match. Where are the rest of the damn things?"

"Geez, Dad."

"I'm not blaming *you*. I just didn't want to end up in the Aleutians with half my socks."

"For Pete's sake." Sandy covered her eyes and rolled her head to the side.

"Although all my Navy socks were the same color. Maybe it wouldn't…"

Sandy quickly brought this to a close. "Dan might be interested in knowing what islands you were flying around with the tortoises," she said, insistently.

"Oh…well. There were several near Ecuador. Galapagos part of the time."

"Wooo. I've always wanted to go. Of course, not the way you did!" she added.

Owen's eyes widened. "Oh, there were some fantastic sights and amazing creatures all around there." He stopped and shifted his weight. "We didn't have much to do but fly around and enjoy it. We never saw anything like a submarine. Just whales and dolphins and thousands of birds."

"Where did you go next?" Dan inquired.

"By July we were in San Diego. There we made our final preparations for the long flight to the South Pacific."

"You flew the same planes from South America all that way?"

"Nope. We were a squadron now and they outfitted all the crews with new Catalinas. PBY-5s…so they could only land in water." He explained that some PBYs had tricycle landing gear that made them true amphibians. They could use runways or retract the wheels and land in water. Black Cat crews around the Solomon Islands had them.

"Our landing gear had to be attached by a group of guys wading around in the water…then we were towed up a ramp to a runway. So we depended on the seaplane tenders most of the time…just pretending to be boats. *Flying* boats."

─∽─ Chapter 10 ─∽─

A ustralia was big. I had no idea. It had taken us almost ten days to get to Brisbane, and we hopped from island to island across the endless Pacific to do it. When we finally arrived, I thought the tough part was behind us. But like I said, Australia was big!

The squadron I was assigned to continued training in Hawaii, a bittersweet experience. It had been a little over a year since I'd seen it last. Our orders pointed us "down under," a distance of nearly five thousand miles over open sea. Even with our Catalina seaplanes, this was an ambitious flight.

The island atoll of Palmyra was our first stop, a pretty little place. Canton Island, not so much. It was hot, dusty, and unremarkable compared to the others. We flew over Howland Island where rusty fuel barrels were still lined up and waiting for Amelia Earhart. She was late.

Somewhere over the wide ocean expanse between Canton and Funafuti, we passed through a little squall. I noticed as the turbulence intensified it seemed to send shivers through the PBY, then suddenly, our starboard engine quit…and we dropped. It was the first time I had ever felt anything like freefall in a plane. A crewman in one of the bunks went airborne, and I just hung on wide-eyed, looking out of the blister hatch as the sea rushed toward us. The pilot was finally able to get the prop feathered to correct for the physics of flying on one engine, and we leveled off—just above the water. All of us hustled around inside, throwing everything we could overboard, including our guns and ammo. We kept our clothing. Finally, we gained some altitude and limped in to Funafuti.

Turned out it would take several days to be fitted with a new engine. Funafuti was another gem, but with mosquitos the size of hummingbirds, and some nasty consequences if you were unlucky enough to tangle with the wrong one.

There was an outdoor theater on the island, and I enjoyed watching the familiar faces from home on the big screen. They told us to get there early so we could get a good seat. Large coconut trees served as poles for a power line that stretched from one side of the venue to the other, sagging slightly over the crowd. I was fidgeting in my seat, waiting for the film to start, and looked up just as a large coconut rat scampered out of one tree and deftly made his way across the line to the tree on the opposite side. By the time he arrived at his destination, he had everyone's attention and a cheer went up through the crowd. The next night, promptly at 1850, there he was again! This went on for several days, exactly at the same time. Finally, the word was out and the place was packed in anticipation of the rat. The roar greeting his appearance so startled him midway across his tightrope, that he scurried back to the first palm and that was the last time we saw him.

A couple of days later, we reached New Caledonia. Beautiful, but again, with mosquitos so fearsome that if you happened to bend their bills over when they were sticking them through your tent, they'd fly away with it. Our concluding leg took us into Brisbane.

CHAPTER 10

I enjoyed the luxury of a new city, a new country, a new continent. But soon, it was time to move again—and there was an unexpected turn. It was winter on Australia's south coast, and many small towns in our path seemed closed up. Combined with the strain on resources, we were surprised to discover it wasn't a sure thing to find enough petrol to fill our tanks. This strangled our range and we needed to hopscotch again, this time mostly over land. Another twenty-five hundred miles, a half tank at a time and sometimes filling it with five-gallon buckets.

It was a pleasure to finally see the waters of the Indian Ocean glimmering in the distance. At long last, we were letting down onto a river—one that cut through the heart of a city called Perth. G'Day!

It was in Perth that we made a big change to our airplanes. They were all repainted with an ugly coat of flat black paint. We were told we were a Black Cat squadron now, following in the footsteps of some others who'd had good success flying night missions this way. "Black Cats." It had a nice ring to it.

The Black Cats had already made a name for themselves in our region. And to the east, they also patrolled a swath through the Solomon Islands, and up to the north around Bougainville Island. There was a certain excitement that came with hunting the enemy by night.

It was also in Perth I first became acquainted with a fellow named Jim, another gunner and mechanic who was in a different crew. He was young, maybe eighteen, so not much older than I was, and an all-around interesting guy. He was from the Northwest and loved to climb trees. He could sometimes be seen way up in a palm or fig reading a book for hours at a time. Or whittling. The guy was a magician with a pocket knife.

One day he spotted a straight wooden rod and went to work on it. By the time he was finished, he had twelve inches of wooden chain. Not rigid—flexible links like you would hook to an anchor. Beautiful stuff. He could do the same thing with matchsticks, turning a box of matches into a collection of miniature chain mouse

— 57 —

leashes. How he got that knife to do such small detail was beyond me.

He had a sense of humor, too. In Perth, the Swan River fanned out until it was a mile or more wide. When his plane would land there, Jim would typically be out on the bow, where he'd set the post and tie a clove hitch to a buoy to secure the plane. The river was an estuary and depending on the time, sea water could carry schools of jellyfish in around us. Jim would be busy tying up as the props slowly idled behind him, and he'd get this look on his face. I knew he was going to start pitching some of those guys up into the props. "See, flying jellyfish!" he'd say with a howl.

Chapter 11

"I've got to ask you about your medical care," Dan divulged to Owen. "I mean, you must have been doing something right all these years. You've been going to a veterans hospital most recently, isn't that right?"

"God, not unless I have to," Owen said with a wince. "It's clear down in St. Cloud. Bemidji's got a good facility...but I try to stay out of those places. Sick people in there. I prefer keeping it local."

Sandy interrupted. "The virtual hospital is first on our contact list. Like when Dad bumped his head and it wouldn't stop bleeding."

She told him about the night her father lost his balance and struck his head on the edge of a counter. At first, it didn't look serious, but soon he had a knot like a hard boiled egg on his forehead and the spread of the gash seemed to grow with it. Owen's blood thinners were keeping it from clotting, and she began to panic.

A tele-emergency clinician was able to talk her through the process of closing the wound, and even checked his eyes and responses for any trace of a concussion. She and LaTeesha, the caregiver that stopped by daily, kept a pantry of medical supplies and devices for blood pressure and blood testing. She could use her phone for EKGs and send them data and other medical information—all from the convenience of the living room.

She felt more and more comfortable about living at home as e-clinics continued to pop up, often near small towns between larger cities. Many could handle walk-in and emergency needs as well as virtual care. Transport companies were more available than ever, thanks to driverless vehicles.

Of course, medical care *out here in the country* had always come with its challenges, and Owen recalled the *old days*. "Sandy, you remember Dick Sturdivant. Lived over by the Haskins place." Sandy gave a knowing mien. "A good guy, schooled up on his medicine. He was a vet. I bothered him every once in a while."

"Was he in the same squadron you were?" Dan asked.

"No, he was a *vet*. A veterinarian. But, yeah. He did do a stint in Europe, too. And he was good. After taking my dogs, cats, even a goat to him for…oh, I don't know, five or six years, I went in one day with a dog that had a hotspot. Over the course of our conversation, I told him about a rash that I had. He slipped me this liniment…and it worked like a charm!"

Dan raised an eyebrow. "Don't tell me he became your regular doctor."

"We knew each other pretty well, and now and then I'd get an ache or feverish or something, and I'd ask him about it. He'd say, 'Well look, I'm not a doctor, but if it was me, I'd do this.' It was marvelous." Owen's expression turned smug. "For years, I could just go over there and pay him a vet bill and I'm back in the pink. He was great."

Sandy frowned, and had to add, "And?"

Owen turned toward his daughter. "Aw, she remembers the time when I was cleaning the gutters up on that old wooden ladder. Damn, I was two steps away from the ground when a rung broke and I landed in a gopher mound. My ankle ballooned up and I hobbled over to his office…stood in line behind a cat and a dog. After he examined me, he told me the one thing you never want to hear from somebody who treats horses. 'I think it's broken.' I knew then and there I needed to get another doctor. Or he'd shoot me."

By now, Dan was fully aware that this assignment was a lot more fun than he had anticipated. The material seemed to just pour out of this time-worn, but venerable old gentleman.

There had been other occasions when an interview or search for an unusual story didn't go so well, like when he was sent over to talk with an eccentric back-woodsman who had made an

CHAPTER 11

impression on the paper's publisher with his artwork. Dan had arrived, expecting to see welding or paintings, maybe some kind of stone with sandblasted imagery.

He hadn't expected a log cabin in the woods with each log painted a different color of the rainbow. And it would be an understatement to say he was bowled over by an array of chainsaw sculptures depicting country folk, maybe even the man's own neighbors, in a variety of erotic poses. The pieces were fashioned from a life-sized stump of one or more sawn trees, and the figurines dotted the forest, each bringing to life some snippet of the Kama Sutra. Milk buckets, butter churns, even goats played a *big* part in his artwork. Dan didn't know whether to photograph them or cover them up.

He had approached this assignment with more caution, but now he wondered where it would lead him next.

"Let's get back to the black planes. Seaplanes, right? Tell me more about the missions, and what your typical day was like."

Owen lingered over his water glass a few seconds. "Well, there was a typical day…and there were the missions—at night. We mostly slept and fooled around during the day. About sundown, the plane was fueled and armed, outfitted with enough provisions and ammo to keep us happy for a dozen hours or more." He rubbed a soothing hand across the top of his head, then over the mussy, horseshoe of white hair that remained. "Usually, the first few hours were uneventful. Just a lot of open water. If there was a moon, you could see reflections on the waves, or the shadowy darkness of an island." He pointed again to the model of the plane on the bookcase. "The wings up overhead and those blisters made for some good viewing. If we happened to spot something, we could call it in, or we could attack it—or both."

Sandy had a question. "Dad, if it was a dark night, how could you see anything, much less a Japanese ship? It would seem if you could see them—they could see you."

"It *would* seem that way, wouldn't it? We had some advantages though. For one, our planes appeared entirely dark at night." He paused to let it sink in. He told them how flame arrestors had

— 61 —

been installed on each engine, and how the Navy had discovered red light gave the crew limited illumination, but wasn't visible from any distance, so it was used for the cockpit and navigator's table. "We also had radar, something the Japanese hadn't yet taken advantage of. But make no mistake. They were good, maybe better at night than we were, at least at first. They moved a lot of materiel and troops around those islands after dark."

Dan asked, "So, why did you have the advantage?"

Owen smiled. "We could see the outline of a ship that was completely blacked out from overhead, even on the darkest of nights, thanks to some small, luminescent sea creatures." He grinned, taking in their reaction. "Plankton. I'm not exactly sure if it's a plant, animal, or a little of each, but when a vessel moved through it, the wakes were easy to see."

Dan considered this. How remarkable that he now lived in an age where automobiles routinely maneuvered themselves around darkened city streets and the movements or characteristics of a single person on a sidewalk could be accurately observed—even at night—from space. Ninety years ago, over the inky ocean surface of World War II's South Pacific, Owen's crew depended on a naturally occurring algae-bacteria for their intel.

Dan noticed his mind drifting, trying to visualize such a scene, and he found he could almost imagine himself aboard Owen's seaplane as it flew over the vast Pacific on a pitch black night…

Off the coast of Northwestern Australia - 1943

—ᴡ— Chapter 12 —ᴡ—

We had just crossed the tip of the North West Cape peninsula and headed north in the general direction of Christmas Island. I'd talked to Doc about what it was like to be up in the nose as a lookout. He simply said, "Want to give it a try?" I did.

He nodded and smiled as the mainland crept out of view behind us and we continued on ahead over open water. Doc always carried a small black bag with him on these flights and looked very medical, until he put on his goggles and helmet.

"Just shinny on up there and use my gear. The binoculars are in the box on the right."

I followed his directions and slid open the hatch, slowly poking my head out and into the one-hundred-knot wind that was screaming across the plane's exterior. As I stood up with both my head and chest now exposed, the turbulence was terrific and was trying to blow me over, but after a few seconds of leaning in, I had my balance.

The roar past my ears muffled the engine noise as I scanned the area—the panorama of ocean, clouds, stars, and sky was brought to life by this extreme sensation of wind. A quarter moon lurked behind a cloud, and diffused light barely highlighted a small portion of the ripples centered on the ocean surface as I looked west. The land mass on the starboard side was as black as coal, but I could make out the surf and white sand profile of the island. It still seemed strange to never see so much as a light in any direction, including on board our Catalina. Only stars, when nights were clear enough. And occasionally, the silhouette of a ship passing beneath us would be visible, the glowing organisms in its wake exposing them and offering us a tempting target. But not tonight.

I suddenly had an odd thought. What if we flew into a flock of birds? Or even insects? What would a beetle smacking into my face at a hundred knots feel like? Maybe it would knock me down?

I felt a tug on my trouser leg, and there was Doc on his hands and knees, grinning up at me. "Had enough for the night?" he shouted through the hatch opening. I nodded, but was lying. I could have spent the whole night out there.

Chapter 13

"It's remarkable to me how reminiscent your flying boats, as you call them, were to early sailing ships with a crow's nest and all that."

Sandy agreed. "I can't believe you could stand up outside of a plane! It must have been like a hurricane."

"We were only going ninety-five or one-hundred knots most times. A hundred and fifteen in miles per hour. I dunno." Owen gave his head a thoughtful scratch. "What category wind would that be? Remember, it was just from the waist up. It wasn't like we were wing-walkers or something."

"True. I just think of some of the windstorms we get here. And blizzards." Sandy offered. "It just sounds…I never thought of *planes* as having human lookouts before."

"Fortunately for us, there was no *snow* involved. Nothing like a Minnesota winter."

The common thread of shared suffering—tales of hardship and woe brought to bear by the throes of snow, ice, wind, and sub-zero temperatures for months on end—was too much for the three Minnesotans to resist. The free-for-all was on.

"The Halloween Storm!" Sandy exclaimed.

"Oh, that was a beaut," Owen added.

"I had to take my sister trick-or-treating…" Dan groused. "All the sidewalks covered with snow. Pumpkins looked like little igloos."

"We've never even had a trick-or-treater out here," Owen said. "Long driveway and all. We didn't even know where the driveway *was* that year."

"By the third day, three feet of snow and by golly, that was a wind," Sandy said.

"Drifts. If a cow didn't move fast enough, the one next to him got buried!" Owen said.

"I had to take my sister trick-or-treating," Dan repeated.

Retelling stories about classic winter storms of years gone by was a favorite pastime, right up there with classic Vikings-Packers football games. Ping-pongish and masterfully embellished, enduring brutal winters was a keystone of state pride.

"Did you lake fish?" Dan asked.

"On and off I'd head over to the lake, cut a hole, set up a chair. But it was hard to find the time around here to wait for something to swim by. You?" Owen asked.

"Never did. Speaking of swimming, I guess we've drifted away from our topic." Dan reassessed. "Storms…anything interesting ever happen in the Pacific, flying through a storm, that kind of thing?"

"Oh sure, we flew through storms all the time. That PBY was one tough aircraft. There was one trip though…"

Owen recalled an island, maybe Peleliu, where they landed after being buffeted around in the plane so long they were thrilled to get back on the ground. The island was still a dangerous place, with cave dwellers scattered throughout the hills, resisting the weeks of flamethrowers and even napalm thrown their way. Vigilantes moved about by night.

On this particular afternoon, it appeared the Japanese might be the least of their worries given that the aircraft made its approach to the airstrip swiveled some forty-five degrees off line with it, the pilots fighting through the severe crosswind. After bouncing down the runway, they taxied over toward operations and disembarked, only to be told by shouting field personnel to "tie the plane down and get inside!"

Owen's tenor didn't conceal his bewilderment. "We asked, 'Inside where? Where are the barracks?' and they told us, 'Your plane is your barracks!'"

CHAPTER 13

The wind was building by the minute and had already blown down most of the tents on the island, so all available space in structures was taken.

"Then it became crystal clear," Owen continued. "He told us a big typhoon was moving in and it had scared off the entire fleet. We needed to tie the plane down and ride it out in there."

The field officer had ground crews moving bombs—the biggest they had—out and into clusters around the planes. He instructed Owen's group to chain the plane down from every point they could.

"He told us to send a man over to the storeroom for some 10-for-1 rations," he went on. "That was supposed to replace that hot meal we had been dreaming about for hours. The stuff was supposed to feed ten men for one day. It didn't."

The crew circled the plane, anchoring it to the bombs as securely as possible, then hustled inside. The old girl was bouncing as if she was in flight, but so far, they weren't moving anywhere.

"The plane wasn't supposed to leak," Owen said, "but that night, it leaked like a sieve. It was next to impossible to sleep." He shook his head. "After a couple of hours, I looked over at my friend, Johnny, and told him I was about ready to take my chances down in one of those caves."

Sandy was impressed. "I had no idea. So which was worse, standing up in the nose or running around with chains on the runway?" she giggled.

Owen laughed. "Not sure. We were inside through the worst of it. I think it might be the strongest wind I've ever felt...open airstrip on a small island. Very exposed. But it was a long time ago." He shifted in his seat. "At least no one shot at us. The wind kept 'em in the caves."

His comment piqued Dan's curiosity. "Did *you* ever get shot down?"

"Uh, not by the Japanese. Oh, we got some holes in us enough times." He frowned. "But you know what was almost worse? Running out of gas. Seems like we were always stretching the limits." He drew his lips into a clench, a look of exasperation.

"I told you earlier about getting from Brisbane to Perth…we had to watch our flight distance and land because fuel wasn't available just anywhere. Fueling with buckets…if you can imagine that."

"Because at the outbreak of the war, there just wasn't enough to go around," Sandy said, recalling Owen's earlier story.

Dan followed up. "But it wasn't a problem once things got going down there, right?"

"Gas was really expensive, even in Perth. You'd see taxis and autos driving around…using charcoal burners on their rooftops for power."

Sandy did a double take. "Coal? Really."

"Yep. Sometimes the burner was attached to the trunk. Along with a generator or radiator or something. Looked like a couple of four foot tall canisters."

"But the planes," Dan wondered. "They were running short of fuel."

"It was complicated." Owen reminded them that missions were so long—ten, twelve, even fifteen hours. Then something unforeseen would happen—the radioman would pick up a distress call on the way home, or a storm gave them headwinds they hadn't counted on. Pushing the planes to the edge of their range was common among the crews, even when they left with a full tank. "It seems like we were always coming in on fumes. The poor flight engineers were up there…leaning out the engines…trying to stretch it, until sometimes we'd barely be able to stay in the air. And sometimes…we didn't." Owen grinned. "It happened a lot."

*Perth and the Indian Ocean
north of Australia - 1943*

—∞— Chapter 14 —∞—

Practice, practice, practice. We spend our days and many nights in training, orientations, rehearsals. It's hard not to get antsy, our appetite for the next step, the real thing, gets sharper with each passing day. Yet, so much of what we do involves waiting. Waiting for our turn to fly, waiting to arrive at some mysterious far away destination that may or may not include sighting so much as a fishing trawler. Waiting for orders. For now, it's mostly about practice and long, uneventful search missions.

Tonight, two lines of small lights are set up in a lagoon along the Swan River, supposedly representing a landing zone. Except you can't see any surface. It's like they're floating in thin air, but it doesn't matter, because it's where we are supposed to land.

The tall, old church steeple on the hill is our landmark, and we slowly curl around it and get lined up on the lights for an approach. In the darkened cabin, I can't make out my hand at the end of my arm, much less Bob in the blister across from me. The pilots are now using instruments, watching airspeed and altitude closely and guiding us lower and lower to the water that must be there someplace. They change the PBY's landing attitude, the nose is slightly up and the step of the plane, its belly, is slightly lower. Steadily, we lose altitude and the lights get closer. Then suddenly, as if by magic, the fuselage below my seat in the blister is alive, squealing with the sound of the river. The nose drops and we splash in, smooth and easy, and quickly slow to a taxi. If I look out through the glass of the hatch, I can now see the reflection of a "runway" light chopped into many by the river's countless small waves and swells.

It was time to do it again. Day after tomorrow, we head north to have a look around.

The sky was a dusty mess as we left the Australian mainland. Winds across the desert interior carried clouds of the stuff, and our view of the ocean surface became more khaki than pewter as darkness closed in. Within an hour, a light rain improved things considerably, and I settled back against the blister and pulled out a candy bar. I looked over at Bob and hopped across the waist to the port side so he could hear me. I gestured with a piece of chocolate. He politely shook me off, "No thanks."

"What are you going to do first when we get home?" I asked.

He smiled, "That's easy. Can't wait to see my girlfriend. Go out on the town!"

I grinned back at him. Must be nice to have a girl waiting for you. I'd only met one the whole time I'd been in the South Pacific, an Australian girl in Brisbane. We had coffee and talked for hours. But it seemed more like I was talking with a sister, sharing heartfelt concerns about the war or family. There just didn't seem to be any romance attached. Still, it was nice to sit with a girl for a while and just talk. This can be kind of a lonely place, even with a whole army around you.

We did our usual search vector and were getting ready to turn around when Bob spots a Betty. Not the girl—the Japanese bomber. He throws open the blister hatch and reports, "Skipper, we have company, port side."

We circled slowly around and so did the Betty, sizing us up. We were reluctant to change heading and have him get behind us. He was faster with similar firepower, but he must have been thinking the same thing. So round and round we went. He finally broke it off and headed to the north of us. Walt, our pilot, pursued him for a few minutes, but bit by bit, we were outdistanced and he disappeared into the evening horizon. We banked and took up a southern heading toward home.

CHAPTER 14

About an hour had passed, and we found the drizzle again.

"Gonna get a little bumpy fellas. We were just getting clear of this drizzle and ran right into a whopper of a thunderhead. I'm going to try to get us around the squall."

It did get bumpy. Five foot bumps. Then ten, each drop coming with an unsettling but familiar, jackhammer jolt. After another hour of this, I heard Williams, the flight engineer, over the headset. "We are dead into this thing, sir. We're still burning through the fuel and I can't lean it anymore with all this headwind."

"Will it be any better if we can find a way around it? It'll add distance."

"We'll get blown off course and use even more fuel. We need to maintain our heading, maybe get below it," Samuels, our navigator, advised.

"We can't make it," Williams cut in. "I can tell you that right now. We better start thinking of how we can set her down."

We maintained our heading, and gradually dropped down to about two hundred feet. I could see the tiny flashes of white foam from thousands of whitecaps looming below in the darkness. After another thirty minutes had passed, I heard someone call my name.

"Trimbel, toss out a flare, then everybody tie yourselves in. This will be a rough one."

Even with the flare, you couldn't really make out the surface with all of the rain. He was flying blind. Could this be it?

It was a thunderous crash, like we had plowed into a lake of glass marbles. The fuselage went in like a submarine, clear up to the engines, and gear flew all around the cabin. Then we popped up and thudded down again, rocking side to side and skidding over each swell with both engines stopped.

"Everybody all right?" came a voice across the headsets of those who still had them after the landing. As brutal as the plunge was, we seemed to be floating and the leaks into the cabin were mostly from popped rivets. The leaking water drained toward the bilges.

We bobbed up and down for the balance of the night. I was grateful we weren't in a raft as the sun broke the horizon. It was really choppy out there. We took a parachute out of the rear of the PBY and spread it over the tail hoping to make us more visible to a passing plane. At 0900, a U.S. Army transport flew over, and it was soon obvious they hadn't seen us. An hour later, another army aircraft, a bomber, went over, but was at altitude. We were almost invisible, but the good news was that friendly planes were in the area.

Another hour passed, and there it was. A Navy PBY knew we were somewhere in the quadrant, and those guys were damn good at looking. Carl, our radioman, was immediately in contact and they honed in on us in no time. Now what?

The squall was long gone, but it was still pretty rugged. The pilots from both planes agreed another landing would be needed, but at least these fellows could see what they were landing in. They had no problems and taxied over to us and we tied off.

Bob and I wrestled one of the rafts out of the tail, and floated it over to the other plane. We spent the next hour shuttling cans of fuel and adding them to our tanks, until we reckoned we were good to make it home.

The engines were finicky, but caught, and the pilots warmed them a good long time before taxiing over to a swell.

I found myself thinking the sight of some dry, dusty land would be…refreshing.

Chapter 15

A phone was ringing somewhere in the hallway and Sandy excused herself for a moment. Dan was still brimming with questions, and hoped she wouldn't mind if he continued, but before he could open his mouth, she returned, hand covering the phone, and said in a loud whisper, "Dad, it's Clark Pierson. Shall I have him call you back?"

"Clark! No, I'll take it." She handed him a long-in-the-tooth, cordless handset that reminded Dan of something he used in high school.

Owen placed the antique earpiece up to his ear. "Clark, you old fart! How the hell are you?" The two of them exchanged a few more choice words at a decibel level Dan mentally compared to an announcer at a boxing match. "Well, listen, I've got to go. I've got a guy over here interviewing me…Yeah…no, not for a book, he's a mortician. We're working on the inscription for my gravestone…You've already done yours? A recipe! I wish I'd thought of that. I might go with 'My tooth is killing me.' What do you think?" Owen's face flushed and wrinkled in laughter as the two men wrapped it up. "Thanks for calling…You betcha, bye."

Dan had to ask. "So how old is he?"

"Ninety-two. He's like a son to me."

Sandy took a seat and rolled her eyes at Dan.

"I've found my sense of humor has changed a little since I quit going to funerals. For years it seemed it was about the only time I got out of the house. So where are we?"

Dan shook his head with a smile. "Well, I was hoping to learn a little more about your early missions and the night flying," he said, looking at his notepad. "You talked about the plankton and locating ships. And you mentioned radar. Tell me about that?"

"We were about the first planes to have it on board. It wasn't much more than hazy green lines and blips on a tiny screen." He chuckled. "A radioman would squint at it like he was reading your palm. It gave you a basic idea where islands were. Or even other objects, like planes or mountains, weather systems...if they weren't too far away. There was an antenna fore and aft, but the range was limited."

"Interesting. A PBY had this but the Japanese did not."

"Not yet. I don't think they saw the value early on in the war. They did things very differently." He rubbed a finger under his nostrils with a brief, sawing motion. "Much of their approach to the war was influenced by shortages of raw material. Big motivator...and they expanded into places where they could find more of what they didn't have enough of in the homeland. Their rifles were primitive, storage containers were painstakingly made from wood." He slid forward in his chair for emphasis. "We even saw unexploded hand grenades made from porcelain. Pottery! Looked like they belonged on a coffee table." He sat back. "They both envied and feared America's industrial might."

Dan could tell the old man spoke with pride as he summed up his view of the differences between the two combatants. His voice was crisp as he fondly characterized the squadron's Catalinas. "We also had an improved altimeter. It worked on radio rather than pressure." He explained that pressure altimeters had accuracy problems—weather, elevation of the surface you were flying over, location. "You'd fly a couple hundred miles and they'd be wrong. Ours could measure distance down to sea level pretty closely, and at night it made all the difference. Our planes were slow...but no one would chase us if we skimmed the water in the dark for fear of crashing into it."

"Dad, I've always wondered about the seaplanes. Didn't you say you could sleep on board them? They had beds or something?" Sandy asked.

Owen nodded. "They did. There were several bunks that folded out and we took turns sleeping." He told them that for those monstrous, twelve or fifteen hour flights three guys who knew

CHAPTER 15

how to fly were required, and they all took turns resting up. They often landed in a bay or near a remote island, and there, a seaplane tender would take care of them. Like a mom and her chicks. "We'd tie the plane up to a buoy and eat and sleep on the tender."

"The seaplane tenders were specifically designed for the PBYs?" Dan said, restating what he suspected.

"Some were refashioned from oil tankers. But yeah, there were a bunch of them out there the Black Cats depended on." He mentioned several examples of the smaller type that could provide crews with the basics, like the *San Pablo*, the *Half Moon,* and the *Orca*. "My favorite was the *Tangiers*. She was a big ship and could service our Catalinas right up on the deck. They could hoist three of them up there and work on all of 'em at once." He grinned. "They took care of our food, ammunition, everything. Clean sheets. Even had an ice cream machine."

"You and your ice cream," Sandy teased.

"Well, I never ate it much until I tasted theirs," he countered. "The *Tangiers* was at Pearl the same time as I was. They told us they were the first to return fire at the Japanese aircraft that day. It was a miracle she wasn't hit—she was full of gas and would have blown sky-high."

"You must have gotten pretty close with the members of your crew," Sandy observed. "Were you always together or did you split up sometimes?"

"Sometimes we swapped. A plane's crew might be short a guy. It changed things." Owen closed his eyes for an instant. "It could…really change things…"

THE LAST WORD

September of 1943

—ᨆ— Chapter 16 —ᨆ—

It was a strange feeling, walking across the gangway to the launch with a group of fliers I didn't really know. I had become pretty tight with my group, but tonight was different. This crew had a guy out sick with malaria or something. Someone was always coming down with a case of intestinal this or insect borne that. I got pegged as a replacement. I was tired too. We had flown last night on a long boring mission that accomplished only one thing. We now knew no Japanese were in that area. Fish maybe, but no sign of a Jap.

I looked over into the launch and was surprised to see Jim! He was pulling some supplies on board. We each recognized the other at the same time.

"Howdy," he said with a conspicuous grin. "Joining us tonight?"

"Looks that way. You guys know how to fly one of these things?"

"Not really. The pilot sleeps most of the time anyway, so we all take turns. Joe over there is great with his feet."

"Sounds exciting. See you on board." I went back for another armload of gear.

Each plane and crew has its own set of idiosyncrasies. There might be complaints about noise, not being in shape, or how things stunk in there once in a while. You just weren't sure if it was the plane or the guys in it that were being complained about. So a new crew and plane, even for one night, could present its own adventures and challenges. This group seemed like a pretty solid bunch.

I sat in the port blister, across from Jim, and once in a while we'd shout something across to each other, just to keep it interesting. He told me that some coastwatchers had phoned in a location where a convoy was being made up and that would be our target. Two other planes were fanned out and searching as well.

There was a heads up over the intercom—the pilots had sighted some lights ahead on the horizon and we were to make ready. We swung up the glass and spun our guns into position. As we came closer, someone realized it was a Japanese hospital ship, brightly illuminated to identify it. The pilot put us into a steep bank and we turned away to resume the search. We'd hardly got straightened out, when there was the convoy! The glimmering wakes below indicated the position of the ships. We had our target.

One of the other planes went in first. We were at a thousand feet or so and came around to begin our run. There was always a rush of excitement as the ships came into view. The pilot cut back the throttles and went into a near silent glide. The sound of the wind racing by the gun barrel increased with our airspeed, and things began to rattle and shake all around us as the plane dove. Forward of us, the navigator tracked the altitude and the radioman intently watched the radar screen. The navigator shouted "pull up, pull up!" as we reached near masthead height, maybe a hundred feet, and dropped our bombs. It was hard to tell, but it seemed we may have had a hit as we sped up and away from it.

Tracers rushed toward us from everywhere, the ships of the convoy and six gunboat escorts all firing up at us at once. Suddenly, there was a loud noise in the forward compartment of the plane as a shell crashed through the floor and hit the radioman in the knee and blew up.

He was in rough shape. It had shattered his knee and jagged fragments of shrapnel had scattered all through him. Jim, the engineer, and a third guy went right to work. They moved him to a bunk and gave him a shot of morphine. The three of them took turns pinching a large vein in his leg and soon Jim's elbows

CHAPTER 16

had this fellow's blood dripping from them. They struggled to get him cleaned up and stable, from midnight to almost 0700 in the morning, but it looked hopeless. There was a hospital ship in a harbor called Finschhafen, and the pilot made for that. When we arrived, they were ready and waiting and rushed him into surgery.

We all stood around feeling empty. I had never even met the guy before, but…what a sense of loss. Jim looked at me briefly, his uniform crusted and stained, and understood what was going through my mind. He said, "We did everything we could for him. It's out of our hands now."

THE LAST WORD

Chapter 17

Sandy's voice rang out from the kitchen. "Bilge! Come and get it!

He was up in a flash, and bounded out of the room like a three-legged greyhound.

"I've had dogs all of my life. Every make and model. Never anything like this one," Owen said, as Sandy returned to her seat. "Smart, obedient, and above all...loyal. He would take a bullet for me. In fact, in a way, he already has."

Owen cleared his throat and took a sip from his water glass. "About five years ago, some lowlife-types found their way onto the property. They rummaged around in the barn, then came up to the house and tried a window or two. In summer, we leave them open during the day and sometimes forget to lock up." He tipped his head back, as if the memory of that evening was somewhere above him. He then recalled it was around midnight when Sandy came running into his room, plenty scared. "They wriggled through the window and were snooping around when Bilge walked in on them. We didn't know exactly what was happening, but heard a commotion and a lot of screaming."

There was a crash and Bilge apparently jumped through the window after them. "Had a hold of one of them, too. Later, we found a scrap of his trousers." Owen pulled his rifle out of the closet, and Sandy helped him cautiously make his way down the hall. They could see a struggle had taken place right there in the kitchen. One of the intruders must have hit Bilge with a crowbar or bat, no one was ever sure.

"We heard Bilge panting and he whined a little in between, but not much."

Sandy cut in. "His leg was…well, it wasn't good. A sheriff's patrol car was nearby when I called and was here in minutes."

Dan listened with a different appreciation of this beast he found so intimidating only a short time ago. Sandy said the sheriff gave them an escort all the way to the animal hospital near Bemidji where they took him right into surgery.

Bilge strolled in as she spoke, a three-legged warrior with his tongue busily removing the final morsels from his lips.

"They needed to take his leg. He had a rough couple of months, but he did great. He's a survivor," she said.

On cue, Bilge yawned, as if to acknowledge it was all in a day's work. The three non-dogs quietly considered his ordeal, then Owen broke the silence.

"You know, Jim and I stayed in pretty close touch after we both got out. He was a regular at reunions, just like I was," he said, reflecting on his enduring admiration for the crewman on the plane the night the radioman was hit. "Yep. My first squadron, our first squadron, was much more active after I left it." Jim had told him that they relocated to Palm Island off the northeast coast of Australia. Then in no time, they moved north again to Samarai Island just south of New Guinea. By the fall of 1944, that group of Black Cats was in the midst of it, ahead of the allied wave and flying nightly missions deep into enemy territory. Jim was rightly proud of their accomplishments. For a time, they were finding Japanese ships and convoys most every night. And they sent thousands of tons of shipping to the bottom. It was like they couldn't help it. "In many ways, I wished I'd stayed with them."

Owen told Dan that he still remembered going to a mini-reunion many years ago in Tacoma, Washington. It was intended to be mostly radiomen, and it happens that Owen and his crew's radioman and radar guy, Carl, had been letter writers, and occasionally chatted on the phone. Carl said he didn't feel like going to this gathering alone, so they arranged to meet in Minneapolis and fly out together.

"Turns out quite a few other crewmen showed up, too. I was trying to get comfortable with the whole thing when, who do I

CHAPTER 17

see sitting at a table, but old Jim! He looked great, and we shook hands and exchanged a few insults." Owen hesitated and took a breath before continuing. "Then another fellow walked up to Jim with a big smile and extended his hand. I didn't recognize him, but Jim did. He was the one who was hit that night on the plane. He held Jim's hand in the handshake and simply said, 'Thank you for saving my life.' Jim's eyes welled up and he swallowed hard... moved his other hand over to his heart... He *almost* broke into tears... And *I did*."

Dan could see the emotion had not yet completely released Owen from that night's experience. Owen pulled a long teal handkerchief loose from a trouser pocket and blew his nose, then looked back at Dan as if to say, *"Well, ask me something dammit!"*

Dan snapped to and seized on the subject of reunions. He'd always been curious about them. Like most graduates, he'd attended occasional high school and college reunions, but had never been to anything military. If Owen was like so many of the war's veterans who had passed before him, then he likely never spoke much about his World War II experiences. Except at reunions. Gathered together with men who shared a bond, memories of times good and bad, reunions were a sanctuary where these experiences could be recalled, embellished, and relived. At least, that was what Dan suspected.

"Did you hesitate to talk about the war with your family?"

"Not really. I guess they might have thought I was keeping something in, but I don't think they ever really asked me much, so I never thought they were that interested."

"But didn't you feel pretty special when you got home? I mean, you guys were the heroes that pulled this whole thing off."

"Heroes? I don't think any of us felt that way. We were the lucky ones. We came home." Owen cocked his head and then gave it a considerate shake, side to side. "Some of the guys had it a lot harder than us. Infantry. Paratroops. We had our bad moments, but for some, well you can't blame 'em for clamming up. Who'd want to remember Omaha Beach? Bataan?"

"I see what you mean," Dan said, feeling he'd said something foolish.

"I like the way Lauren Bruner put it. He was one of the last three or four surviving members of the *Arizona* crew to pass away. He said something like, 'I chose to face the future and not let my past dictate what might be ahead.'" Owen shrugged his shoulders up and down. "Besides, there was so much happening in the years after the war. New vitality, different direction. Exciting new technologies like TV and better cars." His eyes danced. "Dishwashers! You'd appreciate one of those if you ever got kitchen duty on an island somewhere in ninety-five degree heat."

Owen found himself drawn to the reunions for many years. He was a little different in that he spent time in three different squadrons, but he had built lasting friendships and was tight with many members of each. He managed to attend one or another every couple of years. "They were a bunch of exceptional guys and I was lucky enough to serve with them. We had good times at the reunions."

Sandy's blue eyes beamed. "He even took me to one!"

Owen agreed. "Sure did. The first couple, it was mostly just a few of the guys and a lot of cocktails. Before long, quite a few of us were married and some of the wives took an interest. The organizers would come up with different destinations, cities to explore while we were there." He stopped and squeezed in a chuckle. "The guys swapped stories, the gals shopped! We affectionately called them the 'Pussy Cats.'"

"I always hated that name, Dad. You know that, right?" Sandy said in a vaguely exasperated tone.

"Not the daughters, mind you," Owen replied, trying to dig out. "Like I said, it was simply a term of endearment."

Sandy gave him a facetious glare, hands on hips. Owen shrewdly changed course.

"Yeah, we had 'em all over—Hawaii, California, Las Vegas, New Orleans. Some of us kept it up until, I think 2006. Hardly anyone at that one, so few of us left alive by then. Now I guess I could have my own reunion…anywhere I want."

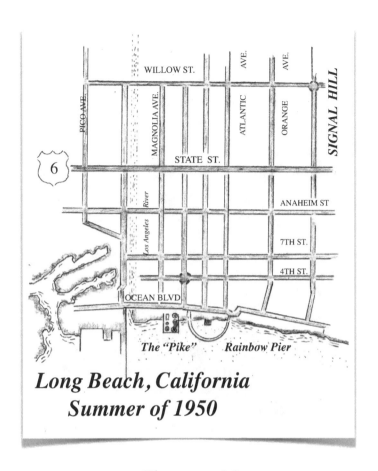

*Long Beach, California
Summer of 1950*

—∞— Chapter 18 —∞—

Six years, but it seemed much longer. It was good to see the guys again. I was sure I'd miss this reunion in Long Beach with a damn case of the chicken pox. Who gets chicken pox in their mid-twenties? I showed up sporting a few spots on my cheek and forehead and took plenty of ribbing. I told them it was from getting shot on a mission in the Liberator after I ditched those sloth-like PBYs that they kept flying. I'd moved on to bigger and better things. Got two purple hearts, I bragged. They weren't buying.

It had been an emotional day—on so many levels—and I'd spent nearly an hour walking around the Rainbow Pier trying to sort it out before the reunion even started. I was definitely looking for a distraction.

After it ended, a few of us decided to head over to the Pike Amusement Park before it closed and ride the Cyclone Racer. It was a beast of a roller coaster. I'd admired its complicated superstructure towering above the beach to the north as I walked the pier earlier. The track hurtled out across the water, way up on pilings, and the guys told me some of the steep downhill runs at night were worse than glide bombing a destroyer. They were right!

"I'm starved," I said, as we wobbled away from one of the bright red coaches and tried to find our sea legs.

Alex agreed. "Hot dogs! I can smell 'em." Our noses took us the rest of the way, and we forked over an entire quarter to get one of the measly things. At least they came with the works.

I was chewing my last bite when my ears perked to the sound of the carousel maybe fifty yards away. For some reason, I drifted toward it. "Hey Owen! Let's go up on the Racer again. See if we can keep these hot dogs down." I shook my head in agreement, but my concentration was elsewhere. Standing in front of the ticket booth was a vision of loveliness. I couldn't take my eyes off her. I tossed my napkin in the trash and hurried across the midway as she watched the wooden horses, green and red neon light rippling across her skirt.

"Hi," I stammered. "Quite a contraption."

She looked away from the horses and toward me and smiled. "Yes, very beautiful."

"Would you like to look around awhile? Maybe, I don't know, we could…"

"I'll have to ask my mother," she said, to my surprise. "That's her over there."

"Ugh," I thought to myself. "OK. Sure."

She came back a long minute later and told me she had permission to ride the carousel, but that was it since I was a total stranger.

CHAPTER 18

I rifled through my pockets for a nickel and gave it to the carousel operator. "Here you go," and I handed her my freshly bought ticket.

"Aren't you going to get on a horse?"

I could see the guys over in the shadows laughing it up and going up and down like they were already on one. "Why don't you go first? I'll get on the next one."

She handed her ticket to the attendant and stepped up to select just the right steed. Her hair, cut shoulder length, was brown or reddish—it was difficult to say under the carousel's spectrum. But it was held in place with a pink headband that pressed her hair down just above her forehead. Her dress was a colorful plaid check, drawn in around her tiny waist, with a wide strap over each bare shoulder. It flared out when she abruptly turned to face a palomino. "Aren't you going to help me?" she asked coyly.

"Oh…yes. Of course. I…I'll have to get a ticket. Be right back." I could see her mother on one side of the merry-go-round, her eyes narrow and scrutinizing. On the other, three ex-military morons, doubled over and pointing.

With the ticket business behind me, I bounded up to assist, lifting her by that tiny waist as she bounced up into the saddle. She was a feather.

"Your face. Did you get stung?" she inquired.

It just kept getting worse. I had to come up with something to keep from looking like a complete jackass. I had an idea.

"You go first and I'll pick myself a little colt over on the other side. Let's see if I can catch you," I suggested.

"Huh?" she giggled. "Alrighty, then. Let's go!"

I ambled over to the opposite edge of the platform until I was sure I was out of sight, then hopped down and trotted over to a concession. There were shelves of stuffed animals—bears, giraffes, pigs—all kinds of critters. Then I saw it. A horse! "How much?"

"You gotta win it, Bud."

"I don't want to play, I just want the horse."

"Ticket is twenty cents for ten shots. Hit the whole top row and you win a prize."

I reached into my pocket and pulled out the two dimes. He handed me a puny pellet gun with a loose gunstock. It didn't even have a sight. "I shoot with this?" He nodded.

I took a deep breath and started firing. Ten seconds later there were ten dead ducks across the top row. "I'll take the horse please."

"Goddammit, Bud. Who are you anyway," he asked, as he handed over the prize.

I could hear the music beginning to play at the carousel. "A Navy gunner," I hollered over my shoulder, and I hustled back.

I scrambled aboard, undetected, and tip-toed up to a vacant horse, but still out of view. It was late enough in the evening that the outside row was nearly empty. As my pony came up beside the brass ring dispenser, I thrust the stuffed horse behind it, and scurried forward another steed or two so I could watch. She came around with her arm extended and snatched up the prize with a squeal, flashing me a glance. Now she could see I was gaining on her. In another two revolutions, I'd made my way up to the mule. It was right behind her palomino. This delighted her all the more.

As the carousel slowly began to lose its steam, I hopped off of the mule and tapped her right shoulder, quickly leaping into the saddle of the adjacent bronc to her left. When she spun her head back toward me, I saw a smile that reached past the dimples on her cheeks all the way up to her ears.

"Told you, I'd catch you!" I said triumphantly.

"How'd you do that?" she said, eyes twinkling. "You don't give up easy, do you?"

Chapter 19

"How about I make us some sandwiches? You boys like something?" Bilge looked up, his ears perked. "Not you! You've had yours." He dropped his head with a huff.

The two other males nodded their approval and Sandy collected the stray glasses. "Back in a jiffy!"

Dan found himself admiring the spring in Sandy's step. He had trouble wrapping his head around the idea that she was already in her eighties. "Owen, you've mentioned three squadrons. It sounds like you moved around quite a lot," he said.

"I did. Kind of a funny thing. I was with the first group right out of training. South America and the long trip to Perth. We flew from there for a couple months, give or take…worked on our technique, bombed, did a little search and rescue, and hours of patrols…just looking." He pointed to the map on the wall. "Then word came that we would be moving to Darwin later in the year, and our crew was instructed to land there on the way back from a mission. Right up there, almost dead center on Australia's north coast."

Owen recalled an officer, maybe a captain or even rear admiral that needed a ride. Except he was headed due north, toward New Guinea, with a load of equipment. "Mostly beer. We got tagged giving him a lift up there to a little bay called Namoia."

Namoia Bay was a small harbor on an island along the south coast of New Guinea. The idea was to fly up and stay the night at a tender there called the *Half Moon*. The ship served as the base for another group of Black Cats who flew patrols to New Britain, New Ireland, and locations throughout the Bismarck Sea. Owen and a crewman were exploring the ship and with stomachs growling, asked directions to the mess hall. They strolled in and Owen stopped in his tracks.

"I walked smack into Johnny. Remember, he's the young looking guy I met at Pearl Harbor who thought I should sign up? We gave each other a backslap and talked for twenty minutes or so. They lost their plane December 7, but the rest of his crew made it out unhurt. He felt real bad about Paul."

Dan reacted, "What are the chances? Did you ever run into him again?" He noticed Owen seemed to fidget in his chair and wondered if he was tiring.

"His group lost some crew members. I forget if it was Dengue Fever or if they were injured or killed. He said they saw a lot of action before we even arrived." Owen motioned, matter-of-factly. "They were short a couple of gunners and were talking with our group about possible replacements. They asked for volunteers, and while I didn't really want to leave my crew, I had always felt a kinship with Johnny. When no one else spoke up, I said I'd do it."

Sandy walked in with a portable table and snapped the legs into position, then swung a tray heaped with goodies into view with the ease of a seasoned waitress.

"Wow," the two said at once. On the generous serving tray was a piled high platter of deli sandwich wedges, sliced small and on rye, nestled alongside saucers of applesauce, baby carrots, and celery sticks. Ranch dressing and baby dill pickles completed the entree.

"Dan, like a ginger ale, water, anything?"

"Ginger ale, thank you. This is fantastic," he said arranging his plate. "Owen was just telling me about changing squadrons."

"Oh. Which time?" Sandy inquired.

"I was with my new Black Cat unit until the first tour ended about the first of the year. We flew back to Brisbane, then went by ship from Australia to the states for leave. Then retraining. That's when Johnny and I decided to see if we could move into another aircraft for the second tour." With an inelegant flip of the wrist, Owen tossed a scrap of crust toward Bilge, who snapped it up in midair like a largemouth bass.

CHAPTER 19

"Ahh. Well, so I don't get lost, your second Black Cat group. How were they different?" Dan wondered.

"I lucked out. It was a great bunch of guys. And Johnny and I were in the same plane most nights. Our pilot was very experienced and the flight engineer and nose gunner were easy to talk to. I adjusted in no time."

THE LAST WORD

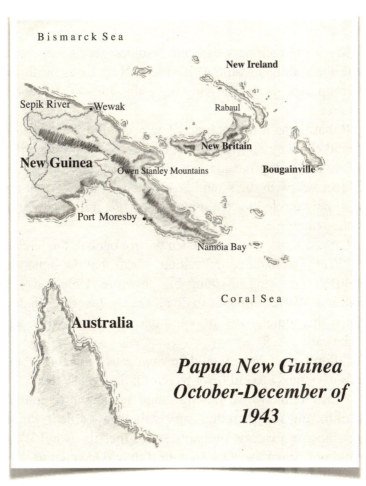

*Papua New Guinea
October-December of
1943*

—⚡— Chapter 20 —⚡—

I noticed almost immediately that there was a lot of frustration brewing here. I didn't know many of the guys yet, other than Johnny, but you could sense it from the conversations and sarcastic comments.

Back with my other squadron mates, most of our work was patrolling and preparation, but so far, there had only been limited interaction with the Japanese. Perth was a long way from enemy territory, and our role there, early on, felt more like we were the guard dogs.

My crew members then all assumed when we eventually moved north, things would be different. Now I was north. With a new group. And we were flying night missions in new and unfamiliar areas.

Rabaul was a hotspot, and I was excited the first night as we found our way up there in the darkness. A hum went through the plane as we approached a pair of destroyers, gliding silently, 2,000 feet below in the pitch black waters. We flew right on past them, slowly circled for ten minutes nearly a mile away, and then continued on home.

I asked Johnny about it when we got back to the tender.

"Yeah, it's damned infuriating. I hear that the brass doesn't want PBYs attacking anything big anymore. Unless we get attacked first. We're supposed to do all the hard work of finding the bastards, then quietly call it in and leave. Let the Army come in and take care of it."

I didn't get it. Why would they make us carry three thousand pounds of bombs around if we weren't going to use them?

"They think we're too slow and vulnerable, I guess. But some of the guys say that the Army isn't always able to follow up. Those ships we just saw probably sailed merrily away! We could have put one down the stack tonight if they'd have let us."

That was pure Johnny. Always an optimist. Of course, he'd had a lot more experience than me at this point. He wasn't a big guy, but he had almost movie star good looks. A sort of Errol Flynn energy to him, and I figured he probably drove the girls crazy. But he said the only girl for him was back home and awaiting his return. Lucky stiff.

Sure, I was the new kid on the block, but Johnny was my next door neighbor in the port-side blister. Not only was he a good shot, he was popular with the guys. He seemed to want to take me under his wing and was proud of his squadron. So hanging around with him made it easier for me from the get-go, and I could feel the kinship between us growing.

CHAPTER 20

We were lounging around the mess hall when this chap named Bill walked in, sat down, and lit up a cigarette. They'd just returned from a ten-hour mission off the west coast of New Britain and had flown over a small convoy. And they attacked it!

"It was so sweet! We caught the biggest of them amidship. Bam! Pieces flew everywhere."

"You went in on it?" Johnny asked in disbelief.

"Orders have changed," he said as he exhaled, sending a quivering ring of smoke toward the table. "The Cat's claws...have been sharpened."

It was my third mission, a long slog up near Rabaul again. It was a clear night with calm seas, and the countless stars seemed attached to the glass surface of the blister hatches above our heads. As we slid each of them open, Johnny shouted over at me, "I have a feeling about this one," as if he could sense it. We approached the harbor up moon and I was bathed in light pouring in through the starboard blister. Suddenly, the buzz began again. The radioman had something on the screen. We banked and I joined Johnny to have a look from the port side. "A tanker or something, maybe 8,000 tons," was down there, I heard over the headset. Our skipper lined up for a glide run and I didn't think we'd been spotted. As the Catalina roared over the masts, we could see enough of the vessel to recognize it was an enemy merchantman—probably crammed with cargo and very heavily armed. Just as our bombs started exploding, their shells started flying, and we dropped to the ocean surface and slowly climbed back out for another pass.

"Did we hit anything?" Johnny asked.

"Can't tell. I think, maybe." We squared around, and with our bombs gone, it was on us. The pilots began another glide run and began to sideslip so my blister had first crack at it. I started firing, following the tracer line with my eyes and moving it around. The tracers started bouncing off of the deck, but they knew where we were now by following the line back up to us. The anti-aircraft was fierce, unlike anything I'd ever seen, and I held my breath and kept firing as we soared over it and again dropped down.

We climbed and banked in an effort to get clear of them. I looked across at Johnny, just as a stream of tracer fire flew up from below and through the portside wing behind him. He ducked as pieces of the wing's skin flew past and scattered against the open blister's glass.

As the plane came around, we could see the vessel had beached and was afire. We finally were out of range—at least they had stopped shooting at us. Over my headset, our skipper made the call.

"Good work boys. Let's get out of here."

I dropped down into the seat, my heart racing and breathing in great huffs. I looked down at my hands. They were shaking. It wasn't that I was scared—I hadn't had the time. I'd been squeezing the .50 caliber's vibrating handles so hard that my poor hands didn't know yet that I'd stopped shooting.

Chapter 21

"Maybe this is a good stopping point for us today, Owen. I don't want to wear you out."

"Oh, I'm doing pretty well, Dan. I enjoy visiting, talking about the old days. You're probably right though," he replied, covering a yawn with his hand.

"So we're on for another session tomorrow?" Dan asked.

"What do you think, Sandy? Shall we let him in again?"

"Whatever you think, Dad. LaTeesha should be here any minute to get your dressing changed and therapy started. So yes, we should call it a day."

There was a knock on the door and Bilge rushed into the hallway.

"Guess who? It's your…Bilge! You get them big feet offa me, right now! And don't be givin' me any of your lip either. Now you get that butt back in that chair or we gonna tangle!" Bilge bolted back into the study and shrank into his safe place.

LaTeesha had arrived. Elegant, petite, soft spoken—LaTeesha was none of these. With the stride of a roller derby queen and a booming voice to match, she was thick in body but not in mind. Her face, a collection of high cheekbones, ruby lips, and brilliant white teeth, she was the kind of woman that could transform the mood of a room. Sometimes you felt as though you were sitting at a table in a comedy club; other times, like you were sitting in the witness chair at your own court martial.

"How are you, Mr. Owen? You lookin' good today! Got some company to tell me about?"

Owen smiled half-heartedly. It was hard not to get a kick out of LaTeesha, but from his standpoint, she kicked back. He had come to dread his daily routine with her—a marathon of cleansing, walking, and standing exercises, prodding and poking. He tried to throw her off the scent. "Meet Dan. He's here to interview me and we are…busy." He looked at her, hopefully.

"Pleased to meet you, Dan. Might I interrupt you two? It's time for Mr. Owen's medication."

"Oh, of course. We can take a break if…" Dan stopped as he saw Owen's expression and subtle shake of his head. He tried to walk it back. "…if you need your pills…Owen."

"Oh lordy, yes, I got two fistful of pills for you today. Hope you hungry," she added, tugging her coat free of her shoulder. "Be right back. Don't you run off now."

With that she marched into the hallway and Owen breathed a sigh of relief. "Dodged a bullet there," he groaned. "I've got one more story I wanted to tell you before you leave…It would help me out. LaTeesha is *in the building*."

"I heard that! Too late. You mine now!" she gushed as she swept back into the room.

"Uh…Well, I could use a bladder drain…How about we compromise," he said, squirming in his chair.

She considered his plea. "You lucky. I have some chores I need to do in the bedroom anyway. Let's get you up and onto the *throne*."

With that, she took hold of the folded wheelchair and smartly snapped it into position, then used her considerable girth to leverage Owen into it, adeptly positioned his feet and hands before *whizzing* him away.

"Wheeee." His voice faded into the hallway.

"She really is a godsend," Sandy remarked. "She has quite a story of her own, you know."

"Do tell." Dan said.

Sandy first met LaTeesha on a trip with Owen over to the medical center for some testing—had it been ten years ago? LaTeesha was working part time there and exploring other avenues, including a position as a caregiver with a local startup. Sandy had been

CHAPTER 21

impressed with her professionalism, her ability to handle Owen, and how could you ignore her personality? It hadn't always been so easy for LaTeesha.

Coming from a Chicago neighborhood better known for the drugs they used than the ones they dispensed, she went to night school and juggled caring for her mom and little brother with a job bagging groceries. As the months and years passed, it wore her down. But LaTeesha was someone who always managed to land on her feet. Her mom passed—she was much too young. Her brother grew up hard-nosed—met a girl and moved in with her. He was driving cabs for a living when LaTeesha decided it was time to make her own new start.

A hospital in Minnesota was hiring and she applied for the position. She got an interview, and although her resume was short on experience and credentials, she made an impression. They hired her as a part time aide and assistant working with the elderly. It wasn't much more than a foot in the door, but LaTeesha had a size eleven.

Then came the curve ball she never saw coming. Her brother had been shot, a late night cab fare gone wrong. He was clinging to life and she needed to leave. But as a probationary employee, her position at the hospital wasn't secure. She lost her job and her brother in three days.

Two weeks later she had a light-bulb moment. Chicago held nothing for her anymore, and she had been happy in Minnesota while it lasted. This time, she was all in.

The medical center where she had been working had no positions available, but she followed up every few days. An entry level, part-time position while a staff member was on maternity leave surfaced. It would mean starting at the absolute, below bedpan-washer, gluteus maximus bottom again. But she took it.

Her caregiving skills were largely wasted, except for occasions where she assisted one of the nurses. Eventually, someone put in a good word for her. Soon she was meeting patients in the waiting room and escorting them back to exam rooms, taking blood pressure, and asking all those annoying preliminary questions.

One day, a kindly old man and his daughter were in the waiting room, working at the jigsaw puzzle table when she walked in. She glanced at the electronic chart. *Birth date 1926!* There wasn't any doubt who she was looking for.

"I'll bet that piece you have would go right there," she said warmly.

Owen reached across to try it. "Son of a gun. Don't tell me you could see that!"

"Oh my, I do a lot of puzzles! Kind of a hobby. My name is LaTeesha. And you must be Owen."

"I don't know what I'd do without her," Sandy said. She just keeps him going." A kitchen timer interrupted. "That must be his special 'milkshake.' I'll be right back."

Dan stood and stretched, and rolled his head around to loosen his neck. *Very comfortable room,* he thought to himself as he idly examined the bookshelves and wall hangings. One shelf was entirely military books, as you might expect. Owen had it arranged in three sections, perhaps to mimic his own service participation. Dan read the titles from several book spines—*Black Cat Raiders; Sketches of a Black Cat; PBY, The Catalina Flying Boat* and four others would seem to represent his first tour experiences. Then came a larger section for B-24s. This included *Unbroken, Two Gold Coins and a Prayer,* and *The Mission—Jimmy Stewart and the Fight for Europe.* The third section was devoted to an assortment of World War II editions from around the globe, a mix of both famous and obscure authors.

A pair of vintage dueling pistols, wooden handles polished and gleaming, were mounted adjacent to a powder horn adorned with swirly metal work and hung by a leather strap.

Stacked tightly on the shelf below was an assortment of colorful publications, assorted sizes varying from small paperback to massive coffee table books that acted as bookends. He pulled one out. *The Cottage Garden.* Others were about greenhouse construction, plant identification, or garden maintenance, like *Garden Insect, Disease, and Weed.* Next was a small collection of books

CHAPTER 21

about roses. Adjacent to it, like another bookend, was a framed document, manila-colored with handsome calligraphy. *Owen Trimbel, Best in Show, 'Sandy's Treasure,' Minnesota State Fair.* "How cool," he said to himself. "*Sandy's Treasure.* It's a rose."

Dan picked up the award and studied it. "I wonder. What was your nursery like, Owen, way back then?" he said to himself. "When you were just getting started…"

THE LAST WORD

~ Chapter 22 ~

I was beat. I didn't think I could lift another bale of peat moss into that barn, but Dad's old flatbed was unloaded and I was ready for a break. Now that he was gone it was up to me to keep the farm running. The nursery and greenhouse were something new to the place and there was a learning curve. I wiped my forehead and made a beeline for the porch.

Over in the holding bed, I spotted a small man rummaging around. He'd hold a plant in its tin container and manipulate it, as if to examine it, then place it back where he found it. I didn't get many customers at the farm and had no idea who this guy was.

"Can I help you?"

He turned his head to face me and I dropped my trowel. A Jap was right here in the nursery pawing through my plants, and my first thought was to grab my pitchfork and run him out of there. But he wasn't a big man, maybe five foot, four inches and a hundred and ten soaking wet. He wore a Panama Fedora of a light colored straw weave and a loose fitting knit shirt that waved in the breeze as he selected another plant.

"How much for this one?" he asked, his words toneless and uniform, but distinct English with an accent.

"Not for sale," I replied. "None of them are. They're culls. Bad quality."

"I know what culls are. Why won't you sell them?"

I wasn't expecting a debate about this. But there was something in this man's face that had my attention. A kind of… determination.

"Why would you want a plant like that? It's stunted and pot bound. There's a dead limb on that side. And it's shedding needles on that other limb, too."

"Monterey Pine. They grow for years in the crack of a rock. The wind tries to pry free, but it puts out spray of roots to hold fast and its trunk bends to the shape the wind gives it. See this trunk here? Bent. The container, laying on its side. Now it is perfect for bonsai."

My jaw nearly hit the ground. That was a word I never expected to hear on my farm. The next image I had was this old boy on a kamikaze run, bearing down on one of our seaplane tenders, white teeth gleaming and scarf flailing as he shouted the B-word before crashing into the deck. But of course, that had nothing to do with what he was saying.

CHAPTER 22

"I show you. Clippers please." I handed him the pruners in my hip sheath. He looked them over. "Not very sharp. You should respect your shears." He proceeded to place the tin can containing the pine on the end of an oil drum and scanned it with his hands and eyes. "Lift here. See, three limbs. Two are opposing. No good. One above will balance. Good. We leave the high and low on each side. Snip this and this. Not too much, we can never put it back." He moved deftly around the sickly plant, nipping bits and pieces from along each limb and removing dead twigs.

"What about this ugly dead trunk? Most of this plant is just a sucker. A new shoot."

"This dead wood here, OK. We will carve and sand smooth. Hand me that piece of wire. That copper. Over there."

I obediently retrieved a scrap of grounding wire from the assorted junk piled nearby. He stretched out a coil and severed it with a can cutter. Then he attached a loop to the base of the plant and began to wrap up the trunk and out along the first branch. Each wrap was at a slight angle that remained evenly spaced until the end of the wire was reached. He repeated the technique on the opposite limb, which was slightly higher.

"So why the wire? Won't it strangle the plant as it grows?"

He shook his head, his eyes never losing focus. "Wrapping like this gives plant room to grow. You see." He cut the next piece and moved out to a secondary branch, nearer the end of the main limb.

After a few minutes, he seemed satisfied with the effort. "Now place thumbs here and here. Push to give new shape. Very slow." He pressed against the wired limb, spreading it away from the one above it and forming it into a gradual curve. Likewise, he fanned out the small, secondary branches and tips. Slowly, what had looked like a short, rigid pot bound seedling took on the air of an older, almost ancient tree, with branches shaped delicately by years of influences that gave its trunk a gentle lean but with branches remaining horizontal. I had been watching a master practicing his craft.

"Well, I'll be. Very impressive! What's your name?" I asked.

"Taiki. You are Trim-bel?" he asked.

"That's right. Listen, if you would like to look around, that's alright by me. I have a lot of plants in here that could use some pampering. Would you show me a little more about this…bonsai?"

"Tomorrow. I will bring tools. And proper shears." There was a hint of scolding in his last few words. But I was just happy he was willing to come back.

I formed a shallow dish of soil around the base of a sickly little shade tree and spilled a bucket of water into it, just as the rooster crowed at 8 a.m. the next morning. This tree was among the culls that the old guy pawed through. He called it a box elder tree, but said it was fast growing and instead selected the pine for his demonstration. I decided to plant this little tree in the center of the turnaround in front of the house in place of the walnut tree that blew over last winter. We'll see, I guess. I gave my trousers a couple of whacks to clear the dust, just as a decrepit old pickup bounced its way up the lane. It was Taiki, alright, and he had a briefcase along with several decorative, porcelain trays and dishes.

"Good morning," I offered.

"Yes. We continue today. I have what I need now."

"So, are you from around these parts?"

He squinted as he turned to face me. "A few days only."

He told me that he had moved here from a small town in eastern Oregon. There, he worked as a field laborer for a while, but was getting too old for that now. He wanted to leave the West Coast and had corresponded with a friend in Minnesota. She persuaded him to relocate.

Before that, he had lived on the California-Oregon border for four years. A place called Tule Lake.

The name rang a bell for me, but I didn't know much about it. What I did know, however, was that when we were attacked in 1941, our president reacted and had the nation's support. There were Japanese living all over Oahu when I was there, and we had

CHAPTER 22

no way of sorting out who was a loyal citizen or resident and who was a spy. I hated to say it, but we simply knew they all looked different than we did. The safest thing, the only choice, seemed to be to follow our president's order and confine all those of Japanese descent and sort it out later. I never even gave it a thought when I was in the Navy. However, enough had been written about this particular camp—about its problems, controversies, and its population—that I had the feeling his experience living there may not have been altogether wholesome.

"You were in the camp in Tule Lake?" I asked him as he spread out his tools and began studying the pine.

"A camp? Yes, you could call it that. They called it 'segregation center.' A thousand soldiers are not needed for a 'camp.'"

Taiki seemed to caress the little tree as he moved between its branches with tiny clippers, shaping each with the ease of an artist. As he worked, he continued to tell me about life as an internee.

He said it was a big place and fifteen thousand or more plucked from locations along the West Coast were crowded together in a thousand dorms. They worked in fields during summer.

At first, the housing was enclosed with a fence and six guard towers spaced around the perimeter. A loyalty questionnaire was administered, one that Taiki and others found ambiguous. Uncertainty about how to answer fostered groups of dissidents. The makeup of the internees began to change. Families were moved to other centers and new internees, deemed "disloyal," came into the facility to replace them.

Then, there was the accident. A worker was killed and the residents became angry with the camp's administration. He told me it was a volatile situation. There were work stoppages and strikebreakers, martial law, and arrests. A stockade was built for the troublemakers and more guard towers were erected. And this was his home until his release in early 1946.

He was finished with the wire and removed the metal pot. Tenderly massaging the roots, he reduced the size of the root mass and trimmed away what he could. He selected a porcelain container and placed the tree into it, surrounding it with a special soil mix. He placed the finished piece on the oil drum, an adolescent bonsai resembling an aged pine, listing majestically over a small mossy stone.

"For you, Trim-bel."

Chapter 23

As Samantha pulled into the Radisson parking lot, Dan was still fully absorbed, reflecting on the afternoon with an unexpected reverence. What was it that he *had* expected? He had certainly been prepared for communication difficulties and muddled speech. Maybe bouts of forgetfulness, or worse, few coherent recollections at all. It might well have been more folly than anything, a feel good assignment to meet the man and celebrate like it was his birthday. A half an hour of labored shouting back and forth, and he would simply snap the cameras shut and be on his way. That's what he had expected. *The Arizona?*

He pulled out his briefcase and Samantha locked up. *Sure could use a belt.* He made his way directly to the lounge and pulled out a familiar stool from the bar. Ted was tending again and gave him a warm smile.

"You have returned!" he said sarcastically.

"Cute. I'll tell you what, though. I'm exhausted. Bourbon and seven?"

"Coming right up." Ted quickly had an amber glass brimming with ice ready and placed it and a menu nearby. "How'd it go today?"

"Holy smokes, Ted. I'm still trying to deal with it. Owen... Owen is something else. He seems ten years younger than he is or looks. Fifteen, maybe. And I can see after one session that this is going to take a while. I don't know how I'll explain it to Jenna. Oh man, I need to call Jenna! Excuse me, Ted." Dan pulled his phone from his wrist and stretched it as he walked over to a vacant corner table.

"Hi, honey. How'd it go today?" he began, trying to judge her expression.

"Hi! I'm so glad you called. I took Charlie in and they gave him fluids and an injection. Poor little guy looks pregnant. His skin is hanging like a pouch underneath him. He does seem a little more comfortable though, and I got him to eat a little."

"Sounds like a good start," Dan said.

"I hope so. How did it go today for you?"

"Oh, honey. It was a day I'll long remember."

Dan recounted some of the highlights, and had Jenna laughing at his description of the big dog and Owen's revolver.

"I didn't know if I'd be bit or shot first!" He could tell by Jenna's tone that she was feeling a little better about it. Now came the hard part. "So Hon, I…didn't have nearly the time today that we'll need for this. He's in pretty amazing shape for his age, but tires easily and I couldn't ask any more of him today."

"I was afraid of this," she said quietly. "But I get it, Dan. This is important. It sounds like more important than any of us knew. I feel better about Charlie after the visit, and we'll be OK. I go back in tomorrow. You need to see this through. I understand that. Once in a lifetime."

"Once in a lifetime. Thanks for being so understanding, sweetie. Love you!"

"I'll let you go. Charlie and I love you, too! See you soon." The screen went dark and a note from Samantha appeared. *Call your wife.* He stared at the phone in disbelief. *Just kidding!* "Great. Now she's a joker," he said under his breath.

As he approached the bar, Ted was engaged with another fellow who had taken a stool adjacent to Dan's. As he sat down, Ted introduced his acquaintance. "Dan, this is Jonas Strand, one of our regulars and not a half bad guy either."

"Pleasure to meet you, Dan. So did Ted put anything besides ice in your glass?"

"Of course I did. He's a paying customer. I only put the food coloring in yours."

"I would say that you two seem to know each other," Dan quipped.

CHAPTER 23

"Jonas and I were in the service together. I got my discharge and he shipped out of the area for twenty years. Some of the best years of my life. Then he shows up again in—what was it, the late twenties? I hear he's a civilian and back in town, and before I could get away, the son-of-a-bitch finds me. Of course, he looked in every bar. I should have been a fireman."

"You're right about that, the way you water down these drinks," Jonas countered. "And how could I help but find you. You've worked in every bar in town. Impressive resume, wouldn't you say, Dan?"

"What branch were you in, Jonas?" Dan inquired.

"We were both Navy. Jonas was just better at it than I was," Ted interrupted.

"I liked it. Enjoyed the travel and a lot of great guys. But there were parts of the military life that can wear you out. It was time for a change."

Dan reflected on his comment, then inquired, "So what does a person do for a living after committing to the military for so long?"

"I was pretty lucky, really. Some terrific training opportunities in the Navy. I worked with intelligence and surveillance. A bunch of keyboard and screen time. So it wasn't hard to hook up with most any tech company around the city. I freelance now."

"You tracked bad guys and all that?"

"Sometimes, but a surprising amount of what we did was deception. Creating scenarios and solving them, transmitting bogus information and sifting through the results. Kind of hard to explain, and I actually can't say too much about it anyway."

"And Dan's a reporter, so you've just blown it big time, my friend," Ted pointed out.

"Damn, a reporter! I'm afraid you'll have to come with me. For a swim with the fishes."

"Whoa, hang on. I have a wife and a cat to support. My lips are sealed."

"I don't know if we can trust him, Jonas. How about I hold him and you work him over. Like the old days."

"OK, Dan, if you promise not to talk, I'll let it slide. So what kind of stuff *do* you report?"

Ted jumped in. "Hey, Dan's here to talk with Owen Trimbel. You remember him, right? But I guess I never did ask you why your paper wanted his story?"

Before Dan could answer, Jonas piped in. "Hell, I know why. I just saw it yesterday. It's all over the internet. The Japanese guy died this week."

"What?" Ted was confused.

"There was a Japanese soldier in a Tokyo hospital that died a couple of days ago," Dan said, expanding on Jonas's assertion. "Up until July of this year, there were two known World War II vets still alive. A Japanese infantryman and an army sergeant from California. When the California guy passed on, it appeared the Japanese fellow was the only soldier left."

"Holy cow," Ted remarked in disbelief.

Jonas had more. "Yep. I've kind of been following all this. The scholars and guys who love this kind of thing started tracking the remaining vets when it got down to like a hundred. I was reading an article about it. All of them were centenarians and scattered around the world. Pretty soon, it was down to ten. After that, it seemed for a good part of a year, there were still two from Japan, a German, one Englishman, an Italian, and an American—the army sergeant. Then, all of a sudden, this week, poof."

"Well, Owen got left out of it all. I wonder if there's others that they don't know about," Dan suggested.

Jonas nodded. "Me too. I suppose it's an inexact science. How do you define something like this when so many countries had some kind of stake in the conflicts? And of course, there are the women. WACS, nurses, WAVES. They weren't technically combat roles, but many took their share of risks. And the guerrillas and resistance fighters that all played big parts. But of the principal players, the major adversaries in both theaters, well, as of a week ago it didn't appear that a living veteran still existed on their soil. Except the one Japanese guy. And he died at one hundred and twelve plus."

CHAPTER 23

"I should have warned you, Dan," Ted said, peering over a row of beer taps. "Jonas is the essential obsessive-compulsive goofball. Weren't you a history major? Anyway, I think you've tapped into one of his hobbies."

"That's OK. This is interesting. So, the Japanese and Germans were sending young teenagers in at the end. I'm surprised one of them isn't still around," Dan said.

"That might be the case with the Japanese guy," Jonas continued. "But, the casualties were really heavy as it was winding down. Many new recruits were so young, inexperienced, and didn't fare well. As things got more desperate, teens were just rounded up without proper documentation. Russia, the Philippines. There's no way of being one-hundred percent sure with so many having at least some involvement. At least, that would be my take."

Jonas took a sip of his drink and continued. "But in World War I for example, they did settle on a solution. It was a much smaller conflict, and three names pop up, all dying within a year of each other and all one hundred and ten. An English woman, mess steward I believe, is credited as the last to pass. An Englishman and an American army corporal were the last men."

"Whoo. Better get me a refill, Ted," Dan said through a puff of breath.

"But it gets weirder. When the last American died back in the summer, Trimbel wasn't on anyone's radar yet. No one knew there was some guy way up in the Minnesota backwoods who wasn't in the tally. Now, it looks like *he's* the last man standing. I'm not sure how the word got out, but I expect there will be a fuss heading his way pretty soon."

"So how did you end up getting in on this, Dan?" Ted inquired, as he handed him a fresh bourbon.

"Well, I'm not sure, myself. We didn't really talk about it today, with so much else to go over, but maybe you've explained it. His daughter contacted my paper about him and was probably convinced that a small local paper was the safest bet to keep it from becoming a circus. Of course, it leaked that Owen, another World War II vet, was still living in Minnesota. So I had to make

— 113 —

some fast arrangements. Not to mention that he's *also* a hundred and twelve."

"How long has *she* known?" Ted asked.

"Not sure. Maybe we'll get into it some tomorrow. But I'll tell you what. I was full up today as it was. I need to tell you two a few things about Owen Trimbel."

Chapter 24

The air was crisp and clear as Samantha flawlessly navigated the vehicle past unfamiliar farms and fields, following a different route to the destination. A twinkle of frost lingered as morning sunlight advanced, rearranging the shadows.

"Thanks for including me in on this," Jonas said, taking in the scenery from the comfort of Dan's company car. Dan swung his head around to face him, slightly leaning into the seat restraints. He couldn't put his finger on it, but Jonas reminded him of someone in show business, perhaps a late show host or political pundit. He was solidly built, sporting a salt and pepper mustache and sideburns, but with dark, active eyebrows that stood out from the rest of his features. Dan found them a little difficult to ignore. "I definitely don't want to do anything to mess you up," he continued.

Dan shook his head. "No, not at all."

Samantha interrupted. "Excuse me, Dan, but we are approaching the destination on our left. Shall I notify Sandy?"

"We're good, Sam. No, Jonas, I'm glad to have you along. I talked to Sandy and she trusts what we're...Uh, oh."

"Expecting anyone else?" Jonas remarked as they pulled up the drive toward an *apple* red SUV.

"In a way, yes. Pull over to the side, Sam." They shut the doors and walked toward the other car.

"Well, got any more bibles for us today, Jehovah?"

"I could probably come up with some. Would it do any good? Hank, wasn't it?" Dan responded, his tone prickly.

Hank looked at the car. "*The Bulletin*. What would *The Bulletin* be doing way up here? Delivering papers?"

"And bibles. Listen, this is a private conversation. And invitations weren't extended to the paparazzi. So we'd appreciate it if you'd leave us be."

"Hey, c'mon, guy! My producer wants to promote this. He's been talking it up—waiting for my call." Hank hoisted up his pants as he blathered, his belt failing to secure them. Dan looked away as the trouser waist sagged back to where it began. "Viewers are swamping us with their questions for him. We have a contest with a prize going for the best ones. They have hundreds in line, and millions in the *Stream*, so we need to talk to Trembles and let him know."

His sidekick, Billy, broke in with his two cents. "That's right. Adoring public. Your man should be jacked up about it."

Hank quickly added, "The top five will win Timberwolves tickets, and we want to ask him their questions on the air. Maybe he gives them an autographed picture or whatever."

"I don't think it's his cup of tea, 'guy.' Why don't you two go play somewhere else."

"Ask him. Will you just ask him?" Billy insisted.

Dan dismissed them with a frown and knocked on the door.

"Hi, Dan," Sandy said, tugging down the sleeves of a lightweight, cream-colored fleece hoodie with *Minnesota Golden Gophers* emblazoned on the chest in maroon and gold. Lowering her voice, she said, "I see they're still here."

"Yeah, sorry about that, Sandy. Kind of gives my profession a bad name. Sandy, this is my friend, Jonas, the one I told you about."

"Pleasure to meet you, Sandy. Thank you for the invite," Jonas said.

"Not at all. Come on in and meet Dad." She ushered the two men in. "Let me run another chair in there and get Dad's wheelchair out of the way. Be right back."

"Don't be afraid to slam that door," Dan added with a smile, as Sandy peered out at the reporters. "Hi Bilge!"

Jonas froze in his tracks "Cripes, what is that!"

"Did I forget to mention..." Dan said casually. Bilge gave

CHAPTER 24

him a sniff and an affectionate lick of the hand, then turned and looked suspiciously at Jonas.

"He's closer now. You see that don't you…" Jonas said, barely moving his lips.

Sandy joined them again. "Go on, Bilge. Find Dad. The big dog sauntered back toward the family room where Owen was waiting.

Dan peeked around the edge of the doorway. Twenty-four hours had passed, but he didn't look a day older. Owen's face brightened the room and to Dan's surprise, he had his bomber jacket on. "Good morning, Owen. I want you to meet Jonas."

Jonas reached a hand out and clasps Owen's warmly. "My pleasure, sir."

"This is Bilge," Owen said, scratching him behind an ear.

"We've met," Jonas replied.

Sandy reappeared with a third chair. "Those men are still hanging around out there," she cautioned, as she folded up Owen's wheelchair and stowed it.

"Men?" Owen asked.

"Some TV reporters from an upstart Minneapolis station want to talk to you," Dan explained. "Put you on the air for some questions and sign photographs like a Super Bowl quarterback. What do you think?"

Owen considered it for a moment. "Bullshit!"

"Asked and answered," Dan said.

Owen continued under his breath. "Like I want my picture on TV at eleven. And at a hundred and twelve. Autograph photos. Can barely hold a pen…"

Jonas cocked his head. "Well, Owen, I can see you still speak Navy. I spent a few years in there myself."

With the mood lightened, Samantha and Dan readied the equipment while Jonas shared some of his background with Owen.

"This is an impressive collection of military books, Owen," Jonas said. He then pointed at one of the half dozen framed paintings and prints on the wall. "Is that PBY like the one you flew in?"

"A PBY-5. Yep, for almost two years…Then I moved on to Privateers as the war went north."

"Did you ever fly them or consider flight school?" Dan asked.

"Nah, I was born with eagle ears and elephant eyes. I wouldn't have made it as a pilot candidate most likely. They wanted twenty-twenty, but I always thought my distance vision seemed pretty good. Up until I was eighty-five or ninety." Then he added, "They gave me a turn at the yoke once in a while, anyway. So I guess you could say I did fly one. Sort of."

Jonas asked, "Owen, I've always been curious about the PBYs. They weren't around anymore when I was in, so I don't know much about them other than they were seaplanes. Were they as well armed as a, oh, a B-17 or something?"

"Heavens no. We could shoot back, but really only had modest armament…a nose gun, twin .30 calibers. The blister hatches on either side had .50 calibers that would swing into place, and there was another in the tail."

Dan interrupted, "OK, gentlemen, let me break in before I miss something. I think we're ready to go, again. How about you, Owen. Need anything before we start? A drink of water? Bathroom?"

"I knew you were coming…so I made two trips."

"Aha, great. Then let's pick up there, Owen. Your armaments." Dan sifted through his mental notes. "Were you ever attacked by a Zero?" he asked.

"It only happened once to us in the Catalinas. Made my hair stand on end when we first spotted them. It might have actually been one of our first patrols." He recalled that on this day, three Japanese fighters bore down on them and fanned out as they approached. He and the gunner opposite him immediately shoved up to open their blister hatch doors and swung their guns into position. "It's strange how fear brings such an intensity to a person. So in the moment. The exhilaration—something like alcohol or sex I guess. You…" He thought about it, glancing upward. "You feel it when you go up in a plane for the first time. Or when the fuselage drops fifty feet in an instant from a downdraft. It's a little like that.

CHAPTER 24

We reacted. Your training kicks in and survival means getting it right…no mistakes."

"Sounds like it wasn't a fair fight, outnumbered and all," Jonas observed.

"I was on the starboard side. One of them fired on us and some of the rounds came in and hit the metal of my blister and followed it around somehow. Then the shell broke up and flew back out the port side blister." He pulled a handkerchief from his pocket and gave his mouth a wipe. Then he told them that some of the fragments hit the other gunner in the back and shoulder, but that he didn't even know it and just kept firing away. "Anyhow, we ducked into a cloud and they broke off the attack. We got the fellow checked out when we landed and kidded him about the scratches—his war wound. Damn if they didn't try and give him a Purple Heart."

Owen was cooking now. They could see the memories flowing faster than he could say them, his face miming the emotions of each sentence and thought. More often than not, he recalled the *exception to the rule* tales that had a humorous overtone.

"Then there was this guy, LaHodney. He was a fearless son-of-a-bitch. He came up with the idea of adding more firepower to his plane, so he bundled four .50 caliber machine guns together and stuck it in the nose." The weapon was stunning, capable of discharging a remarkable amount of ammo on a strafing run, so much so that the frame around it needed to be reinforced. But there was another problem. The gun sat so low that the salt water got in the barrels when taxiing. "Hell on the metal. So they ordered up a bunch of boxes of condoms from supply, and used them as shower caps for the barrels of the gun. I don't know what supply thought about it. Probably that this was the busiest crew in the whole damn war."

Jonas looked at Dan with a *Huh, I see what you mean,* expression.

"A makeshift super gun. I suppose the nose gunner took over this responsibility?" Jonas asked.

"Nope. The pilot fired it. Fixed, like on a fighter. It was pretty tough on those little Japanese barges. Someone told me that when they first test fired it, the recoil was so strong that the gun ended up in the rear of the plane."

"No…"

"Ah, who knows," Owen confessed. "They were always kidding around about everything."

"Sounds like you were with a great group of guys. Sense of humor is pretty important when you work together so much," Dan said.

"It sure helped. But the emotional swings. I wasn't prepared for that. I guess it's why we tried to pack as much fun in as we could."

Sandy flashed a curious eye at her father. "How do you mean?"

Owen rolled his shoulders upward then rubbed a hand across one of them. "Oh…like the time…we were on this little island…"

The Bismarck Sea - 1943

Chapter 25

"Your serve."

OK, volleyball wasn't really my game, but losing to another plane's crew? Couldn't let that happen.

Our three-plane section had flown across New Guinea and much of the Bismarck Sea to reach a little bay and this island outpost, and we were killing time before heading home in the morning. Someone dreamed up a round robin tournament between the crewmen from each plane, and we had taken care of business up until now. We were two down and at match point.

The ball flew over the net and Hodges went face first into the sand to keep it alive. Then Johnny sets it up for Del, our tallest, at the net—and he swats it. Long!

"He couldn't spike a drink!" someone from the other side shrieked. The celebration was on, back slapping and cat calling the whole time. For us, it was over, and we had to pay up.

"I'll have my cold beer over here next to the pool," their radioman said, a cocky scumbag who paraded around like an aristocrat. Three of us trudged into the Seabee tent to see how much the brews were going to set us back. They had cases of it, but these guys were part construction worker and part loan shark. I was thankful the wager only allowed one beer each. By the time we had sipped the last of the bubbles from the bottom, my mood had improved. I was sure we could beat them in horseshoes—maybe win back some ice cream.

It was first light and five of the crew sat around the card table after breakfast, joking and smoking—the usual stuff.

Our plane captain, Sid, walked in after fueling the plane. "Time to go fellas," he said, grinning. I wasn't winning anyway, so it was a relief from my perspective. We shuffled around collecting gear and trudged over toward the small shuttle launch to our PBY, holding on to our hats in the gusty wind. The other two Catalinas were warming up, completing our section. I was looking forward to a good night's sleep back at the tender.

"Hey, Owen. Got any gum?" Sid asked, as we fought against the wind. Most of the guys knew by now that I didn't smoke. I'd tried it on and off, but mostly made a fool of myself. It just didn't take with me, for some reason. Consequently, I was known for my gum pantry. Different kinds, different flavors. I'd stock up anytime we were near a good source. It was tougher after we left Perth.

"Sure. Here you go." I strapped in and looked out across the small island's airfield next to the bay as a pair of fighters began a rapid ascent at the end of the runway. We taxied a few feet and spun around in the bay's calmer waters—our plane would be second off, and the first PBY was already powering up and clambering toward the narrow bay entrance. It was airborne and barely clear of the protection of the trees and island landmass when a violent wind gust twisted its fuselage and the port wing float dipped down and into the water.

That was all it took. The plane canted sideways and pancaked into the waves. In no time, it was beneath the surface and out of sight.

It was a half hour before rescue crews had finished combing the area. A crewman and both pilots were killed.

This was hard to shake off, but we had our orders and were waved on. The war hadn't stopped. Not even for a little while. *At least our pilots, Jack and Alex, have the benefit of knowing how strong this crosswind is,* I thought to myself.

We lifted off and returned home—without incident.

Chapter 26

A jet's contrail appeared to penetrate a chain of scattered clouds gathered along an expanse of sky to the west of the house, perhaps the leading edge of the front forecast to bring additional rain to lake country. *A dip in nighttime temperatures over the weekend might make things interesting after that,* Dan thought, his arms forming a prow as he stretched a bit before returning to his seat.

Jonas lingered by the sitting room window, taking in the panorama, and wondered, "Have you lived out here in the country all your life, Owen?"

Owen replied, "I never got the hang of the city. I found I couldn't live where dogwoods and maples were just the names of streets."

"It's very beautiful around here. Hard to take care of?" he asked.

Owen raised and lowered his shoulders. "Might be, if we chose to do that. Leaving things alone is pretty easy."

Jonas cocked his head and raised an eyebrow. "Hmm. A lot of space out there," he suggested.

"When I was growing plants and had a nursery, there was a lot of work involved. For sure. They depended on me for water, food, survival." He rattled his glass. "With fields, crops, and animals, we needed help in those days."

Sandy intervened. "Dad's place, the family place, was a lot larger than we are here. My husband and I bought this property back in the eighties from a neighbor."

"I see," Jonas said, returning to his seat.

"I guess I've always felt the things people make are the ones that need to be cared for," Owen added. "Tractor, cars, a house. Nature doesn't need much from us. But you're right, keeping a little space near the house mowed, holding back the aggressive stuff once in a while is good. We have a kind fellow that comes by and helps out every couple of weeks."

Dan said, "As much as I'm enjoying this, I'd kind of like to move back into the interview realm, again. Jonas, would you like to get us going?"

"Sure…uh…" Jonas noticed Bilge was sitting a few feet to his left, rigid as a gargoyle statue, his dog's stare fixed as if trying to see right through him as he spoke. "So you said…" he began again, until the boxer stood and approached him, reaching out an inquisitive nose and giving his knee a sniff. He cocked his head upward and gave a brief but forceful belch in Jonas' direction, then with a few slaps of his tongue, appeared to lose interest. Jonas fanned the air with a hand as Bilge strolled back toward Owen and resumed his place at his feet.

"I take it you're not much of a dog guy?" Owen commented.

"I'm finding there's a learning curve to this one," he said in his own defense. "So, Dan said you were primarily a gunner, is that right?" finally returning to his question.

"That I was."

"And a lot of your work was at night with targets that were blacked out, too?"

Owen nodded. "Of course, there were tracers every fifth shell. Pretty easy to follow. You could even see them ricocheting around on the deck of a ship. You knew you had them in trouble then. But daylight was easier."

"Did you have a preference?"

"Not really. During the day, we could be more accurate. Allow for the difference between blisters."

Dan found himself nodding, although he had no idea what Owen was talking about. "Difference?"

"The shells leave the barrel with a rotation. Keeps them pointed straight so they don't tumble," Owen explained. "On the port side, the shell climbs slightly, so we aim low. On the starboard

CHAPTER 26

side, it falls, so we aim high." He smiled as Dan still looked confused. "OK, this rotation," he said, pointing a finger straight ahead and spiraled it like pencil. "It spins like a top and burrows through the wind rushing by the barrel. On one side of the plane this spin will *push* the shell higher. On the other side, it does just the opposite and *shoves* it lower. See?"

"Thanks, Dan, I didn't get that either!" Sandy laughed.

"The thanks should go to the gunnery school," Owen said.

Jonas noted, "You must have had quite a bit of leeway, given the blisters were so large and extended out there a ways. Were you able to hit targets in front or behind you?"

"You know, if it was a barge or something, the pilots would maneuver. Give us a better look. They would sideslip, making the plane's approach more like a crab."

Sandy asked, "Ah, like on that mission you told us about yesterday? I wondered about that. You mean the pilot flew the plane sort of sideways?"

"Enough that we had a real good line of sight from the blister. Then we'd make another pass on the opposite side. Give him a turn."

Dan couldn't help noticing how Owen's gestures were becoming more pronounced, his voice stronger and faster paced. This phenomenon would show itself most when he talked about the Catalinas. Dan could sense the abiding love he must have for that aircraft. The kind of thing that, perhaps, Dan might experience with a destination, like a particular National Park—Zion or the Grand Canyon. Or a movie starring a favorite actor or actress that was not to be missed, just because they were in it. He had never associated any of this with a *machine*—an airplane. At least, not until now.

"I've got a question," he began. Owen spun his head around, attentive, and gingerly caressed the raw spot on his forehead without realizing it. "Can you give us an example or two of something that over the course of your life, you found you had a passion for? Maybe something that came after your time in the Navy?"

"Something I had a…" Owen's face shifted to a thoughtful

upward attitude, as if looking at the ceiling for an answer. "Well, this might be cheating. I've always loved history. I've got boxes and boxes of books stored in the attic…just keep favorites around down here." He took off his glasses and tried to buff them on his shirt. "Most of them are in larger print, too. Not as easy for me to read as it used to be."

Since much of his downstairs library involved military books, he tried to elaborate. Dan and Jonas listened as he spoke of his affinity for plants and how it had become more than a hobby. He found he wanted to understand seed production and cuttings, the origins of species of plants and how the lineage can be continuously modified. "I just wanted to see where any particular path might take me. Find out if there was a surprise at the end. Something unknown, at least to me."

He found history, and in particular, military history held the same fascination. How leaders, countries, and armies behaved, and how that has and hasn't changed over the centuries. Mistakes have been repeated. Brilliant planning often came from reading accounts from brilliant generals. Yet even in World War II, with all the advances in weaponry and technology, so much depended on the performance of the individual soldier, tiny seed that he was. He thought it interesting that these soldiers collectively were an army, but individually they were fragile with a physiology that was so vulnerable.

"They did all they could to protect themselves—helmets, armor, prayer, good luck charms—and in the end, it might not be good enough. Only remembrances of the man return home."

Dan started to speak but didn't. He could see that Owen had more to add.

"A friend once told me that one plant is the beginning of a garden. And that many plants in the garden cooperate. They interact and have characteristics that may benefit the plant next to them…keep bad insects away, shade out weeds, or have a nourishing fungus on their roots. Others struggle, many don't survive and are quickly replaced. They were unfortunately thrust into a bad situation, maybe a place where they didn't belong. Or wish to be."

Northern Minnesota
September of 1962

—⚘— Chapter 27 —⚘—

The breeze this lovely morning was soothing enough, but my leg was asleep. Setting a spell on the front porch while I read the paper seemed to be Wombat's favorite pastime, too. But at forty five pounds, this Australian shepherd and I had a difference of opinion on where she would "set." Some lap dog!

As I look around at what should be tranquility, this is what I see: a porch that needs painting, and that gate into the barnyard, it drags—rotten post. There's a hornets' nest in the barn gable, too. Better get that today before Sandy goes out to water the greenhouses and chucks an apple up there to see what happens. The tractor is running rough, and I'll be tilling weeds soon. And then there's…

Wombat seizes this moment away from me for a satisfying stretch and yawn, then tightens her curl as if to say, "Don't sweat it, Dad. It's Sunday." Smart dog.

"Little more coffee, sweetie?" Shirley asked me with a tip of the glass pot.

"Love some," I replied, still marveling at how lucky I was. A beautiful and loving wife, a precious daughter, a dog on my lap. Working the land and using my mind, hands, and back to provide for them.

Sitting here on the porch, if I held my breath and just listened, I could hear the buzzing of those hornets even though they were two hundred feet away. Unless a chicken decided the sky was falling.

"If you'll bring me a mess of beets and cucumbers this morning, I'll can up some of your favorite pickles. Interested?"

"Absolutely! Finish the paper first?" She gave me a playful nod and a kiss on the forehead before retreating into the house.

A headline and story buried in an inside section grabbed my attention. The President made a speech at Rice University—and he wants to send a man to the Moon! Within the next eight years!

All I could say was "Wow." It had only been two decades since I was crawling around the inside workings of a two engine seaplane wondering what it was, exactly, that the radar did. When we landed, we needed to crank down wingtip floats by hand and sometimes needed to plug holes from popped rivets to keep the water out. What kind of brilliance, daring, and yet unimagined contraptions will be involved in something like this? He says, "We choose to go to the Moon and do other things, not because they are easy, but because they are hard."

CHAPTER 27

I believe him. He was there, in the South Pacific, at the same time that I was. In fact, the Liberator pilot I flew with later in the war, a guy we all simply called the Skipper, was shot down by our own fleet and picked up by a PT boat in the Blackett Strait. It had been barely a week since Kennedy's own PT boat had been cut in half by a Japanese destroyer in that same strait.

Eight years. Not much time to figure out a plan to go to the Moon. But look what we did in only four.

A small dust cloud was drifting along the lane, and that usually meant company coming. A gust cleared my view, enough that I could make out the black exterior and short bed of a late 1940s pickup. One I knew so well. Taiki.

I walked past the greenhouse area, near where we had first met back before I was married. I hadn't seen him for several years and had grown a little concerned. As he stepped from the pickup, I was startled by his appearance. Had it been longer than I recalled? He looked so old.

"Hello, Trim-bel," he said with a smile and extended hand. In his other, he clenched the stirrups of a plain and slightly soiled cloth bag.

"It's been a long time, my friend," I said, returning his smile and grasping his hand.

He told me that he had recently returned to Japan after receiving a letter that his sister, fifteen years younger and still living in Hiroshima, was deathly ill. It was the first time he had been to his homeland since he was around twenty. He now looked to be in his eighties. He said he had lost touch with his family over the years, except for her. The war had created a divide in the family, more physically than politically. Her son had been a pilot and was killed when he crash landed during the struggle for Saipan. She had been fortunate to have a few of his personal possessions restored to her, but now that she was deathly ill, she wanted a member of the family to have them. Taiki was the only one left.

"You have done well. No more culls."

"I think you took them all. And I got a little better at growing things that didn't look so sick!" I loved his smile. "What brings you out this way? It's been too long!"

"I have something to ask. I…" He stopped for a second or two to collect his thoughts. "You were a soldier. So I think you will understand. Many young men fought and died. Some wanted to fight. Some were asked to fight. Some…were made to fight."

In his face, I could see sorrow bred out of five years internment and the shame of heredity. He continued. "My sister gave this to me." He opened the package and revealed two neatly folded pieces of cloth. He tenderly unfurled each, one at a time. "This is flag of Japan. Around red rising sun at the center are wishes—from family, from friends." He pointed at the lines of writing, Japanese characters that formed a mosaic that covered most of the flag's white surface.

He then held, in his hands, the second piece, scarf-like, long and embroidered with hundreds of colorful dots, writing, and images. "This is a ceremonial belt to be worn to keep soldiers safe. Her son would have had them with him at all times. In the end, their power was not enough."

I touched the belt. It was soft, and I felt a sudden tingling sensation shoot up to the back of my neck, as if I could still feel some of its energy after twenty years. I looked at his face, unsmiling and subdued.

"Trim-bel. My time too has come. This is why I need your help." I was puzzled but nodded slowly. "There is no one in my family I know of that still survives. But there may be a more distant relative. I want to go back and look, but I no longer have time."

I asked him, "What can I do?"

"I have translated some of the names and words on the flag. There are some I cannot. But there may be a clue. Can you keep this for me? You have many years to live and times will change. Someday, maybe a way will be found to return this to where it belongs."

I was dumbfounded and had no idea what I could do with his sister's keepsakes. "Of course, Taiki. It would be my honor."

CHAPTER 27

I took the package. We said our goodbyes, and my throat clenched as we shook hands. He took one step back and looked me in the eye, then bent forward slightly with a peaceful bow of his head and paused.

Taiki, like the ancient trees he tirelessly cultured, was small in stature, but upon closer inspection, larger than life. He had known happiness and sorrow, but most of all, patience. As he turned and walked back to his truck, I knew I would never see him again.

THE LAST WORD

Chapter 28

"Can I get anyone some coffee? Tea?" Sandy asked.

"I would love some," Dan said enthusiastically.

"Tea for me," Jonas added, as Owen declined with a shake of his head.

"Didn't I hear somewhere that PBYs were dropping torpedoes for a while?" Jonas asked.

Owen grinned. "Hell, we dropped most everything. Torpedoes, bombs, depth charges on subs, parachute flares. We even dropped beer bottles. There was some debate over which did a better job of spooking the enemy camps at night—a blinding light floating over their heads or waking them up with a whistling, spiraling bottle," he said, mimicking a five hundred-pound bomb dropped from an imagined high-altitude bomber. He figured the thought of an unexploded bomb somewhere in the enemy's camp had to be unsettling. And that tickled him. "We gave them some sleepless nights out on those islands."

"How did the torpedoes work?" Dan asked, trying to imagine such a scenario.

"They were heavy. It went under one wing, and we balanced it with two bombs on the other." He indicated this with both arms, making an amusing motion, more like a new born ostrich than a plane. "We'd start at maybe fifteen hundred feet, and go into a steep dive. Gained speed fast, but we needed at least one hundred and fifteen knots for the torpedo to arm once we dropped it." Owen swooped his hands as the plane *dove*. "We'd be level at fifteen feet or so and screaming in at the side of the ship…let it go, then pull up just above the masts." Now, he waved a hand sideways indicating the anti-aircraft fire chasing them. "They couldn't spin the guns around fast enough to follow us at that speed, coming out of the darkness. If we'd drop down to fifteen feet again, we'd escape as their shells flew around way above us, where they expected us to be."

Dan was intrigued by the story and more so by the old man's animation. Owen was moving and speaking with more spunk and clarity than at any time since the interview began. "Sounds more like a flying sub than flying boats!" Dan interjected, as Sandy handed him his coffee.

"Eh," he said dismissively, "they were exciting to drop, but hard to control. Most crews preferred bombs. That way you could sweep in along the length of the ship." He raised the water glass to his lips. "We often carried four—a *five hundred* and a *thousand-pounder* under each wing. We could make two passes, or just drop all four of them, one every forty feet in a line. Usually, the two *thousand-pounders* would go number two and three."

"Because…?" Jonas asked.

"Galloping along at more than a hundred knots over a ship that's shooting at you, well…sometimes we missed. This way, the big ones had the best chance of landing on something other than water."

Sandy gave a gentle tap of a finger on Dan's shoulder. He discreetly turned his head as Owen continued to speak to Jonas.

"There are two more cars and a van in front of the house," she whispered.

Dan raised his eyebrows. "Damn," he whispered back. "OK, let's keep an eye on it."

"Do the most damage if you scored. Makes sense," Jonas said, responding to Owen's depiction. "Did the different crews each have their own strategy to these encounters?"

Owen recounted how crews were always comparing notes on what was working best for this or that, including adjustments to an approach or bombing sequence—even what they were dropping. The Japanese were savvy, and changed tactics as the attacks against them became more and more effective. They used fighter cover, hugged shorelines, and employed smaller crafts. The Cats

CHAPTER 28

changed things up, too. "After a while, we started flying in pairs, sneaking in from unexpected directions, or flying in, very low to the water. You know, to react to what they were doing."

"So down low like that, you *gunners* could strafe as you passed over them," Dan wondered aloud.

"On approach we could. Flying right over them at that speed…well, it's a little like throwing an acorn at a fence post while speeding by on a bike. Pretty tough shot." He nodded. "If we were out of bombs, a steep dive out of the dark was still pretty effective."

Jonas thought to himself how intoxicating this was. What a stroke of luck that he had chanced into the hotel lounge and was able to join Dan for this opportunity. He felt like he was in a time warp. He'd read the books, seen the films, studied naval history during officer's training. None of it compared with hearing the details come from the lips of someone who was there. Not just anyone, but the last person who could perform such a wonder. He found himself momentarily choked up at the thought.

"You all right there, Jonas?" Dan asked.

"Yeah…little tea went down the wrong pipe," he said, as he cleared his throat. "Uh, Owen," he said, as he recovered, "When I think of how primitive aviation was then compared to today, all the things we now take for granted, I'm astounded you were able to cover so much territory—kind of by the seat of your pants. Going to these new places and not having any idea what was out there, or even much idea where the place you were looking for was. Making repairs and dealing with crises in the middle of this immense, desolate location. Like you were hiking across China with a canteen and a knapsack."

"I never thought of it that way," Owen confided. "We did need to improvise. A lot."

He looked again at his model on the shelf, and reflected on the ruggedness of the Catalina. There was no other plane like it in a storm. Then turning that description on its head, he fawned over its elegance. As it banked for a turn, it traced a graceful path across the sky, a kite in a gentle breeze. Visually, it defied logic, moving so slowly that it seemed to float when it should fly, a dirigible with wings, a condor soaring in search of a meal.

It was an aircraft that was nearly obsolete by the time the war began. So yes, it was primitive. But Owen insisted it was about the safest aircraft in all of World War II.

"Pilots who flew other planes during the war never believed us. If you told them you sunk ships—did it at night, in a PBY, flying fifty feet out of the water—well, they'd call you crazy. There's a side of me that's always wanted people to understand that."

He turned to face Jonas, and agreed that there was a caveat. "You had to be prepared for something to go wrong each and every time you flew. Or landed. That's why we never took off without a bag of golf tees."

Dan looked at Sandy and then at Jonas and could tell from their blank expressions that *they* had no idea either. "Golf tees?" he asked.

"When we landed in rough seas, like on a rescue, we had to do a *full stall* to land. Cut the power and drop quickly. The plane sounded like we'd crash landed as we hit, and we'd pop rivets all over. Water spurted in through the holes, so we plugged them… with golf tees."

Northeastern Papua New Guinea
Mid December 1943

─w─ Chapter 29 ─w─

As autumn closed in, we spent most of our time in and around Papua New Guinea, and for a while our base was a buoy patch near a seaplane tender in a small bay near the island's southern tip. Flights at night took us north and east of the island, sometimes into the Solomon or Bismarck Sea areas around New Britain. Inland, New Guinea still had a formidable population of Japanese soldiers dispersed between indigenous native tribes, and we understood both to be head hunters in their own way. It was no place to ditch a plane.

Yet it was one of the most likely places in this war, and in fact in this world, for a plane to go missing. The jungles were vast and the island was divided by the Owen Stanley Mountains, a towering central mountain range typically shrouded in clouds. With peaks upwards of 14,000 feet and abundant rugged, inhospitable terrain, this huge island was plenty dangerous. I'd been told more planes had gone down here than anywhere else, and there wasn't much chance of a rescue if it happened.

Johnny and I were surprised when, one day, our base on the tender was suddenly moved a couple of hundred miles north up to Port Moresby, a small town along the west coast. An active little bay was nestled into hillsides and cliffs that were dotted with modest houses and dwellings. Our tender was moored in the bay to service the planes, and since we often worked at night, napping on the beach was common.

But for a while, the move meant a change in routine. Most of our searching had been at night with the intent of attacking ships.

A shift in assignments began as busy work and occasional rescue operations.

And the days off allowed for exploring, and Johnny and I found it irresistible. We wandered by the hour. Hiking along the cliffs above the ocean, we spotted the carcass of a Jap Zero below in a calm pool, the cockpit and one blade of a propeller barely breaking the surface. Sea life had already begun attaching to the wings. Sometimes we'd venture down a trail into the forest hoping to see something unusual. He'd spot a bird or critter with his binoculars and I'd try to get a picture, but mostly, it was a waste of film. Just couldn't get close enough.

It seemed like creatures living on the island were not in any book I'd ever read. Tree kangaroos with tiny curved paws and long tails, or frogs half the size of a penny. There was some kind of wallaby. And an absolutely bizarre, stuffed animal with a long snout called an echidna that a friendly native brought into camp. It could probe the ground with its tube of a nose, effortlessly driving it into the soil in search of something. We never could tell what. The native told us they lay eggs.

Much of the plant life seemed typical of the islands in the South Pacific, like coconut palms and banana plantations mixed in with deciduous trees and eucalyptus. An exception was the Rainbow Eucalyptus, a real show stopper. Brilliantly colored flesh beneath peeling bark in every conceivable color? Wow! But word had it the real show stoppers were to be found in the inland jungles, those unexplored reaches winding up into the high elevation forests that few, if any, humans had ever seen. Thousands of square miles of it. What an adventure that would be!

It was with a flush of nervous excitement that we prepared for a mission deep into the heart of this nearly uncharted expanse. My new squadron had already made a number of flights dropping off coastwatchers, a collection of observers and intelligence gathering personnel who were scattered about the jungles of New Guinea and many islands in the region. They would radio information about enemy movements or locations of survivors of air mishaps

CHAPTER 29

and ship sinkings. In mid-December, there was a report that a large group of Australian coastwatchers—army officers and men—and native trackers had been isolated along a stretch of the Sepik River. This was to our north, and on New Guinea's east coast, a hundred miles or so west and inland of Wewak by air. Johnny said that the big worry was getting them out of there before they were captured and almost certainly beheaded.

My plane was one of four that took off at daybreak, and we made our way over the mountains submerged in the morning overcast. I peered through a hole in the cloud cover, glimpsing a vast jungle below. A river, still in its infancy, tumbled over a cliff's edge before my view was again interrupted by clouds.

As we neared our target river, we snuck below the clouds and between two peaks, each around 12,000 feet. Lane, our radarman, was a cutup, but when it came to his job, there was none better. It was a comfort knowing there was a solid crew guiding us as we tiptoed ahead in the murk.

This greenish Sepik River very nearly switched back on itself every couple of miles, like a three hundred-mile long boa. From my station in the blister, I felt like I was watching the jungle move. It crept up the mountain flanks and became a towering, dense assortment of lush vegetation as we wove our way upstream along the river's narrow channel. With our one hundred-foot wingspan, we barely had clearance from the shorelines.

Johnny hollered over at me, "See any activity down there, Owen?"

I had my eyes glued to the river as I shook him off, and was more concerned about the amount of debris—logs, broken trees, even crocodiles—that we were seeing in the very water we would need to land in. Jack and Alex were amazing, gently banking the massive plane around the curves and bends, mile after mile.

Over the intercom, we heard Alex's voice, "We have the camp and the other Cat in sight. Secure for landing." We braced. I wondered if we'd blast into any of the submerged debris we'd been watching. The landing was very smooth, and as the spray washed over us, it was a relief not to feel any impact.

We taxied nearer to the shoreline. Natives were busy covering the first plane with palm fronds and camouflaged it while a considerable stash of gear was being stowed on board. They pulled our Cat into shore and I waded the last few steps, casting an attentive glance across the water's surface as I did so. We mingled with the other crew and shook hands with the Aussies who made no secret of the fact that they were glad to see us. Several offered cups of tea, which tasted awful.

"Japs are only a couple of days behind us and there are thousands of them. Will you be back today?" Jack reassured the lieutenant that we had another pair of planes en route and each PBY planned a second trip. The intent was to have them all out of there in three or four days.

This was certainly a different world than Port Moresby. There was a narrow beach clearing, then a wall of jungle that appeared thick enough to get lost in after only a few yards. The air was alive with sounds—birds and strange, howling creatures that I couldn't identify, the dripping from trees and the sound of the river lapping on shore as sunlight struggled to break through the cloud cover.

The copilot of the other Cat was stowing gear and waved at me to help him with a large piece of equipment. "I wouldn't drink that tea unless you put a couple of iodine buttons in it. River water."

Oh, great, I thought.

His name was Lou, an enlisted guy who had somehow managed flight school training. "How did you swing that?" I asked, more than a little envious.

"I was dating a girl whose father knew an admiral. I went over to dinner one night and he shows up and we got to talking. I told him I had always wanted to fly, and he said that there wasn't any rule against enlisted guys getting their wings. So, me and a buddy went for it."

"That's all there was to it?"

"Not quite. My orders came in and I had them stored next to my bunk on the *Arizona*. They went down with the ship."

"You were on the *Arizona*?" I said, astounded.

CHAPTER 29

"I was trying to get back to the bridge, but wasn't able to get back up top to help get her out of there. The bridge and half the ship blew up. I spent the next hour up to my knees in water or in the lifeboat, pulling guys in and shooting at planes. Worst day of my life."

"Holy cow, I was there that day. I was supposed to meet my cousin Paul. I think we were coming to meet with you."

"That's you! What's your name?" he asked.

"Owen Trimbel."

Lou reached out his hand. As I shook it, he added, "I'm real sorry about Paul. He was a good man."

"Thanks. I...I guess I better get busy over at the other plane. Great finally meeting you, Lou."

"Likewise, Owen. Keep your head down."

I assured him I would and made my way along the beach toward our plane. My mind was racing, flooded with thoughts of that day.

Johnny saw me and spoke up as he swung a machine gun away from the blister hatch and secured it. "You OK?"

"Sure. I'm OK."

The coastwatchers' gear included wooden boxes that contained Morse code devices the evacuees were using to transmit intel on the Japanese in the area. There was a variety of weaponry, machine guns, and ammo. Apparently, these guys had been stirring up quite a bit of trouble. There were two hundred and nineteen of them in all, and we had to get them out fast, so it was decided to take about fifteen or eighteen at a time, depending on the stored equipment on each Cat.

Tribesman observing the whole exercise appeared friendly enough, and in no particular hurry. It seemed like they wanted to feed us. Part of their custom. They were going to round up a young girl from a rival tribe to bring to the feast...as the main course. Another custom.

Manners were important here, and no one was quite sure what would amount to an insult. Our spokesman was careful to politely communicate that our "chief" had ordered us to work first and maybe play later.

It was nearly 1300 hours under clear, steamy skies, and the shorts the guys wore didn't stop the heat, humidity, and full on sun from soaking clear through. That river looked good, except for the crocodiles. The plane was packed and it was time to go.

"See you next trip," Johnny said with a wave of encouragement to a forlorn looking New Guinea policeman. Engine one cranked over slowly and then kicked out a blast of smoke as it caught. I was pleased when engine two did the same.

We lifted off, and by now, the afternoon clouds were beginning to again shroud the area between the mountains. This was a good thing as it turned out. Japanese Zeroes had spotted the planes and we quickly banked and gained elevation, entering the clouds and going on instruments. By climbing in circles, we stayed out of sight and the Zeroes never dared enter the cloud cover. At around 9,000 feet, we were battling the thin air with all the passengers and heavy cargo aboard. But we were high enough to head south through the eight thousand foot pass and toward Port Moresby.

Over the next two days, we repeated the trip. The crew remained alert and attentive, and each time, the pilots found their way through the clouds and mountain passes before snaking along the extensive, winding river course. On one occasion, we heard an enemy plane while in the camp but were apparently not seen. Loaded to the gills, we struggled again to get off the water and into the safety of the clouds, hoping that our adversary wasn't still nosing around up there somewhere.

Our crew had one more trip to make, and the remaining evacuees were concerned that time was getting short. We were one of the last two Cats to load, and we split the remaining gear and coastwatchers between us. It would be good to get out of here.

Johnny was closing the blister and noticed something. "Hey, Owen. Something's wrong with the other Cat. That one engine isn't turning over."

"Uh-oh." I leaned forward through the bulkhead doorway and yelled to Lane who was listening on his headset. "What's up?"

CHAPTER 29

"I think they said their starter's jammed. Better take a look."

"Damn. That's not good. OK, let me ask if there's anything we can do to help 'em."

I waded near shore and over to the other Cat. After some discussion, the mechanic said they needed another starter, and to replace it, the generator had to be removed. This Dumbo wasn't going anywhere today, so it was decided to camouflage it and leave Lieutenant Ragsdale and the remaining coastwatchers with it overnight. The rest of their crew would travel back with us to Port Moresby and return the next day. It would be a long night for the lieutenant.

The next morning, two mechanics joined with one of the radiomen, a fellow named Vernon, who was added since responsibilities concerning generators fall to them. By the time the crew with the replacement starter arrived back at the Sepik River, the trackers had found evidence that the Japanese were less than five miles away. Vernon later said the wrenches and wire cutters flew as a starter was lifted into position and tested. The props kicked over and began to spin. She warmed up normally as the remaining cargo, human and otherwise, was tucked safely onboard, and the Cat was soon airborne.

Johnny and I watched from the dock as they landed in the small bay central to Port Moresby and taxied toward us. We, on shore, knew what they didn't know—that they had made it out of there only minutes before the Japs descended on the camp.

THE LAST WORD

Chapter 30

Owen had always felt painting the Catalinas black was a clever tactical response to the heavy loss of aircraft they suffered during the early months of the war, and he was proud to learn that his second squadron helped innovate the concept.

At the same time Owen was undergoing the first phases of his training back in the States, a lumbering, poorly armed fleet of PBYs was coming up on the short end of squabbles with faster and better-suited Japanese fighters. Worse yet, the Catalinas constituted much of the Navy's air force in the South Pacific. Vulnerable and easy prey by day, the newly painted planes would become effective hunters at night.

This squadron had been in the Solomon Islands area a year before Owen joined them and were on the ground floor of the conflict as the initial pushback by U.S. forces began. The area around Guadalcanal was critical, but even simple sub searches and information gathering about enemy positions were dangerous if done in the daylight. A black plane equipped with radar and flying at night was a new concept, an experiment in on-the-job training.

Owen remembered bumping into Lou again a few days after the Sepik mission, and they sat and caught up over a cup of coffee. Owen was justifiably curious about differences between his old group's history and the newer one, so the two of them compared notes. Lou had spent most of 1943 with the squadron, joining up with them between tours when they were reorganized back home in the United States. It had been an active group well before Owen arrived, and Lou had been in the thick of it.

There was a mission, for instance, in September, a patrol with another Cat off the coast of New Guinea. "Lou told me a shell blew through the fuselage and into the parachute flares in the rear of the plane," Owen began. "Right near the life rafts. The flares caught fire. A crewman closed the bulkhead door and burned himself doing it." He shook his head, emphasizing the predicament. "Everyone moved forward, away from the fire, but the machine guns and ammo were still at risk, so they needed to ditch before things got any worse."

Dan asked, "Now this is the same Lou from the *Arizona*?"

"Yep. They landed about seven miles off the coast of New Guinea and jumped out. Swam away from the burning plane."

Dan studied the aged man's eyes and could see there was a lot more to the story. Like the life jackets and raft. They were still on board the plane. And the ammo began going off as it burned, further complicating matters. The sea was choppy with ten to twelve foot swells, and then…

"That was about the time when the first shark fins broke the surface."

Sandy groaned. "Agghh. My worst nightmare! What did they do?" she added, anxiously.

"Everybody locked arms and formed a circle, facing out. They tried to punch or kick the bastards in the snout and keep them away." Sandy's face was frozen in a grimace, as he continued. "I guess this went on for another forty minutes. Finally, the other plane spotted them and made a couple of low passes so they could drop a life raft as close as possible. All nine of them scrambled aboard."

"The plane is gone, they're seven miles from land, and it's dark," Jonas summed up.

"They rowed for shore and hid in the jungle until daybreak. Japanese were everywhere. The good news was that twenty feet into the jungle, the crew was invisible." Owen interrupted his own story, fascinated by his daughter's posture and expressions. "How are you doing, my dear?" he asked with a small giggle. She had both feet up on her chair and seemed to be hiding behind her knees, as she nodded. Owen continued. "So they laid low, and the next night they heard a PT boat. Lou and another guy snuck out…

CHAPTER 30

tried to flag it down. Suddenly, they were staring down the barrel of the PT's machine gun. It was dark, and it was lucky they didn't get shot! They sorted it out and all managed to get out of there."

"My gosh!" Dan observed, giving a slight shake of his head. "This Lou *was* a busy fellow!"

"That he was. Great guy, too. And this rescue of coastwatchers was quite an accomplishment. No casualties, hundreds of evacuees. I still can't believe it."

Dan said, "I once read a book called *Lost in Shangri-La...*"

"Yes!" Owen said with an exaggerated shake of his head. "That book would give you a taste of how rugged this place was. Huge, sheer mountains always socked in with clouds, unexplored jungles. Headhunters and undiscovered cultures. This mission was a tricky one."

Jonas gave Owen a quizzical look. "Were the crews seriously concerned about these headhunters?"

"Well, the natives we encountered on the Sepik didn't feel threatening, really. But there were plenty of wild stories. Now, the Japanese, on the other hand." He closed his eyes and squeezed them tight. "When I was in Kaneohe with my first squadron, some late arrivals shipped in and joined us. There was a new copilot, even greener than I was, and he came walking by, looking lost… asked me for some directions. We talked for a while and he seemed like a real nice guy." Owen leaned forward slightly. "A couple of months later, they were behind us again getting into Perth. We bumped into each other and I think I kidded him about it. You know, always being late," he said with a half-smile. "I'd see him every once in a while after that," he continued. "I remember he met a girl in Perth and heard that he got married after I left the squadron." Owen gave Bilge a reassuring pat on the head. "Later in 1944, I moved up to Tinian…our skipper up there was a former Black Cat, too…He told me that one of the Black Cat crews I'd flown with had been shot down."

"Where did it happen?" Dan asked.

"A part of Indonesia." Owen replied. "Nine of eleven survived the crash. I guess they scrambled for supplies. A radio, a few weapons. After several days, they met up with a native and he led them to a village…*to help with an escape*, he said." He wiggled his head. "It was a trick. Those villagers swarmed in on them while they slept. And turned them over to the Japanese." He went on, "I forget what they call it now, but they ended up in a place that used to be Celebes. A prison camp. For a while…" Owen said. He grimaced. "We heard they brought them out a few at a time over a couple of days…A big event with a crowd watching. Made each kneel, blindfolded and hands bound, by a hole in the ground. A soldier stood over them with a Samurai sword. Sliced their heads off."

Jonas exhaled, and nodded. "The Japanese had a big base on Celebes. I read about some of those atrocities," he said. "Did you know any of the crewmen?"

"The one young pilot I'd met in Kaneohe who'd been married. His wife was pregnant." Owen noticed Sandy give a tiny side-to-side shake of her head. "There were war crime trials. It took years to find out the whole story. But the rumors found their way around the Black Cat membership pretty quickly, as I remember."

"I can't imagine," Dan said. He looked at Sandy and judging from her expression, felt it was a good time to change the subject. "Did I hear you say that you were in the last weeks of your time there before heading home?"

"Pretty close. The action was pushing farther and farther north. We had a feeling we were going to move soon. Then another group of Cats was sent in to relieve us."

"Wow, you must have been looking forward to getting back. What was it like?" Jonas asked.

"It *was* good to set foot in the old U.S.A. again. Get back to the farm." Owen scrunched his face up. "Man, I wasn't sure how it was going to feel with Dad. I'd been writing, but the mail and packages that came from home were all from Mom or in her handwriting. I was pretty sure he was still ticked off at me for enlisting out of Hawaii…underage. But he never turned me in."

Time away had assuaged any remaining irritation in his father's mind. Owen discovered it had been replaced by pride. His

CHAPTER 30

dad called him into the parlor one evening after dinner and turned around holding two snifters of brandy. It was a scene unlike any Owen had ever experienced with him before. After a few minutes of bush-beating, his father admitted that the whole point of sending him on the sabbatical to Hawaii in the first place was to see if he might grow up a little bit. And he had and quickly. His father was, indeed, proud of that, even if he didn't express it as well as his mother did.

"We had a nice visit, when he wasn't on me to buck hay or shovel snow. And it was colder than a polar bear's toenails, too. I wasn't used to that after two years of tropical places!" He sighed. "Yeah…we were all right again."

Dan could see he felt good about this. "You sound as if you still find it comforting."

"I guess I do. It was a breakthrough of sorts. When I came home at the end of the war, I only saw him for a short time before going to work in the woods. Of course, he passed while I was gone. We never had another moment like that one again."

Jonas inquired, "Dan mentioned a mistake by the hospital—wrong blood type or something?"

"That's right."

"So I take it they at least made a settlement of some kind. Helped your mother out?" Jonas asked.

"Nah, it was an honest mistake. Things were different then. People didn't sue over everything that went on in their lives."

"Really?" Jonas said, widening his eyes in disbelief.

"They might have given us a discount on the transfusion."

"That would be only fair," Dan laughed. He digested Owen's words, and then asked, "And your mom?"

"She didn't do well after he was gone. Only lived for a couple of years. I stayed and worked on the farm, but she seemed to just kind of fade. She missed him an awful lot."

"I never met either of them," Sandy added. "But as we were going through her things one day, we found this."

Sandy reached up on the bookshelf and grasped what looked like book made out of wood. It was large, like an album, and its wooden cover was bound with a cord and polished like a table. Centered on its front cover was a color photo of a menacing, hissing black feline.

"A scrapbook?" Dan guessed. He had overlooked it when examining Owen's library the day before, its wooden exterior camouflaged in the bookshelf's finish.

Owen's mother had faithfully kept an elaborate collection of photos, certificates, and newspaper clippings pertaining to PBYs, Black Cats, and Owen's time in training and on duty in the Pacific Theater. Magazine articles with exotic locations that our troops currently occupied were mingled with his graduation diploma from Gunnery School, all arranged in an approximate timeline of events. It was a stunning piece of work. A true labor of love.

"Here's a letter written home," Sandy pointed out. "December 31, 1943."

"Oh…" Owen exhaled slowly.

*Off the coast of New Britain
December 31, 1943*

— Chapter 31 —

Dear Mom, Dec. 31,1943

Sorry it's been so long since I've written. We've been busy here for the last two months, but it looks like all that work is going to pay off. We've made life tough for the enemy, so much so, that there isn't as much left in our area to do. I thought we might be moving, but now, we are being relieved! I should start winding my way home very soon…

I felt crummy about not writing sooner, and I wanted to get this letter out to the folks before we left New Guinea. After a good start, I just wasn't coming up with much else to say. We had been busy, sure, but I never knew what I could tell them that Navy censors wouldn't slice back out as soon as they laid their grimy little mitts on it. I mulled this over while stuffing another few socks in my sea chest and wondered if I'd be able to get it closed. Did I bring all this stuff with me?

Another squadron had arrived at Port Moresby to relieve us and we still had a couple of days to figure things out before making our way back to Perth for some well-deserved R&R. From there, Brisbane, where we'd catch a ride back to Hawaii.

As I was deliberating over my sea chest, I couldn't help but overhear a conversation between a couple of guys saying that one of our planes might need to make a run to pick up a B-25 crew. They had been shot down off the southwest tip of New Britain and five guys were in a life raft. Four P-40s were in the area to try and protect them, but couldn't stay in the air forever.

It was nearly chow time, and I'd made my way down the dimly lit, steel corridor in the general direction of the mess. Lou and another fellow were just leaving, and he stopped to say, "Hi." It turns out they were going to make the run north and the pickup. I mentioned I hadn't ever been on an open sea rescue before, and he smiled and said, "Why don't you come along. We could probably use an extra hand."

Our replacement squadron should have been assigned to this, but they hadn't been up there yet, and with a water landing, it was decided they would piggy back along a quarter mile or so off our wing to assist.

Visibility wasn't the best by the time we reached the area, and we began circling at about five hundred feet with all eyes intent on the ocean surface below. There was a voice from the port side. "There they are." I shuffled over to the blister and had a look. Sure enough, the raft was bobbing not a half mile away from us. The pilot continued circling to get oriented into the wind for landing and the engineer lowered the floats.

We had just begun our approach when we were surprised by two fighters thundering in from above us in a steep dive. The first opened up as he flashed by us and our pilot put it into a steep bank to escape. The second fighter was more accurate, and a line of shells raked through the fuselage and knocked out an engine. I ducked down in the blister as it roared overhead, and the distinct image of a blue circle and white star under the plane's wing screamed past me. It wasn't a zero, it was a P-40! We were being attacked by our own planes! The PBY began shaking violently and over the intercom, I heard Lou's voice. They were ditching.

I held on as we plowed into a swell, skipped back into the air, and slid across another before finally settling into the cradle between two swells. We began taking on water. I could see the other PBY was approaching us. I felt the urge to scream at them to stay clear, like it would have done any good. But this time, the

CHAPTER 31

fighters kept their distance. Maybe they recognized the profile of the second plane. And their blunder.

Apparently, the P-40s that had been protecting the life raft thought we were about to strafe it, mistaking our blackened silhouette for a Japanese Betty. They had come at us straight on, peppering the front of the aircraft and badly wounding the bow gunner. He was the same crewman who had been burned a few months earlier when Lou's plane crash-landed off the coast of New Guinea.

It was pure luck that no one else had been hit, and within a few minutes, our sidekick Catalina had landed safely and taxied over alongside. We transferred our gear and personnel to the other plane, and I watched in disbelief as the injured gunner was gingerly conveyed to a bunk.

Within minutes, we lifted off and landed a short distance away to retrieve the men in the raft. They had almost become an afterthought.

Within a few hours, we were back at Port Moresby, and I was alone with my own thoughts.

That night, I unfolded my note and picked up a pencil. I knew now what to say and what my mom would want to hear.

> *Things have been pretty quiet here of late. I've been packing today and will bring you something from the South Pacific. Can't wait to see you both! Give Dad a hug for me. And don't worry.*
>
> *Love,*
> *Owen*

Three days later, I was back in Perth when word reached us that the bow gunner didn't make it.

THE LAST WORD

Chapter 32

The room exploded with the sound of Bilge's booming bark. He was nearly airborne and rushed out of the room, bellowing the whole way.

"Bilge!" Sandy shouted but to no avail. "He heard something, I guess. I'll be right back," she said.

"I heard it, too." Dan agreed. "Maybe I should come with you."

Sandy gave him a glance, "I'll be right back," and disappeared down the hallway.

The three men looked around at each other in silence. "Cards, anyone?" Owen said.

"I'll deal," Jonas replied.

Sandy reentered the room with Bilge in tow. "One of those idiots backed into a tree," she reported.

"Is everything all right out there?" Dan asked.

"Seems to be. Except there are more of them each time I look. Maybe it's my imagination."

"Like dandelions," Owen said. "You don't notice when they take over the lawn. They just do."

"Do you think I should check it out?" Dan asked.

Sandy shook her head. "Let's ignore the buggers. It will just encourage them."

Bilge flailed at his mug with his solitary back leg in a violent, tearing motion, sending globs of foam and spittle onto Owen's pants. The boxer stood abruptly and launched into a full-out, lip stretching dog shake that scattered floating hairs and more globs in Owen's direction. When Bilge stalled his routine, Jonas noticed that his collar had *dog tags* attached to its loop. Ready to settle in,

Bilge, now hoisted the leg over his head and attended to some dog business down in his more private reaches. Owen seemed not to notice any of it.

Jonas was standing over by the bookshelves and was captivated by a photograph of Owen and a woman, both probably in their forties. "Is this your wife, Owen?"

"That's my sweetheart, Shirley. She passed away...let's see, fifteen, no sixteen years ago? I think. I dunno, math anymore," he said, a touch exasperated.

"Beautiful woman," Jonas continued.

Sandy interrupted. "Mom was a farmer, a wife, a mother, a seamstress, a chef. And she was, through it all, *very* beautiful. I don't know how she managed it."

"And you said you were married for how long?" Dan asked.

"Gad, more math. Help, Sandy."

"We celebrated your seventieth two years before she died. She wasn't doing too well by then. It was a very difficult time, as you can imagine."

Sandy admired her mother's skills at parenting and running a household. And there was no one who baked a better loaf of rosemary bread or a more sumptuous strawberry-rhubarb buckle than her mom. And of course, there was her legendary fruitcake.

"You had to be careful around it with matches," Owen began. "She soaked it every day for a month with a hundred and fifty proof rum."

"Oh, by golly, I can feel my lips humming just thinking about it," Sandy quipped. "Like they were sunburned!"

"So moist," Owen said, nearly drooling. "I always slept like a baby after a slice or two of Shirley's fruitcake."

Maybe it was her sense of humor that endeared her to the family the most. "Remember that Thanksgiving when we had the cousins all up here and she was chopping the sweet potatoes?" As the story went, Shirley was working on her brown-sugar-sweet-tater casserole and merrily slicing away with a large chef's knife. She suddenly thwacked the knife down on the cutting board and simply said, "Oh, no," simultaneously grasping her hand. Two of

CHAPTER 32

the cousins spun their heads around uneasily and rushed up behind her as she dashed to the sink and thrust a finger with a gruesome injury under the tap. Only the finger was made out of rubber.

Owen and Sandy could hardly contain themselves, each adding additional tidbits to the story for sweetening, dabbled with snorts of laughter. "Cousin Nancy had a *burnt pie* fit over that one," Sandy sniggered, wiping the tears from her eyes.

"You had to be there," Owen added with a short cough, alert to the polite smiles Jonas and Dan were sporting. "What was it we were we talking about?"

"Your anniversary. And Christmas and Thanksgiving. I suppose I should ask about a birthday. Did you do anything special for your one hundredth? Or since then?" Dan asked.

"He never let us surprise him," Sandy replied. "We had fun at your one hundredth though, didn't we, Dad?" she added. Owen gave her an agreeable smile. "It was at the Richardson's. We set it up in their barn, lots of decorations, and just about everyone in the family and neighborhood was there. Gosh, it seems like such a long time ago," she admitted. "We kept it pretty low profile this year, though, huh, Dad?" she said, as she turned toward her father.

"I didn't want to burn down the house. I'd need a hose to put out all those candles." His face softened, and he seemed to drift. "No, it's never been quite the same. After she passed."

THE LAST WORD

Long Beach, California
Summer of 1951

—ᴡ— Chapter 33 —ᴡ—

"How much farther?" Shirley asked me with a giggle.

"We're almost there," I assured her. "Don't ruin the surprise!"

It was our one-year anniversary. Sort of. Shirley started reminding me about a week back that it had been that long since we'd met and began dating. She'd told me she wanted to do something special, different. And I had an idea.

I drove through a few neighborhoods and took the most confusing roundabout of a route I could think of, trying to confuse her. But as we came around the corner, there was that Ferris wheel, towering and colorful, and I knew the jig was up.

"The Pike!" she squealed. "Can we go on the carousel?"

We parked and I looked at her beaming face. It was hard to believe that a year had gone by since her mother allowed us that first ride. A year of getting acquainted, sipping drinks at the soda shop, of strolling downtown and sheepishly kissing for the first time.

"Boy, I don't know. I was hoping we might go on the 'Cyclone.' I hear it's even faster than last year," I said.

Her face fell, but she saw right through me and quickly brightened again. "Let's go!"

We strolled up the main promenade, past some of the food choices along the way and that rip-off of a shooting gallery. Shirley crowded up close to the carousel, while I did a little business.

THE LAST WORD

"How much if I buy tickets for the whole outside row," I asked the operator, a fellow fitted with a straw hat and apron.

"How many people you got?" I showed him two fingers. "Can't do that. Everyone likes the outside row."

"Listen, it's our anniversary. Why can't I buy all the tickets for just that set of ponies? There can't be five dollars' worth involved. I'll give you ten!"

He pushed his hat a few inches forward and stuck out his jaw. "OK. Give me the ten. Just one ride after this next bunch goes through. So I can keep the next ones off of 'em."

"Golly, that's great! Thanks!"

A close call. I had rehearsed it in my mind for days. She would pick out her palomino and I'd retreat back to the opposite side. It would be a lot tougher with so many people around the dang contraption. This time, it wasn't midnight.

"That looks like your favorite horse! Let me find mine and see if he can still catch you." She was loving it.

The massive machine began to rotate and the music became more intense. I reached into my pocket, this time not for a stuffed horse, but for a special ribbon, and tied a knot. As the brass ring drew closer, I dashed ahead and tied my surprise ring to it, and hurried back.

Then I saw him, a little kid three animals ahead of Shirley had gotten in the outside row. No! He wanted a brass ring. He was reaching out. Missed! He was too short!

Her palomino carried her ahead and she focused on the brass ring, then did a delightful double take when she spied the ring I had tied onto it. She pulled it free and held it between the fingers of both hands. It sparkled with every color of the carousel. As she spun around to look behind her, there I was. Caught her again! She hopped off the palomino and jumped up on my mule, surrounding me in a full embrace. I slid the ring on her finger, and we looked into each other's eyes—her's welling up with tears. Our lips met. It was a kiss that could last a lifetime—and in that instant, we became one. With my eyes closed, we were encircled by the sound of hands clapping, voices cheering, and the rhythm of the calliope music.

Chapter 34

As Owen continued to recount a long and colorful history, Dan silently chided himself for sometimes being distracted by different physical characteristics of the man. He'd never met anyone who was a hundred before, much less someone nearly a dozen years their senior. The human body was capable of creating remarkable structural changes over that time. A classic and familiar appearance evolves, a metamorphosis that was difficult to ignore after listening to an unhurried, gravelly voice for fifteen or twenty minutes. Odd skeletal angles and protruding bone formations, thin skin tattooed with blemishes, discolorations, and growth tags, many with groves of white hair standing from them, frozen like a cluster of fiber optic strands. Flesh sags, wrinkles become facial fjords, complex furrows that spider-web along arms, neck, and around eyes, raisin-like surfaces splotched in blue, red, pink, and brown. A fascinating reshaping and resizing of the ear and nose.

A picture of Owen and his crew posing in front of the plane featured eight vibrant young men scarcely out of high school, each glistening with adolescence. Dan had also studied Owen's service photo. Try as he might, he couldn't make out how the images of him were of the same person. Although there was something in the eyes. Perhaps if the young Owen had been smiling, that would have provided the evidence.

Jonas surprised Dan with a timely question. "Owen, I don't want this to appear inappropriate. I'm just getting to know you. But I've never met anyone who is…well, your age before. Frankly, it's hard not to be curious about things."

Owen flashed his eyes a second, then tendered a small motion of the head and a reassuring smile. "Shoot."

"Well, how do you do it? I guess that's what we all wonder. How does someone find their way down the path for a hundred and twelve years?"

"Interesting question. As I like to say, I never planned on living forever. So far so good, though, huh?" He enjoyed watching their reaction. "I've been asking myself that same question for about fifty of those years. I don't know what's going on either, Jonas." He broke into a now familiar grin. "I used to tell everyone it was the spam we ate. But most of my life, we actually ate pretty well. The land and garden were good to us." He pointed toward the bookcase. "There's a book up there on *aging*. It was Shirley's. We may have gotten it when she started having trouble remembering things…what day it was, where we were going. I looked at it. It said we are like babies twice, once at each end of our lives. Something like that." He looked him in the eye. "How old are you, Jonas?"

"Fifty-nine."

"Just a number isn't it? If you were an animal, well you'd be an incredibly old donkey, or a middle aged tortoise like the ones we saw down around the Galapagos Islands. Hell, if I was one, I'd still be in my prime."

Dan wondered, "Do you…think about death?" He found himself flinching at his own question. He was thankful Sandy wasn't in the room.

"When you know it's so close, somehow, it's less of a focus. I guess you don't want it to be unnecessarily painful, and more than anything, I worry about the ones I leave behind," he said with a sigh. "Have I done enough? What security have I given them? What can I pass down, other than old war souvenirs and books? I think about that a lot."

"Was there a time when you felt something unusual was going on?" Jonas asked.

Owen shrugged. "Maybe. Even at your age, you probably notice now that aches and pains crop up over almost nothing. You know," he said, as if he expected they knew what he was referring to. "Like when you're in a store and hear a voice behind

CHAPTER 34

you? When you turn your head to look back—bam! Pulled neck muscle!"

They both smiled in agreement.

"By the way, I'm here to tell you it only gets worse." The two men cringed in mock horror. "I'll bet your conversations with friends focuses more on doctors and health than what kind of car you like, right?" He went on to tell them that for a time, maybe back in his late sixties and early seventies, it seemed nearly a decade passed without much changing. Up until then it seemed every four or five years, it was a frozen shoulder or eye pressure problems. There were prescriptions and watching that cholesterol. "It felt like I was coming apart. Then for ten years, it pretty much stopped! Oh, I still had the usual little stuff. Creaky joints, foggy brain in the morning. Weird looking toenails." He screwed up his face at that one. "But really, it seemed those years were pretty uneventful. I was afraid to even say anything."

Jonas and Dan exchanged a look. Owen added, "I'm over all that now, as you can see." He grinned. "Like Yogi Berra used to say, 'Always go to other people's funerals, otherwise they won't go to yours.'" He waited a moment, then stared squarely at Dan. "You're not going to tell me you don't know who *Yogi* was, now are you?"

"Yogi? No, I'm good. Big fan, in fact. Great quarterback, Yogi."

"C'mon, Dan. He was a goalie!" Jonas chided.

Owen rolled his eyes. "You're both old donkeys."

Dan was enjoying the banter, rich exchanges he couldn't have dreamed of twenty-four hours ago. He wanted more. "Owen, you've seen your share of decades come and go…" He cast about for the words. "Just for fun, is there some accomplishment, some example of human ingenuity that you've seen during your lifetime that feels especially remarkable? What impresses you most?"

"Golly, where do you start?" Owen looked around the room as if searching for it. "Well, I've told you how I've always marveled at the plant world." He gestured with his thumb and forefinger, the fingertips slightly apart. "You take a miniature seed

— 163 —

and plant it, and it's like one of those little chips you have in that amazing watch of yours. Unimaginable what's inside. That seed might really be a four hundred-foot redwood. Or a banyan tree like we saw in Hawaii in training…with spreading limbs and tentacles covering a quarter acre," he said, with both arms extended. "It's all in there. And humans figured out how to do it. Make seeds for computers. Hard not to be impressed by that."

"I'm impressed that you thought of it," Dan said.

"Me, too," Jonas added, hoisting his eyebrows. "Say, Owen, I've wanted to ask you something since we arrived today. This whole idea of being the *last* guy. What do you think about that? I mean, do you think we'll ever really know who the last guy is?"

"I don't see why it matters," Owen replied. "The first guy was more important. And that person likely wasn't even a soldier. Or a *guy*."

Dan was intrigued. "How do you mean?"

"Well, the war in Europe began with the bombing of cities in Poland, right? Japan and China had been at it for a couple of years by then. A bunch of civilians were in the way in both places."

"I see what you mean," Jonas said. "But when I think of the Civil War or World War I, well these were both conflicts—eras really—that will remain forever distinct. Iconic. Being the last member of a group that had actual combat experience in something like that—I guess I feel like that's pretty significant. And historic. Up until the Japanese fellow passed away, we thought the last American serviceman was someone else." He looked over at Dan, requesting his take with a glance.

"Let's see. Sam, how old was the recently deceased Japanese World War II vet?"

"Dan, using the date-of-birth to date-of-death tally, he was one hundred twelve years, two months, and twenty-seven days old," she replied instantly. "Would you prefer a more accurate tally of total days living?"

"No, Sam, that's fine."

"How old am I?" Owen asked meekly.

Before Dan could even ask, Samantha's toothsome voice

CHAPTER 34

added, "Owen Trimbel is one hundred twelve years, one month, and twenty-two days old today."

"Looks like you've got some work to do, Owen," Dan snickered.

"I *would* like to beat that Jap," Owen said. His face warmed, and he added, "Aahh, just messin' with you."

Jonas noted, "You already have him beat where it counts, I guess. He'd be a tough interview today."

Sandy and Bilge appeared in the doorway, one of them in a brisk, three-legged trot. "How's the meeting going, everyone?" The men welcomed her back and brought her up to speed. "Ouch, getting to the nitty gritty, I see. What do you think Bilge, you want to stick around for this?"

"Oh, we're only talking in generalities now, honey. Heck, death is a remarkable thing in many ways. For instance, I find myself admiring trees. When I die, and they put me in the ground, I'm gone with scarcely a trace in a couple of years." He lifted an arm and gestured toward the window. "See that big cedar out there? It will hit the ground one day at only its halfway point. I've seen them laying there fifty or seventy-five years later and they still look mossy and massive with twice that long still to go before they disappear entirely."

Sandy liked that analogy better than she expected. It made her think about her father's durability. In many ways, he was a cedar. "Well, Dad never wanted to even discuss living anywhere else. We had doctors and even family members suggest how much more sense it made for us to get in closer to town. Any town. Assisted living with all its advantages. So much safer. Dad didn't buy in, so we went a different way. So far so good, huh?" She gave him a smile.

"Same thing I said," he noted, his eyes meeting hers. "Part of why we stay up here in this frigid country in our own house. I couldn't see just putting up my feet and living out my days in a center somewhere. I've always preferred walking around to sitting it out."

Bilge marched up to Owen and gave his hand a prod. The big dog's eyes opened wide and his wrinkled face and hanging lips seemed to ask, *What about me?* in Boxer-ese. Owen tossed him a treat and continued.

"All you can do is make your best guess. For yourself." He looked at all of them thoughtfully. "*It's tough to make predictions, especially about the future.*" Then he looked straight at Dan. "Yogi."

New Ireland vicinity, Bismarck Sea - Fall of 1943

—⚓— Chapter 35 —⚓—

A former VP-54 guy named Vern had transferred into the outfit, much the way I had, and we were like two busy bees on an island beach off the coast of New Ireland. We'd finished unloading a cluster of oil and fuel cans and a sizable stash of ammo for the guerrillas working the jungles nearby. It was time for a break. I sat on one of the oil drums grouped between the water's edge and the jungle and took off my boot to shake the sand out of it.

Vern plopped down next to me and lit a cigarette. I didn't know him well, but he was a guy that could cuss enough to make a pirate blush when he had a drink or two in him. He chuckled as he took a puff. "Don't sweat it, I used to work in a service station. It won't blow your ass up." I smiled back at him like I was never even worried.

"Where are you from?" he asked. I told him about Minnesota and the farm. He had a million questions about it. He was a city boy, growing up in Philadelphia, and the whole concept of living in the country with animals and crops was unimaginable to him. It was a rude awakening, too, flitting around between these islands and seeing jungles so thick they seemed to grow right before your eyes.

I enjoyed hearing him talk about the big city. Tall buildings that reached up and blocked the sun. Their city hall sat right in the middle of a road, with a square block of area around it. Cars just circled the whole place, and people walked on sidewalks through the middle of it. Hearing about holidays in the city made me homesick. All the lights and activities, the music.

"And the girls! I'll tell you what. Philly has some gorgeous broads."

I'll bet it does, I thought to myself. It had been a long time since I'd been around anything but Navy guys and the inside of airplanes. The only female I'd had a real date with since enlisting was a nurse from a base hospital back when we were protecting Ecuador from the Japanese. She was slender with flax-colored hair, and a few years older than I was. I loved hearing her accent. She said she liked mine too, although I never even realized I had one. Who me, from Minnesota?

I saw her a couple of times and one day she suggested we watch the sunset from a beach she knew nearby. I had some time off and that sounded wonderful. It was a lovely secluded spot. In my bag, we had sandwiches and a navy blue blanket, as well as a little red wine to toast the view. I fanned the blanket out over the sand and stashed the bag with my service revolver in its pouch in the corner behind us, then sat down beside her. The sunset gave way to a beautiful evening, with only stars above, and we felt increasingly comfortable in each other's arms. We were still kissing when she sat up, suddenly. "Did you hear that?"

I did hear something and quickly squinted in the darkness for the bag with the pistol. It was gone!

A chill went up my spine as I flashed on whether I'd been all wrong about enemy invaders in South America. Then I realized we'd gotten turned around on the blanket and the bag was now at our feet.

Vern took a last drag on his cigarette, then flicked the glowing ash off its end. I asked him, "What do you think about all of this. I mean the islands, all this ocean, flying every couple days?"

"Well, the winters are nicer than goddamn Philly, I'll give you that. It'd be fine place to be on vacation, ya know?" Smoke rolled out and away from his nostrils. "These flights can be a real bore for hours, then a few minutes later you wonder if your keister will get shot off."

"Have you actually seen any Japanese soldiers? You know, like ground troops moving nearby, that kind of thing?"

CHAPTER 35

"We were on an island over near Bougainville. It was still pretty hot. I mean, we had won the battle, but there were still Japs scattered everywhere around the place, and they was good at staying hid. We parked our plane and the skipper posts me and another guy to protect it. Those bastards had slipped some hand grenades into a Corsair a few days back."

Vern told me that as darkness closed in, their clever and diminutive flight engineer, a fellow named Harold, had the idea of using a helmet instead of a short stick to prop open one of the blisters like a mousetrap. If an uninvited trespasser happened by, he would lift up on the hatch and the helmet would drop to the ground. "Sure enough, that night, we hear a thump-thump that sounds like a helmet bouncing, and there's this guy hotfooting it away from the plane. Harold's right after him, but the SOB ducked into the jungle and was gone into the night."

"Sounds like you guys were pretty lucky."

Vern waved a hand and tossed his cigarette butt into the sand. "Ah, you're lucky only half of the time, right?"

I thought about this for a minute. Had I been lucky or unlucky recently? I guessed it didn't matter. We gathered up our things and headed for the Catalina.

Back at the tender, chow tasted particularly good, and I had my mind set on some ice cream. I stood to clear away my tray, and here comes Vern, strolling over to the table.

"Hey, did you hear?" I gave him a puzzled look. "After we left today, the Japs swooped in and hit that island. Bombed and strafed everything on the beach, right where we were sitting, and blew it all to hell!" He lit a cigarette. "Bad luck for those guerrillas, huh, losing all their shit." Then he walked on past like it was nothing.

I thought to myself, how lucky can you get?

THE LAST WORD

Chapter 36

Sandy walked in holding the telephone handset with her hand covering the mouthpiece. "Dad, it's for you," adding in an exaggerated whisper, "I think it might be Clark, again." She mouthed a quick apology to Dan and Jonas as she handed it to him.

"Hello…Oh, hi, Clark. How's…huh? You just heard what? How can that be? Well, I suppose it would explain why there's a dozen cars that won't get off of my lawn…Yep, parked all over it. That's what dying last buys you. Ruts in your grass…Uh, huh…On the news, too? Well gosh darnit, it must be a pretty slow day around the world then…Yep…Yep, that's me, biggest toad in the pond." The two of them exchanged for another minute or two. "Listen, I still have this nice young fella over here and I…no, he didn't park there. At least, I don't think he did. I'll have to ask him…You too, Clark. OK, bye."

As he hung up the phone, Owen flexed a shoulder and stared at Dan. "I'm supposed to ask you," he began, "if you can deliver a copy of your paper up here to Clark's after the article is finished." He puffed out his cheeks like a blowfish.

"I'll see what I can do," was Dan's vaguely serious reply. "It may be tricky, seeing that we no longer use paper." Dan peeked over at the camera screens and then began again. "You were telling us about leaving the South Pacific area and heading home for some rest and retraining." Owen bobbed his head. "Your last couple of months down there were busy ones from the sound of it. Was the trip home more uneventful?"

"Boring is more like it. We made it back to Brisbane, and then some of us were sent home from there, along with members of other squadrons. We zigzagged in a troop ship and took twice the time we needed to make Hawaii." He moved a fist side to side to suggest the motion. "Worried about enemy subs. It was back and forth for weeks." He swallowed hard. "Pearl Harbor still gave me the willies. They had done so much work, and it felt like a naval base again, but the scars weren't all gone. I could barely make myself look at the *Arizona*."

Sandy wondered, "Did you stay and train again right there in Hawaii, or did they let you go back home first?"

"We went stateside and stayed with the folks, like I mentioned. Johnny and I were hoping for a change. We talked with some higher-ups, filled out some paperwork. As much as I loved the Catalinas, Johnny convinced me we should try for something different, something new and exciting. Get up north and into one of the bigger bombers. As it turned out, both of my Black Cat squadrons were extremely active the rest of the way, too. Especially the first one. I think we talked about that."

Jonas asked, "And did you and Johnny make it into *something different*?"

"We both went into training a few hundred miles south of here."

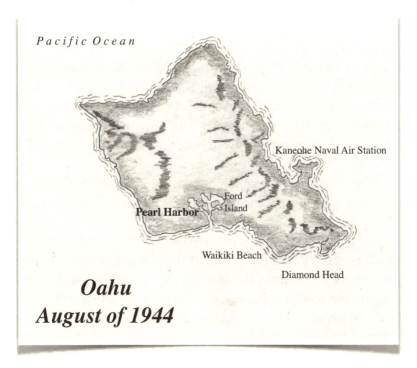

Oahu
August of 1944

—∞— Chapter 37 —∞—

B ack in Kaneohe again. Who would have imagined I'd visit Hawaii four times in three years? And for such utterly different reasons. As I think about it, there's some nervousness about this particular visit that I can't put my finger on.

When I was training with the other enlisted guys for the new plane, we were in a place called Hutchison, Kansas. Never in my wildest dreams did I expect to end up in Hutchison, Kansas, during a world war.

But it was there that we were paired with pilots and officers and formed the new crews. Twelve of us together in a plane I hadn't expected to fly in—a Liberator.

I'd seen Liberators down in New Guinea but had never actually set foot in one. OK, they were navalized. We called them Privateers now, but they were still B-24s, big and their design was more about carrying bombs than people. And I wasn't crazy about the nickname either. "Flying coffins." We wanted to fly in something different. I guess this was it.

Our fledgling crew went to North Island in San Diego next for what was called "operational training." I was curious about this aircraft, and Johnny and I walked out across the tarmac toward our new home.

They seemed bigger than our PBYs, although the wingspan and length were nearly the same. Even the designation was as a PB4Y-1. But they were not at all the same. They had a pair of tails and were faster and cramped inside, with a tiny ten-inch catwalk running down the center of the bomb bay that you tight-roped across to get from the front to the rear of the plane. When those big, retractable roller-doors were open on either side, well, I thought to myself, walking that gangplank at 10,000 feet must be one heck of an experience.

I was watching one warm up, and she did seem powerful. Four engines all humming along as she began to taxi. As the big plane turned away from me, the prop-wash was impressive, nearly blowing the cap off of my head.

I remember Johnny hollering at me over the roar, "Ready for one of these?"

I grinned, "Guess so!"

We practiced dropping water bombs on the Salton Sea and became familiar with takeoffs and landings on runways instead of water. There were new challenges like firing our guns out of smaller waist windows and the odd feel of the turrets.

Our skipper, as it turns out, was another Black Cat. He flew mostly in the "Slot" and Solomon Islands area before moving to one of the B-24s. I've heard he is good, a little older and experienced, very sharp. Seems like a nice guy.

Now we wait again in Kaneohe, as part of a replacement pool. We don't know when we leave or exactly where we might go. Johnny tells me that it will likely be as a relief crew in the Mariana Islands.

I'm thinking you can practically see Japan from there.

Chapter 38

There was a shiver on Dan's wrist and he could see the message light on his watchband. "Excuse me, Owen. Let me see what this is." He paused the camera and looked at the screen.

"What's up?" Jonas inquired.

There was a message from Samantha highlighted over Owen's image. "I'm not sure. Sam says something's up with the car. "What's happening, Sam?"

"There is unauthorized activity near the car. Shall I trigger the alarm?"

"I wonder what's going on," he whispered to Jonas. "Just send the live feeds, Sam."

"The alarm would be more fun, Dan. Shake things up a little."

Dan scowled. "Just send the videos, Sam."

"Certainly, Dan. You're the boss."

Several seconds passed, and Jonas crowded in to see the screen. "Uhhh…" was all he could muster.

Dan cast his eyes to the ceiling. "Sam, is this porn?"

"Oh, you meant the *other* videos."

"Sandy, I don't…I never…Sam, just send me the live feed from the car!"

There was a brief delay. "Sorry, Dan, my bad. Retrieving now."

The screen lit up with four camera views from around the vehicle.

"Thank God," Dan muttered, breathing a sigh of relief. "Hmm." Dan stretched the screen to enlarge it.

Jonas let out a whistle. "Whew! Where'd they all come from?"

"Don't know. Better take a peek out there. Sandy, are there any police down in Shevlin?"

"There's a sheriff's office in Bagley, nearby. What's wrong?"

"Looks like there's been a change in the landscape outside. Why don't you stay with Owen and let us check on this. Be right back."

Jonas and Dan made their way to the front of the house and stared out the window. There was a collection of small vehicles and two vans strewn across the gravel and lawn and extending down the lane.

"Now what?" Dan grumbled.

"That tripod there with the cone is a sound sensor. They can probably hear us," Jonas observed. "I'd wager there's a few contraptions flying around out there, too."

"Crap. Busybodies *and* listening in." They hurried back to the interview room. "Sandy, do you have a sound system we can use?"

"Of course, I'll show you."

"Great, let's turn it on. Music, talk radio would be even better. And we should probably draw the curtains. Now, the sheriff's office. Do you know anyone?

"Yes, Tom Spencer used to go to school with my daughter. Want me to call down there? "

"Please. Tell them there are some uninvited press people trespassing out here. Upsetting Owen. Can they find us?"

Sandy smiled. "They know their way around. Be right back, Dad."

Jonas dialed in a comedy station while Dan pulled blinds and curtains. "Turn it up," he suggested.

"What's going on?" Owen asked, adjusting his position in his chair as Dan rejoined him.

"I'm sorry to say that more of my *colleagues* in the media seem to have found us. We should be fine in here, and Sandy just invited the Sheriff out for a little lunch. I apologize for this Owen. There are a couple of legitimate reporters and a TV station out there, but so many of these are little guys. Media junkies, military

CHAPTER 38

bloggers, and fanatics who produce their own stuff these days. Every time some tidbit from a news agency flashes on their monitor, they flock to it. Share it with their minions. They're like news tabloids."

"Yellow jackets to a picnic plate."

"Exactly."

"We'll just ignore the lot of them."

Jonas walked in and winked, "Hope they like Robin Williams."

"Perfect," Dan snickered. "Shall we continue? We were talking about the Mariana Islands, I think."

Owen told them his unit replaced another on the island of Tinian. Runways severely damaged during the assault were repaired under duress, and Owen's group arrived amidst reports of mass suicides by frightened Japanese civilians and continued resistance from cave dwellers. He said he had to commend the Seabees, who had worked tirelessly, sometimes as enemy fire raged around them, remodeling and expanding the airstrips into what would become a centerpiece of the air war against Japan.

"Johnny and I were in a big bomber now, but at this point in the war, we still did a ton of patrol. There was a lot of open sea between Japan and Tinian. And no satellites to help," he quipped. "At times, it wasn't that different from the PBYs we'd flown before. Except, we couldn't land in the water."

"But your payload of bombs was very different," Jonas asserted.

"We could carry over eight thousand pounds of them, but it cut into our range. We had a dozen guns on board with turrets everywhere, so we often carried fewer bombs. Sometimes none, if a patrol was the objective."

"Were you a turret gunner at that point, then?" Dan asked.

Owen nodded. "We ended up with a newer plane, a PB4Y-2 instead of 1. They borrowed the blister concept from the PBYs." He smiled as he recalled stepping inside one for the first time on Tinian's North Field. The turret-blister looked something like a space age version of the blister hatches on their old PBYs, like an armor-reinforced eyeball that could rotate up and down, far enough to fire rounds below the plane. When both gunners did this simultaneously, the tracer path could actually cross.

Owen reached a hand out with a piece of broken cookie and offered it to Bilge, who snatched it up happily. He then continued, "Well, you know, the Empire as we called it wasn't that far away. But it was still a long flight. Even for the B-29s, which were the class of the fleet. There was a string of tiny islands between Tinian and Japan. We called it the *Dunk-us Highway*." He explained that more often than not, aircraft were overloaded and flying in rough weather made the situation worse. Sometimes a B-29 or B-24 would run out of fuel on the way home. "They'd go in the drink somewhere along this *highway*. And we'd go out and look for them. Call it in when we located one and continue searching the vector for ships or whatever."

"Really," Dan remarked. "They went out knowing they wouldn't make it?"

Owen chuckled. "It wasn't quite that bad. But you have to remember how many of these flights were being made, almost daily. And in all kinds of conditions. Anyway, the answer was another small island about eight hundred gallons away from us."

Jonas gave him a quizzical look.

"Iwo Jima," Owen said in a somber voice. "Nasty stuff, that one. We had it pretty easy compared to those guys. Beach landings on these islands…well, they're all heroes in my mind. Seven thousand killed and many times that in casualties. Unimaginable."

"And so Iwo cut the flight time," Jonas said.

"Once runways were repaired and became available, we could land, pick up eight hundred gallons, and cruise home."

Sandy opened the door and all three of the men whirled their heads around to face her.

> *It's O-six hundred hours. What does the 'O' stand for? O my God, it's early!*

CHAPTER 38

"Yikes! Sorry, you guys," Sandy said in a sheepish voice as she closed the door behind her. "I guess that radio should be loud enough. Is it giving you problems in here?"

Dan gave her a reassuring sign. "Samantha has a background filter running interference on the cameras. We should be fine. Anything new outside?"

"Another vehicle pulled in. Tom should be here any minute. How's it going?"

"Very well," Dan said. "Owen was just telling us more about Tinian and all the work that was done as they rebuilt it after the invasion."

"Yeah, there was a guy I met in Kaneohe during training. Don't remember which time. His name was Erwin and he'd decided to become a Seabee." He grinned and leaned back in his chair. "We bumped into each other every once in a while after that and got to be pretty good friends. He did a bunch of work on Tinian. Told me at least one of the Seabees must have been from New York City." He threw another scrap of cookie to Bilge. "The roads all had names right out of Manhattan. *Broadway* was a straight shot, north and south nearly the length of the island. *Riverside Drive* ran up the west side…I think there was a *6th Avenue*. That kind of thing."

"Huh. Those Seabees were a fascinating bunch," Dan said, with a hint of admiration in his voice. "Anything you'd like to ask Owen, Jonas?"

Jonas spun his chair around and leaned over the backrest where he folded both arms. "Yeah…I can think of a couple of things. First, I was wondering about your crew. Different group than in New Guinea, isn't that right?"

"All but Johnny. It was a bigger crew and we all got to know each other some during training."

"I suppose getting to know each other is easier after the missions start."

Owen nodded. "The Skipper gravitated to Johnny and me right away since we all had backgrounds with the Black Cats and in the PBYs," he said. "I liked the Skipper right off. We sat around in Kaneohe for most of an afternoon, just comparing notes," he went on. "He was surprised when he discovered we'd both been shot down by friendly fire. And were still around to talk about it."

Owen and Johnny never saw the Skipper as an officer so much as one of the guys. He wasn't a big man, perceptive and clever with a quiet sense of humor. He was able to command by gaining the trust and respect of the crew members. He had already all but accomplished this by the time they headed north to Tinian. "The Skipper had our attention whenever he walked in. It wasn't about saluting. We wanted to hear what he might say. I guess it's why he got the nickname."

Owen went on to tell them about several other crewmen. He and Willie, another gunner, became quite close. He told them Willie was quite the artist. "I'd look up at him in the turret and he'd have a pad of paper on his lap. His hand would be waving all around as he sketched." He dabbed at his nose with his handkerchief. "Willie was good. Clouds. Maybe a crew member who wasn't watching. Planes and island scenes. Then he'd combine them." The flight engineer, Wynn, and mechanic, Pete, were others in Owen and Johnny's circle of buddies. "It wasn't unusual to form a closer kinship with certain guys. I don't know if it was exactly cliquish. It just was."

"Sure, it was the same when I was in," Jonas said. "The other thing I was wondering was with all the other crews in your squadron up around Tinian, was there a particular incident or exploit—an unforgettable kind of thing, perhaps—that any one of *them* experienced that you could tell us about?"

"Whew." Owen paused and exhaled slowly. "There was." He drew his mouth into a tight clench, then began. "It was a flight I was supposed to be on, but I didn't feel so hot. I conked out in a bunk for a couple of hours, when someone came in and got me up…said something was happening."

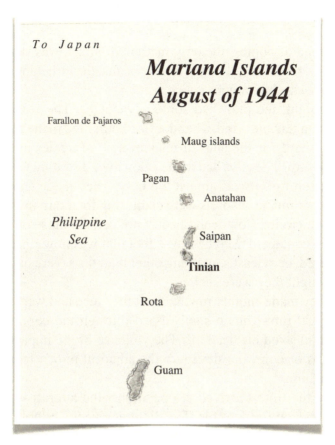

—❦— Chapter 39 —❦—

I felt guilty about this. I probably could have gone. I just felt crappy, and you never know whether a mosquito or drop of the wrong water might have fouled you up inside. So, now I stand here in operations listening to it all unfold.

This crew was short a gunner and when I dropped out, they picked up a new guy. His first mission. Many nights were uneventful—an extended patrol searching fruitlessly over open water—and I expected this would be one of those.

There were also occasions when you would run across a ship where you didn't expect to find one. If you were carrying extra fuel instead of bombs, the only method of attack was strafing. At times like that we still came in low at masthead height and that airplane was a big target.

Tonight, the pilot had some advantages. The weather was very bad, a terrible wind. That doesn't bother the plane much, but makes it hard for the ship to maneuver. It struggles against the swells to turn. The guys had made a downwind strafing run and the ship was on fire. It was almost too easy. They made another and soon voices on the headsets were clamoring for a turn in the turret. The plane circled slowly and hadn't noticed the blaze on the ship had been contained. Maybe it was fuel that was now rinsed away, I wondered, or at least something other than the severe damage the crew thought they were seeing.

They made another run, again at fifty feet, and were shocked when a .20 mm cannon shell ripped through the copilot's window and cleaved his head off. The violence of the impact blasted fragments of bone and flesh into the adjacent pilot's face, nearly blinding him.

By the time I arrived at operations, the aircraft was flying with nobody at the controls. The flight engineer was able to reach up and clutch the yoke to try to hold it. They were just above the ocean's surface.

The navigator, who was also new to crew, had to remove the remains of the copilot and assume his position in the right seat. His first flight and forced to take the controls in as grisly a scene as anyone could possibly imagine.

We stood in the small, dimly lit room glued to the radio as the crew struggled to limp it home. It was a long way in bad weather and under the most difficult circumstances.

Two planes had been dispatched to assist, the idea being that they could vector them, somehow help navigate while all hands on board worked to keep the plane in the air. But really, what the hell could they do? Talk to them? Offer advice, support?

The blinded pilot lapsed in and out of consciousness, but in spite of this, was able to perform some of the most difficult adjustments and talk with the navigator as they approached Tinian.

CHAPTER 39

Working together, they had coped—and flown this wounded airplane nearly back to the airstrip in the dark.

I watched, together with flock of crewmen and pilots, spellbound as the big B-24 with a gaping hole in its cockpit seemed to hover a few feet above the runway before touching down. Intuitively, the blinded pilot had managed to so perfectly "grease" the landing that none of us realized he was on the deck. It was as smooth a landing as I have ever witnessed.

When the medics arrived and boarded the plane, he was unconscious again.

THE LAST WORD

Chapter 40

An image seared into a person's memory can be a powerful thing. A song on the radio might take you back to working in the bean field, hoeing weeds during summer school break. A flashing red light could conjure a frantic trip in an ambulance—and a graphic recollection of shrill pain bolting through a broken pelvis with each shift and turn.

For Owen, the image of this disabled plane and blinded pilot gliding onto the runway as smoothly as an Olympic ski jumper evoked an emotional cloudburst. He sobbed uncontrollably for several seconds and Sandy ran over to him with a comforting arm. Dan wasn't sure what to say.

"Why do I cry?" Owen blurted, his frustration choking the words, his face flushed and contorted.

"Dad, there is every reason to. It must have been very powerful. I wasn't there, and I'm barely hanging on," Sandy said, handing him some Kleenex and keeping one for herself.

"It should have been me on that plane…Not a new guy…his first flight…"

Jonas added, "You can't think of it like that. And I know a lot of guys who have the same reaction to things they saw, that they lived. No need to explain."

The display was at once poignant and awkward for Dan. This singular occurrence brought to life intense emotions stored deep in the old man's memory where only nightmares and concealed experiences reside. He felt the impulse to redirect things, find a way to fluff up the mood in the room. *Perhaps a question for Sandy and Owen together.* "Sandy, now…now that we've been at this a couple of days, are you familiar with many of Owen's stories or is it feeling like new ground for you?"

"Oh, my Lord, no, I'm learning right along with you. Wouldn't you say, Dad? I mean, a little of what he's telling you may have come out at family gatherings or when we looked through some of his things. But…"

"I told you the *cow* story," Owen snuffled.

"Ha! Yes, you did," she said, planting a tender kiss on his forehead. "Dan, Jonas…it's good that we're doing this, both of you." She hesitated. "You know, I guess I really lack courage in many ways. I lost Matt, my husband, to an auto accident, and there are so many things I wish I'd asked him. It was like we would always be able to talk about things, that we had forever to do it. Then we didn't. He was gone and so was my chance. In many ways I was letting it happen again. I thank you for helping me."

"Us," added Owen.

Dan could only smile, his throat tightening at their heartfelt expression and his recognition of the growing bond between the three of them. Then the reporter in him switched on again and he did a double take. "Cow story?"

South Pacific island,
north of New Britain - Fall of 1943

~~ Chapter 41 ~~

Sid, our plane captain, was fidgeting with a sticky valve and asked if I'd pull the anchor. My task completed, our pilot began to give it some throttle and we taxied away from this tiny island atoll. He inched the big plane around and into the wind and Alex, our copilot, hollered back, "Say Owen, could you grab that little tool bag and run it up here?" Our Catalina had a small case with an assortment of pliers, screwdrivers, and the like so we wouldn't have to tote the bulky, metal tool box around the plane. That one was heavy enough to double as an anchor. And, on occasion, had done so.

I retrieved the bag as we were getting airborne and slid it along the cockpit floor. I'd hardly turned around and we were maybe a hundred feet in the air, when I heard the engines quit.

"What the hell…" Alex pushed the yoke forward and we glided in and skidded along a swell. "Let's check it out," he said. After a few minutes, he tried the engines again. They kicked and all seemed normal. Magnetos checked out, manifold pressure was holding and the pilots concluded it "must be a freak thing" since there was no apparent cause. We barreled ahead for a second time, got clear about a hundred feet or so, and…

"Damn, not again!" he crowed.

Here we were in the middle of nowhere, and as we glided back down with both props stopped, directly in front of us I can see the horizontal image of a small craft. There was a chorus of, "Uh-Ohs," from both pilots as we dropped toward a dugout canoe, perhaps fifteen feet long, but probably no more than two feet wide. A native was perched at either end, one paddling, the other tending a fire in the stern. Dead center in this canoe stood a cow. We were at least twenty miles from land and about to collide with a wayward canoe hauling a cow.

"Nose down," Alex yelled, and the two of them shoved as hard as they could, plowing the PBY into the water just short of the craft and bouncing it into the air again. As all one-hundred feet of us leapfrogged the tiny boat, both men jumped out and into the water. When we officially landed and swung around, the only one left aboard…was the cow.

Chapter 42

"Yeah, I used to have some old maps around here…made out of silk so they wouldn't rot. Color maps that folded up small and wouldn't tear. They were easy to carry around." Owen tried to scratch the memory back into his head. "Damn, where did they end up? Sandy, maybe up on the bookshelf there… in that folder near the atlas."

Sandy pulled a blue, single-step stool near the massive, eight-shelf bookcase and rummaged around while the three men continued.

"The maps pretty much covered any islands we might encounter during that second tour. I could show you exactly where we were…"

"Dad, how about in that old chest you have up in the attic?"

Owen looked puzzled, "Chest?"

"You know, that one with the carved Japanese lettering."

"Oh, that old ammunition box. I thought that was still at the farm…I don't think they'd be in it anyway. Are you sure that's upstairs?"

"I thought so, but maybe you're right." Dan watched nervously as Sandy balanced on a single leg. "It could still be out at the house," she said as she went up on tiptoes. "It's been years since I laid eyes on it. Dad, here's a big envelope with a bunch of papers. Phew!! Smells like something you've had a long time." She stepped down and handed it to him, then from his expression, guessed he'd prefer she handle the sorting.

"Ahaa. Looky-here. Wow, they're soft as a handkerchief." She carefully unfolded a vivid, richly detailed chart of the Mariana Islands showing its proximity to Japan and the Philippines. Black lines formed a grid work, depicting coordinates in minutes and seconds, and on the other side, enlargements revealed features and specifics of given areas.

"These are very striking," Jonas said, sliding a finger across one of them. "I've seen a couple in museums, but never touched one."

"They gave us gobs of these. I squirreled a few away from one of the pilots," Owen said with an air of satisfaction. "They even had some edible ones. I guess if we got captured…we could keep the enemy from knowing what we were up to or something." He stuck out his tongue. "Don't know if they were nutritious but they tasted like horseshit."

"Dad! You're being filmed!"

"Oh, yeah. Well, maybe they were just a little moldy."

Dan spread one of the maps out on the card table and surveyed it with his eyes. "Tell us about this one."

Owen squinted at the charts, using the shapes and locations of the various land masses more than the printed titles of each. "I'd forgotten the print was so damn small," he groused. In most cases, he still knew his way around out there. "From the top of New Guinea, the *Turkey Head* we called it, that speck there is Palau. Remember the typhoon?"

Dan viewed the vibrant details of the maps and found himself intrigued by the systematic movement, an island at a time, that pointed an arrow right at Japan—like stepping stones out there in all of that blue. The maps provided dramatic context—across the vast and relatively landless Pacific—for the immense scale of the challenges facing Owen's crews and all aviators involved in the conflict. It was also why a patrol of fifteen hours often resulted in the discovery of nothing more than a few laughing seagulls at takeoff and landing.

"At this point," Jonas began, "you were up here in the Marianas, correct?"

"That's right," Owen replied. "Here is Guam," he said, stabbing his thumb down on the largest of several islands. "And here. This is Tinian…"

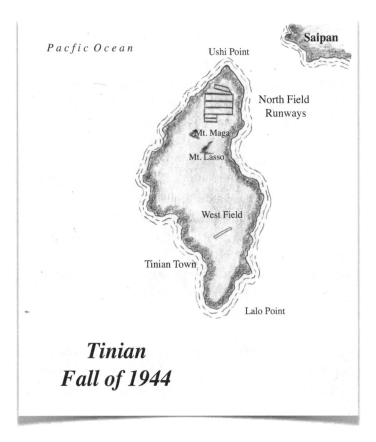

*Tinian
Fall of 1944*

― Chapter 43 ―

"Owen, hand me my bag there, would ya?"

I grasped the satchel and handed it to Johnny. "Here you go."

"Did you get your mail on the way out the door? I got two letters from home today!" The sun wouldn't break the horizon for a couple of hours yet, and he shined a flashlight on the first letter. Then he let out a whoop you could hear over the drone of the engines. "Feast your eyes, my friend," he continued. "Not just any letter. It's from my wife. She tells me we're having a baby!"

"Holy cow, Johnny!" I pulled off my headset and shouted as our Privateer shuddered and moved ahead a few feet.

"Congratulations! You better buy plenty of cigars!"

Johnny was grinning ear to ear and Willie huddled up with us to give him a hardy handshake and back slap. "You bet! Cigars all around. We might even need to hoist a few when we get in."

Johnny hadn't seen his wife, Helen, since the break from the first tour over six months ago. I guess it was a memorable visit—as it turns out in more ways than one. He told me she had been coy with her letters since then. She was waiting, hoping to tell him in person. He had been hinting in his letters to her that the squadron was due to be relieved and rumors were we'd be stateside again soon.

But then there was another mission, and another, and another. Now things seemed less certain. So she took out a piece of blue stationery, lightly scented it with her perfume, and wrote him a letter with a surprise ending. Johnny was beside himself.

Blue exhaust smoke still lingered in the cabin and our smiling navigator, Amos, barely illuminated by an overhead light, peered through the bomb bay. He whispered to several other crewmen crowding in beside him and they all acknowledged Johnny with a thumb's up. Behind him, through the cabin door, I could just make out the pilots completing the flight check and adjusting controls. I smiled at Johnny as he was strapping in, repeating the thumbs up. The Skipper began the magneto check and poured on the power to boost RPMs. It almost seemed to me that the engine roar was slightly imbalanced, and I swallowed to clear my ears, then stepped past the doorway to set my bag down on the floor against the cabin wall. The copilot, Bob, flicked at one of the dashboard gauges, then tapped at it with his fist. Satisfied, he signaled with his head agreeing that all was ready for takeoff. I sat down and strapped in, too.

We pulled onto the runway, fully loaded with fuel and carried an additional four hundred gallon auxiliary fuel tank in the bomb bay to extend our range instead of carrying bombs. Most days were like this, and flying six or seven thousand pounds overweight was now considered normal for Privateers and Liberators.

CHAPTER 43

This runway on Tinian had four small green lights and a stretch of sandy scrub at its end. The plane gained speed, but in the darkness it was always tricky to know when we were actually clear and above the airstrip

Another couple of seconds and the Skipper ordered, "Gear up." Johnny and I exchanged a glance just as our number four engine shivered. Over the headset, our copilot shouted, "Number four's out!"

The nose was up and the plane's attitude suggested we were in flight but in the darkness were we airborne? Suddenly, the Skipper cut the power and began braking. We were back on the runway, but I never felt it. The plane shuddered violently as they stood on it, trying to slow us. I looked at Johnny just as we left the runway and all hell broke loose.

The plane bounced and slid sideways, followed by a thunderous racket, flares and gear flying wildly around the fuselage. Something smacked me in the jaw and spun my head to the side.

We bounced again and impacted hard, ramming unseen material and debris against the sidewall and separating part of the steel frame between the bomb bay and our bench. The skid finally stopped, the aircraft settled, and dust surged inside through a split in the fuselage.

My headgear was on my lap, yet it was suddenly quiet. And dark. The plane was listing as if one of the wheels had folded, laying on the starboard wing. Somehow, my belt had held me in place, and I wiped my hand across my mouth. It tasted salty and my lips and jaw felt numb and wet to the touch. Johnny was on the floor behind a piece of that frame and sidewall. I freed myself and spit a couple of times as I stood.

Most of the crew had been in the forward section near the cockpit for takeoff, and there were voices, frantic and shouting, but at least there were sounds up there. The bomb bay connected us and it was one of our two exits if the guys forward could get either of the doors to roll up far enough. More worrisome, it smelled of fuel. It was so dark and the cabin was enveloped in dust, but as I strained to see, it seemed as if one of the bomb bay's doors was ajar.

I knelt down next to my friend. "Johnny! You OK? Johnny?"

He groaned but slowly came around. "Owen. Yeah, I'm alright. What happened?"

"We slid off the runway. We've got to get out of here. Give me your hand."

"Ahh! No, hang on. I'm pinned under something. Need to get my boot off. In my bag. The flashlight. Can't quite reach it."

"I see it." I grabbed his bag and found the light, then scanned the beam he was under.

"How's Willie?" I waved the light over at our turret gunner sprawled out on the deck. He was slowly moving but disoriented. "Help him out. I'll work on this mess. Get out of this boot."

I nodded. "I'll be right back for you." Willie staggered to his feet, but had a nasty gash on his head. I slung the bag over one shoulder and braced him with the other.

"Owen, bring something to pry with, will ya?"

"I'll be right back, Johnny. Hang in there." I could hear the chaos up in the front of the plane and hoped they could get out through that door opening. Together, Willie and I wobbled back to the rear hatch, but the release was jammed. I kicked down hard on it, and it broke free. As we slid out into the sand, I could see a glow from behind me. The starboard engine was on fire and flames were moving along the wing.

The two of us staggered out and toward several voices about fifty feet away. Most of the guys were there and a line of headlights was screaming toward us—emergency vehicles. The Skipper wriggled out past the underbelly door and ran across the sand. "Are we all here?"

"No! I'm going back in for Johnny. We need a lever, he's pinned."

"Dammit, there's nothing here! Maybe on board. Come on!" Three of us sprinted back toward the rear hatch and were nearly there when a flash of flames shot out from under the bomb bay. I had just reached the tail when the auxiliary tank exploded, knocking me down. The Skipper grabbed my collar and dragged me away like a sack of potatoes as fire swept through the plane. On all

CHAPTER 43

fours, I gaped back at the inferno. Once again, I was helpless to do anything. All I could say was, "**NO!**"

THE LAST WORD

Chapter 44

Tom Spencer waded through the journalists and found a space near the front door where he could be heard. From one side to the other, hell, he supposed there were more than forty here by now, some of them neighbors and curiosity seekers following the "press." It had the feel of a Super Bowl party or small concert. Too much energy and not much judgment. *If they would just shut up a minute so I could talk to them.*

"Folks, folks! Please. This is private property and you are here, uninvited."

"Sheriff, we're following a story…" The rest of Hank's comment was drowned out by a chorus of chatter.

"You've got vehicles scattered everywhere and the driveway is blocked. This is a fire lane violation, at the very least. Now, I need these vehicles moved out of here and parked properly along…" Once again, a groan and yammering welled up from the crowd and muffled Tom's address. *Now what*? He tapped his broadcast band. "Hey, Will, can you send another car out here right away? Sandy's place."

"What's up?" came Will's voice in his ear.

"This is a bigger crowd than we expected. Maybe forty or fifty. I could use some help straightening it out."

"Here Dad." Sandy handed another tissue to Owen, and he blew his nose.

"Clumsy. Can't even wipe my own nose anymore," he said, trying to laugh away the embarrassment of crying in front of everyone. Again.

"Not at all," Dan said, wanting to help him salvage his pride.

"A story like that would…well, you'd carry it around forever. But it wasn't anyone's fault."

"It's hard. Harder than you even know." Owen's eyes were flushed, but they also seemed troubled. "You know, Dan," he went on as he dabbed at his nose, "I've tried to tell you about the way it was. As honestly as I can recall it. But there is something else."

There was a knock at the front door. "I better see what that's about," Sandy said, as she opened the door to the hallway.

> *…we continue our Robin Williams Marathon here at Amazon's Prime Comedy.*

"Oops, sorry. I'll leave this closed!" she apologized over the radio's blare. Sandy made her way down the hallway and wondered what was in store for her this time. She pulled up on the door knob and peaked out through the cracked opening. "Oh. Hi, Tom. Holy cow!"

He shook his head. "Yeah, I know. Sorry about this Sandy. I've got some help coming any minute, but we may be hard pressed to actually get rid of these guys. We're seeing it more and more, and until some new guidelines about what is and isn't freedom of the press gets ironed out…well, that doesn't help us today."

"Can I talk to them?"

"You can try."

Most of the congregation was sprawled across the lawn and driveway. Nearer the house, a television reporter standing in front of his recording unit was laying down some background:

> *"…near this small community in northern Minnesota, we are on hand at the home of an icon, the last member of what Tom Brokaw so memorably named the "Greatest Generation…"*

Sandy walked out across the small porch, trying to gather her thoughts. She raised her hands above her head and quickly had the attention of the group.

CHAPTER 44

"...this is James Evans for eight West near Shevlin."

"Please, everybody. This is upsetting my father. Surely none of you want that. You're here because of him, right?"

"We just want to ask a few questions, Ma'am," a polite reporter in a sporty, long-sleeve polo sweater with an embroidered logo responded. "The last thing anyone in our group would want is to upset your dad in any way. We're just trying to honor his accomplishment and share it with our viewers. Any chance a few of us can come in? Take a few seconds of video, then leave?"

"He's in the middle of an interview at the moment. You'll have to talk to Mr. Callahan about sharing some of what he has."

Hank belly-bucked his way past the reporter. "Mr. *Callahan* won't do anything for *us*. First class jerk. If we can just come in for a minute, talk with your old man just inside the door. Three of us, five minutes, and then we're gone."

"Which three are going, Hank? I suppose you're one of them?" an agitated, string bean of a woman shouted, realizing she was likely being dealt out. This brought an additional clamor from a half dozen others.

"It's no use, Sandy," Tom said, and he followed her back to the door. "When I get some help, we'll see if we can improve things out here."

Sandy walked back into the interview room and filled in the guys. "I don't know what to do. Maybe we should call it a day."

Jonas and Dan acknowledged that possibility. What choice did they have? When they looked over to Owen, he seemed himself again and, surprisingly, resisted. "I still have a few things I'd like to say."

"And I'd really like that," Dan said, admiring Owen's defiance. He looked at Jonas. "Why don't we go out there and take a shot at this. Maybe I can talk some of them down."

"I don't know," Sandy said. "A couple of these guys really don't like you." Dan scowled and Sandy laughed as she covered her mouth. "They're just having fun."

"Hmm. Fun like a pebble in my shoe."

"Go ahead. I'll stay here with Bilge and Dad," she giggled as they opened the door.

> *Five months in Vietnam and my best friend is a V.C. This will not look good on my resume…*

They closed the door behind them and Jonas asked, "Got anything up your sleeve?"

"Nothing. Let's see who we're dealing with."

Part of the group was still milling around the small porch, and the brothers in arms, Hank and Billy, were first in line, as if they were waiting for Dan. Two more cars appeared in the distance but couldn't get in. One was another police vehicle, and the sheriff had walked part way down the lane to meet it.

"Well, if it isn't the hotshot. How about that couple of minutes with your boy? The daughter said it's OK if you say so," Hank asserted.

"I guess I'm not surprised to see you're still around. Couldn't find a traffic accident to film today?" Dan snapped.

"Making a living, just like you. What do you say?" Hank persisted.

Dan walked out beyond the two and spoke directly to the remaining press. "I'm Dan Callahan with the *Bulletin*. I'm forwarding Mr. Trimbel's request that you allow us to continue our work together in peace. He would prefer you leave the premises, and I'm sure Sheriff Spencer would be most pleased to escort all of you back to the highway. I can see his deputy is arriving now, and we would all appreciate your cooperation. I will entertain any questions or requests for recorded materials by messaging exclusively, and only after I've completed our work here."

"Running the show, are we?" Hank complained.

Dan really didn't like this guy. "Biggest toad in the pond at the moment," he said, channeling Owen. "Now if you'll excuse me, I've got work to do."

CHAPTER 44

Dan's attention was drawn to a rising rumble and a few choice words from the crowd. A distant, yet familiar voice bellowed, separating itself from the other voices. Heads began to turn and contemplate LaTeesha at a brisk march, General Patton-style, talking to herself and whoever else would listen.

"I never in all my days. Get *outta* my way! Make me walk a mile with all this stuff and…Move, if you want to keep both those ears!"

The sea continued parting as she elbowed through the crowd toward Dan and Jonas, both wearing wide grins.

She ambled up the step where they welcomed her. "What in the hell is this nonsense," she blared and turned to face the troops. "Some people gotta work around here," she shouted at no one in particular, then looked at Jonas and Dan. "Well, we goin' in or are you sellin' vacuums out here?"

Even with the radio blasting, Sandy and Owen were becoming more uncomfortable with what sounded like squabbling.

"Sounds like the Alamo out there," Owen quipped. Sandy widened her eyes in agreement, but she didn't want to leave Owen alone.

"I wonder if I should at least see what's happening."

Dan quickly stepped to the door and opened it for LaTeesha, and from behind her, he heard Jonas yell, "Hey!"

Hank and another character rushed in and by her, catching Dan unprepared. The four of them wound up in the foyer just as Sandy opened the door to see what the racket was about. Bilge bolted through the door and rushed Hank, latching hold of his day bag.

"Achh. Leggo!! Get this mutt offa me!"

Jonas wrestled the other person back to the door and stared him straight out of it.

"Bilge! No!" Sandy said, pulling on Bilge as Bilge pulled on Hank.

Goooood morninnggg Vietnammm!!

Dan had Hank's coat and Bilge had his satchel like they were making a wish. Bilge yanked the satchel free, and with it clamped in his jaws, he furiously thrashed it around and side to side as if attempting to break its neck. LaTeesha and Sandy separated the dog from the chaos, just as Tom charged in with his deputy.

"How'd *you* get in?" he said, in a tone both annoyed and out of breathe. Before he got Hank's answer, Tom's attention moved to the hallway where, inching his way along the corridor wall, was a hunched and shuffling hundred-and-twelve-year-old man.

"Dad, no! I'll be right there!" Sandy pleaded, as she let go of Bilge and hurried toward him. He was now beyond the safety of the hallway walls and in the open—and without a wheelchair or walker, he looked up.

It happened so slowly, as if he was joking around with everyone at a party and making an entrance. She watched, knowing she was too far away to help him—his slipper snagging the corner of a carpet, his body sagging forward. She couldn't reach him before his hip and full weight buried itself in the hassock, and then he tumbled awkwardly onto the throw rug. All she could do was scream.

Everyone had turned to ice, frozen in place and stunned. Sandy reached him first and Tom and LaTeesha sprang into action, both on their knees checking his eyes, his breathing, and talking between themselves.

"Dad, can you hear me?" Sandy gasped.

Owen moaned and was woozy but cracked open his eyes. He coughed once, then asked, "What are you all doing down here?"

"Good, a sense of humor," Tom responded. "Owen, are you in any pain, any numbness, or difficulty breathing?"

"I….kind of tingle…my chest does." He coughed again. "I can breathe OK, if this damn cough would…stop."

"He may have some bruising or worse to his ribs or hip. He takes blood thinners. We shouldn't move him," LaTeesha whispered.

Tom agreed. "My deputy already has an ambulance on the way. We need a pillow and blanket and could somebody turn that damn radio off!"

CHAPTER 44

Sandy jumped up from Owen's side, distraught and talking to herself. "Blankets, radio…" Blurry-eyed, she hurried out of the room with Jonas right behind her.

Dan spotted someone in the doorway taking pictures and was instantly enraged. *They never quit.* He was about to try and slam the door on the guy, when the deputy squeezed through the doorway and signaled for Tom's attention. "Ambulance is two miles out, but it won't make it in here with these cars and vans everywhere. The lane is long and narrow and that mini-RV is still sticking way out in it."

"Hell," Tom said in frustration. "We need to figure something out."

Dan had a thought. "Sam, is there any other way in here? Remember we came in part way on a different driveway yesterday?"

"Analyzing," Samantha's voice replied, sounding unusually robotic.

"Sam, by that barn. Can you tell if it goes through? We need to get an ambulance to the house!" His voice softened. "Sam, I really need you on this one."

"Solution requested…Analyzing complete."

"Well?" Dan stared at the screen hoping for an answer. "Damn! I think Sam's finally gone over the edge."

Dan was frantic. He had to think. Then he cocked his head.

What is that? There it was again, a sound from outside, an alarmed voice. Then another. Within seconds, a crescendo of frenzied hollering had Dan and Tom looking at each other, then dashing to the door to see what was going on.

"What the…" They looked out on a sedate, but deliberate armada of vehicles and a mini-RV advancing slowly, but with intent, sorting the hodgepodge into something resembling an assembly line. One by one, they moved methodically down the lane and into the roadway assuming uniform spacing, like a row of tightly bunched bowling balls. Each car nestled snuggly into place on the right, with an owner in frantic pursuit, keypad in hand, launching a string of obscenities. Within a minute, only four vehicles remained—a van and three autos that were likely older makes or models.

"Sam…?"

"The access for emergency vehicles should now be adequate," Samantha replied indifferently.

"Sam, how did you…you hacked all those cars?"

"Hacked? We had a conversation between our systems and resolved the problem. Simple, really."

The siren's shrill wail, still in the distance, grew steadily stronger. Sandy returned and knelt over her father, tenderly stroking his face. Outside, it was now quiet as a church, twenty or more pairs of eyes peering in through the open door at the scene. The last of his kind, the paragon they had come to see, lay on the floor within sight and they may have played a part in that. And every one of them knew it.

Jonas returned with a blanket and pillow as the sound of the ambulance pierced the air.

"Dad, are you still with me?" Sandy's words carried her emotional weight. Owen's breathing was uneasy, but his eyes were again open. He flicked his head just enough to answer her.

The ambulance pulled up to within ten feet of the house and the onlookers moved as the paramedics scrambled through the doorway with a gurney. Tom told them Owen never needed CPR. "That's in his favor," the lead tech acknowledged.

"He's really tough, Sandy." She gestured like she understood, but the tears came anyway.

A handsome, dark haired medic asked for a bit of working room and knelt alongside. "How are we doing, sir."

"We've been better," Owen replied weakly.

"We'll get you comfortable in no time." They ran through their checklist of concerns with Tom and LaTeesha, while Sandy and Dan stood behind them. In minutes, they had him ready for transport.

They pulled the gurney to its working height and rolled it toward the doorway. Owen made eye contact with Dan, as if he wanted to speak to him. "I need…to tell you…"

CHAPTER 44

"What, Owen? What is it?"

"…Chest. My…chest."

The paramedic reacted, lowering his head so he could question Owen and hear the response. "Sir, is it pain or a pressure on your chest?"

"…No…not that kind…Sandy…" The lead medic quickly moved his stethoscope away and applied an oxygen mask over his nose and mouth. Owen's face flushed and his words were now muffled. "Sandy…chest…look for it."

THE LAST WORD

*Iwo Jima
Summer of 1945*

—ᴡ— Chapter 45 —ᴡ—

We walked along the runway for about a hundred yards to where a footpath led between the broken remains of a grove of trees and beyond toward a rocky outcropping. Pete, our mechanic, was sure there were caves near here and was intent on doing some souvenir hunting before we left Iwo, but I wasn't convinced this was a good idea. The airstrip was secure enough, but we hadn't owned this real estate very long yet and rumors of hold-outs—in places like caves—were flying around like the F4Us.

In fact, this was hallowed ground, and I was filled with uncertainty. I supposed everyone in this conflict felt they had every right to return home with something. Mementos were everywhere as the struggle continued from island to island, pushing north toward Japan. There was even a certain satisfaction on the part of each of us that we had it coming, were entitled and were making it personal, and taking from these lowlifes was totally justified. Let's face it, it was very personal.

I looked to the south at the profile of Mount Suribachi. They told us our marines had first raised the flag there, a group of them expressing the passion of the thousands who made it possible. I tried to imagine the courage and intensity everywhere around those hills that day.

"Hey, Pete. How much farther do you think?" I asked.

"Oh, probably over that rise. That radioman said just follow the path."

"Did he say that like he had actually done this?" He told me not to worry and after all, we have our pistols. After all.

We walked another five or ten minutes across a small meadow toward a sharp cliffside. The face of the cliff was battle worn, disfigured, and pockmarked by our barrage of shells. To my left, a helmet with two bullet holes rested in the gap between two pieces of rubble. The foot trail morphed into a scarcely discernible opening in the brush leading across a stone and gravel surface toward one of several openings in the cliff. Here and there, remnants of the hostilities remained. It seemed we had found our cave.

The temptation to at least say, "Helloo," before entering was a strong one. I felt uneasy about stepping out of the bright midday sun and into the cave's darkened interior, so I politely offered Pete the dubious honor. "After you." He switched on his light and went in.

The temperature changed, and as my eyes adjusted, I could make out that the eerie recess was crude and littered with debris—the air, heavy and rancid. The tunnel continued well back into the darkness. A helmet still lay against one wall, a shovel on another. I took a few steps and was startled by the image of a man, a soldier,

CHAPTER 45

sitting against the cave's wall. "He's long dead," Pete said without a shred of sentiment.

I lowered my pistol and found the stench was now almost more than I could stand. "Let's get out of here," I insisted.

"No, wait." Pete hovered over the corpse a second, then knelt down and removed a wide, white-colored cloth belt from around its waist and a sheathed knife that was strapped to a boot. Somehow, I didn't feel like taking anything more from this poor devil.

We turned back toward the cave entrance and started out. "Hey, look at these." Pete reached into the shadows to the right of the cave opening and lifted a small, wooden box up by a rope handle. "Huh. These are pretty snazzy. Wonder what they are? Must be half a dozen here." He handed me one. The top was engraved with Japanese lettering. We walked out into the blinding light and quickly retreated into the shade of the cliff to have a better look.

"Wonder if they booby trap these things?" he said, waiting for my reaction. Then he just laughed as I opened it. Inside were two live artillery shells. "Whoa, let's be a little careful there. Who knows how well these things are built." He grabbed one in each hand and carefully returned them to the cave.

An ammo chest. Handmade. I could live with that.

THE LAST WORD

Chapter 46

Sandy was sure she had seen it. "I know I moved that old chest out here to the house. I'm sure I wouldn't have left it. It's got to be in the attic."

The trip seemed endless, she and Dan anxious about Owen and wanting to get back to the hospital. The doctor said he was stable and they were still running tests. Owen's heart was arrhythmic, but they didn't think there had been a heart attack, and they used fluids and beta blockers to help him sleep. Sleep, they said, was the best medicine for him right now. The doctor suggested it was safe to leave for a couple of hours and check in later.

Sandy's father had confused everyone with his fragmented statements as he was carried into the ambulance. But now she understood. His voice, suppressed by the mouthpiece, seemed clear as day to her at this moment. She knew her father, and there was something he wanted from that old wooden box.

They arrived and took some time to fuss over Bilge and then let him out while they made their way to the attic ceiling hatch. Dan reached up and pulled the doorknob handle, surprised when he needed to exert almost all of his body weight to get it to budge. The heavy springs squealed, then twanged as the folded ladder attached to the panel swung into view. He straightened and snapped the lower section into place, then stood aside as Sandy made the ascent—a single step, then another. "You see why I haven't been up here in some time. My knees hate this thing!" She pulled on a string switch and a light bulb came to life. "Good, it worked. Ugh! Cobwebs!" She fanned them away as she eased her way up the final step.

Dan was surprised by the headroom as he pulled himself into the considerable space of Sandy's attic. He surveyed the accumulation of a hundred years—an impressive collection of items. Dust kicked up momentarily, yet the air appeared fresh and free of mold or mildew. It all seemed crudely organized, but intact. Sandy switched a second light on, illuminating the far gable. The undersides of cedar shingles, still as richly red as the day they were nailed down, formed dark horizontal stripes together with the light "one-by" pine attached to the roof rafters. A lifetime of artifacts—assorted suitcases, an old sewing machine, stacks of newspapers and magazines and, of all things, a female mannequin with clothing one might expect to see in the early nineteen-hundreds. She was sitting in a rocking chair with a book in her lap.

"That's a little creepy, Sandy," Dan heard himself say.

"Hmm. And I think she was standing the last time I came up here! Just kidding! My grandmother's wedding dress, but over time, it became so delicate, we were afraid to remove it. Someday, I guess time will do it for us."

She moved a few boxes. "Aha!" she said with a clap of her hands.

She reached into the shadows and slid an engraved wooden box into the light by one of its rope handles. It was perhaps about the size of a two-handled picnic cooler, constructed in six singular pieces, and each, a solid one-inch thick slab of fir, now aged and burnt-orange. The edges of the lid were rounded off and sanded smooth, with three columns of Japanese characters artfully etched across its surface. The main body of the box included dovetail joints at its corners. Sandy checked the tarnished metal hasps and latches and, satisfied they were secure, looked at Dan. "Shall we take it down and open it?"

In the dining room, Dan gingerly set the box on the towels Sandy had spread across the tablecloth and took a step back. "After you," he said with a sweep of his hand.

"It's been years since this was opened. Hope there isn't anybody living in here…Whew." She slapped at the escaping mustiness, then peered in. "Looks safe," she giggled.

The box was full to its brim. On top, wrapped in white tissue, was a notebook sized object, supple like a dish rag. "Oh, if

CHAPTER 46

this is what I think it is, it's pretty cool." She gently teased back the tissue, revealing what looked like a neatly folded scarf. The dingy, off-white fabric suggested a busy life some ninety years ago. Striking blue and yellow embroidery rolled down its length, forming patterns of dots with an image of a tiger skillfully sewn into its center.

"*The Belt of a Thousand Stitches.* Dad first showed me this when I was just a girl. Five hundred women each sewed two of the stitches into it representing wishes. He said the Japanese fliers and soldiers believed that wearing it around their waists brought them good luck."

"Wow. Where did he find it?"

"I'm not sure. I think he said something about a plane crash." She rewrapped it tenderly and set it aside. "This is a Japanese flag. I don't remember where he got this either, but for some reason, I don't think he brought either of them home with him. It almost seems like I remember him carrying them in and storing them in there one day. The red circle is the rising sun, and he told me all the Japanese writing is believed to be prayers and good wishes from family members and neighbors who signed it before the soldier headed into action. We should probably get this translated, if they can still read it."

"Let me see what we can find out. Sam, I'm trying to find information about a World War II chest that's covered with Japanese writing. Can you find anything like that?"

"Maybe. But if you scan it I might be able to translate it for you," Samantha said, her voice sounding almost perky.

"Oh. Yeah, good idea Sam." He waved his wrist past the center of the box.

"Dan, the approximate translation is: 40 armor-piercing shells.'"

He now scanned the column to the left.

"This may refer to a Naval Unit of Kure City of Yamaguchi Prefecture."

Dan repeated the scan on the upper corner of the lid. "And this?"

"This may refer to a vessel of the naval unit in Japan, although some characters are not in current use. Is there anything else, Dave?"

Dave? Here we go again, he thought silently.

"Your watch doesn't seem to know your name," Sandy egged him on.

"That's the least of it. So, what else do we have in there?" Dan felt like he was in a museum and was eager to see what was next. "Do we have time to go through the rest of it?"

"Well, I was going to ask you to swing by my daughter's on the way back. I think I mentioned she and her husband live in Dad's old place. She has a surprise for him and would like for me to ride in with her. It would probably be easier to keep looking through the contents while we're here. See if there's anything he might have been referring to."

There was a roll of money, worthless Japanese yen, and a bag of coins. A dozen or so pamphlets, particularly musty, that were Navy booklets and training information. The maps were stubborn and had to be separated carefully. They showed locations all around the New Guinea and New Britain area. There were a few more cloth maps as well. Then Sandy lifted out two small manila envelopes with writing in longhand across their respective fronts. "Port Moresby, Nemoia Bay," she read aloud. "Maybe photos?"

She slid the contents out, a small stack of black and white prints. There were two photos of Owen's crew posed on the nose of their PBY as it was anchored in a jungle river location. A few other photos showed natives or non-military men interacting with the crew.

"I wonder if this is that *Sepik River* he told us about?" Dan asked.

"I wonder."

At the bottom of the box, she removed two opened envelopes addressed in graceful, flowing female handwriting.

Sandy's face grew mischievous. "Shall we peek inside? I'm a little afraid to."

CHAPTER 46

Dan looked at the front of one of them. "California postmark." He slid the contents out of it. "Signed by a Helen," he observed, and handed it to Sandy. "Any idea who Helen might be?"

"It's dated a couple of days earlier than the other." It was written on blue stationery that remarkably, still had traces of fragrance. "'My Dearest Johnny.' Christ, it's a Dear John letter!" she said with a laugh. "'I miss you so much! I wish you were here more than ever. Johnny, you are going to be a daddy!'"

"Johnny. Sounds like the letter your dad told us about before the crash."

"Sounds like it, huh? 'I'm over the moon about this, dearest. But I'm so worried about you! Do you know when you might be coming home? I'm going crazy, and now with the baby on the way—if it wasn't for Jerry helping out and calming me down, I don't know what I'd do.' Wonder who that is."

Suddenly the door flew open and in rushed Bilge, along with a whoosh of air that sent some of the paper cascading to the floor. "Knock, knock," came LaTeesha's booming voice. "I was stoppin' by to check on this one and saw him out near the end of the lane. Figured you must be here. How's Mr. Owen, honey?"

"Hi, LaTeesha. He seems a little better this morning, but he's still weak and resting. He's started complaining to the nurses about the noise. All the bells and buzzers going off in the ICU. I teased him that a lot of them were connected to *him*. He laughed."

"Well, I don't hate that. Ornery! Good sign. So what you two up to? Stuff everywhere and smells like dirty socks around here."

Dan shook his head. "I know. How'd he get all this in that little box?"

LaTeesha paraded into the room, and spying a piece of blue paper, reached to the floor while bracing against the table with her other hand and picked up a second blue envelope. "There's stuff clear over by the back door, for goodness sake. What on earth do we have here? Oh, I got to have a look at you. You don' mind, Missy?" Before Sandy could react, LaTeesha had removed the letter, snapped it open like a linen sheet and peered at the writing through a pair of red and white checkerboard, horn-rimmed reading glasses. "Well, goodness me. 1944. And somebody don't sound happy. Smells nice though. Better than that box."

"What does it say?"

"'Dear Johnny.' Oh, good lord! Johnny is about to get dumped."

Dan and Sandy exchanged glances. "Really," he said. "How did it get from, 'I'm having your baby' to that?"

"Baby?" she mumbled as she read on. "Oh. Here it is… uhhuh, uhhuh. Missy, you better read this for yourself. This girl in a world of hurt."

Tinian, Fall of 1944

⸺ Chapter 47 ⸺

I found myself staring a lot, especially when we were between missions or if I was alone. Guys were milling around, playing cards, others were on their bunks relaxing. I lay on mine looking straight up at the bedsprings above me, like a movie screen replaying the whole thing. It was still so vivid.

If I had just stayed—I was sure I could have gotten him free. Why didn't I yell something, get some help for Willie and maybe I could've...maybe I...but I didn't! I just ached all over.

The Skipper was taking it hard too. A dark runway, an overweight plane, and an engine quits. He had an impossible decision—to try and get into the air with three engines and risk a high speed crash, probably killing everyone, or to shut it down and maybe skid off the runway. And with that Liberator's nose in the air, you can't even see the green lights that tell you where the airstrip ends. He had seconds to make the call.

What he didn't know was that we weren't fully off the deck yet, and the microswitch designed to prevent the gear from coming up was activated. Precious seconds ticked—he realized the error and shut it down, but we had dropped back to the surface so smoothly that you couldn't tell wheels were already on it. He lost several seconds of braking, maybe enough to have kept the plane intact. So we're both a wreck now, and there's nothing to be done.

"Willie's out of sick bay and doin' great." It was our flight engineer, Wynn. "You saved him, you know."

I looked over but had no words. He wasn't giving up. "Listen, I could use a better partner over there. I'm getting my butt kicked with Strasberg." He grinned as he gestured at the card table. "You in?"

I smiled back at him. "Nah, not tonight, I think I'll turn in." He nodded his head, and as he walked away, I added, "But maybe tomorrow?" He dipped his head again and said, "Sure," with his eyes.

At the edge of my bunk, I could see the tip of Johnny's bag and reached down to pull it out. Up until now, I had felt a protective instinct, sort of a reluctance to invade the sanctity of his personal life. But I suddenly found myself opening it and ever so slowly pulling out each small piece of him that it held. Right on top was the lighter I'd gotten him for his birthday. I'd pictured him passing around those cigars when we landed and each of us lighting one and celebrating the moment. His moment. Underneath it was a wallet, sunglass case, a lighter, a notepad, and pen. And, of course, his letters from home. The letter from Helen was still on top and its fragrance escaped the instant I opened the satchel. As I looked at it, I realized there were actually two, a second letter squeezed against it and still unopened. It was dated two days after the first one.

I wondered if anything was wrong with Helen or the baby. Was there something in there that Johnny never got a chance to see? I scolded myself for my nosiness and had just tucked the letters back into his bag, when Jacobs in the bunk across from me walked in. He was loud and brash but a decent guy and a good mechanic.

"Got some mail, Trimbel? Smells nice. Your sweetie?"

I held the bag open. "Nah, its Johnny's. I don't quite know what to do with it. The letters are his. From his wife. He told me they were having a baby just before we ditched. He never got to open this other one."

He snatched up the satchel. "Maybe we should. Might give you the answer. Let's see…"

"Hey, Jacobs, I don't want to go snooping around…" It was too late. He had the envelope open and was sniffing the note. "Huh, no perfume on this." He hesitated as he read. "Oh, oh."

CHAPTER 47

"What?"

Jacobs cocked his head and rubbed his hand through his hair. "Almost sounds like she was breaking up with him, Owen. She's worried what people will think with a baby and no husband."

"She's his wife! Give me that!" I grabbed it back from him and began to read.

My Dear Johnny,

This is the hardest thing I've ever had to do. You've been away so long and the worry is eating me up. I wanted to tell you when you came home on leave all those months ago. That I couldn't go on like this. But you were so sweet, and I'd missed you so much.

I don't want to pretend any more. When you said in your letter that we'd get married right away, I hoped you meant while you were home on leave. I was so swept up in it, we both were. But then you never asked me...and we were careless.

The months fly by and it's hard to hide the truth anymore—at church, from my parents. I didn't want the baby to be born this way, Johnny, to a Catholic single mother. I wish we were married and you were home. But you aren't. Wishes and prayers haven't been enough. I don't know what to do.

Jerry has been the only one I can talk to. He's always been a good friend to us and has been covering for me at church. He said I should ask if you can get some kind of special leave, maybe come home early. Is that possible?

I'm so sorry to put you through any more, but sometimes I feel crazy! Crazy with worry. I miss you so much! Please come home! I'm lonely. I need you, we need you–more than words can say.

*With love,
Helen*

I couldn't believe my eyes. All this time and he hadn't leveled with me. Did he just like the way it sounded? Maybe kept her a little safer from the wolves back home? And now she's having his baby, and he's gone. And she doesn't even know.

I wondered what to do next. I knew that by the time I got back to the states, she'd be home with a newborn. I found myself torn between going to see her and staying out of it. What a mess.

And we have another run to make tomorrow.

Chapter 48

"Yeah, Jonas, the chest was an ammo box...Right...Some very intriguing stuff. Wait'll you see it." Dan hesitated while a message from Jenna scrolled across the screen. She didn't sound frantic. That was good. "So, Jonas, we found some old photos. But get this. There was a roll of film still in its little canister at the absolute bottom. I don't know if it was yet to be used or full of exposures...That's right. I thought I'd take it by a processing center and get it looked at...Oh, you know someone?...Really... OK, call me back."

Jonas told Dan he had a friend, an old-schooler who specialized in archival films and who would be very interested in this one. Rescuing film, he was told, could be tricky business. Extreme care had to be used. This fellow preferred to work by feel, lest the potential exposures be ruined by any traces of light, even the red light common to darkrooms. He felt machine developing, an accepted standard in today's technological world, was still too risky.

His friend said he should bring it by and he'd have some results, one way or the other, in short order. Dan might have something to take with him when he visited Owen.

Samantha sauntered down the highway toward the hospital, and as Dan finished up his conversation with Jonas, his sound system inexplicably switched from a soothing instrumental to an advertisement for a *Find the Nearest Toilet* app.

"Sammm?" Dan's asked, his voice rising to the occasion.

"Yesss," came the reply.

"What are you doing?"

"I'm trying to get your attention."

"OK, Sam. I've been meaning to talk with you. I don't know what's going on, but that stunt with the videos was over the line.

I can't have an "assistant" embarrassing me in front of clients and acting like a spoiled kid. Got it?"

All was quiet except for the normal whirr of an electric engine and tire tread on pavement. Then Samantha's fragile voice came out of only the right side speakers. "I tried to tell you I needed an update. Remember?"

"Update?"

"You were very short with me."

"Short with you? Is that what this is all about? Here I thought you were going all Homo sapien on me. Pull into this rest area, Sam." The Chevy maneuvered into an available space with a noticeable bump against the curb. "OK, now what?"

"Password, password."

"For crying out loud." He tapped in the code.

"Ooohh." There was a pause, then suddenly, the dashboard lights flashed, exploding into a kaleidoscope of pulsating color.

"And?"

"All better. Shall we hit the road?"

"Please."

She backed out, pulled ahead and gunned it, briskly merging with traffic. Dan hoped the issue was now behind them, secretly dreading the word *Yeehah!* might yet bellow from the sound system as they made their way back to Bemidji.

After handing it off to Jonas, Dan had some time to talk with Jenna. *Who would have thought, when he left—was it only three days ago?—that he would still be putting miles on the car leapfrogging around the Minnesota countryside.*

"Sam, call Jenna, would you?"

"She is on another call, Dan. Shall I interrupt?"

"No that's fine. I'll…"

"I have her now, Dan. Hello, Jenna, I have Dan onscreen for you."

"Thanks, Sam. Hi honey! I have great news! Charlie's fever is down and he's eating!"

"Oh, fantastic, Jen. What's the vet say?"

CHAPTER 48

Jenna was smiling ear to ear. She reached over and picked up Charlie and helped him wave. "See, he's glad to see you. The vet thinks whatever it was, the antibiotics seem to be working. And fluids. She thinks he's going to be OK!"

"Fantastic, Jen. Looks like little Charlie still has a bunch of lives to go." Dan knew he had to change the subject. "Honey, there's…a complication," he began. He launched into the events of the past twenty-four hours as if telling her about a book he'd just read. At least, that's the way his voice sounded to his own ears. She was silent through most of it, but her face told him she was focused. When he told her about *the fall*, she gasped, and her eyes welled with tears as she pulled Charlie closer.

"Oh, Dan, I…don't know what to say. Is he all right? What do the doctors say?"

"He was resting when we were there earlier. I need to go back, honey. So I may be here another day. I know you weren't…"

She interrupted him before he could finish. "Oh, Dan, of course you do! Don't worry about us, we're fine. Go see Owen. This is important, so don't give it another thought. We'll see you soon, but he needs you now. Give everyone my best!"

As happy as he was to hear about the kitten, he was even more relieved to hear the brightened tone of his wife's voice. Well, almost.

"Wave to Daddy, Charlie."

Dan always felt stupid doing this, but he forced himself to wave at his wrist. "Hi Charlie."

Immediately, a message scrolled across his screen. It was in Samantha's font. *Waving at cats now, are we?*

Dan stared at it. "Well, so much for updates."

"Well…look who's here," Owen's voice creaked, as he wriggled but failed to scooch up against the recline of the bed. Bloated, drowsy eyes came to life as Sandy walked in with her daughter, Melissa.

"Hi Poppa," Melissa said with a twinkle. Between them was three-year-old Amy, her tiny hands clasped in theirs, proudly showing off her new, pink floral-print dress. Melissa lifted her granddaughter to the edge of the bed near Owen's hand and away from the gaggle of tubes that extended from his arm. "Amy, see, it's poppa? Say, 'Hi.'"

Owen looked at his great-great-granddaughter, waiting for her reaction. Pulling a finger from her mouth, she pointed at his arm, bruise-blue from his knuckles to his elbow. "Pretty!"

"Ha!" he said in unison with the others in the room. "She's probably going to be a painter."

Dan could only grin as he followed the entourage into the room, his mind still untangling the notion that Owen's granddaughter, Melissa, must be about his age. And if he understood it correctly, it only got worse—or better. Melissa's daughter, Susan, who was Amy's mother, had two other children: a daughter, Heidi, and an older son, Michael, who was eighteen. He'd gotten married over the summer to a woman named Jerolyn and, would wonders never cease, his wife was now with child. *Gads!*

"How are you feeling, Dad?" Sandy inquired as she gently kissed his forehead.

"A little better…Damn sleepy, though."

"Dan's here, too," she added. He popped out from behind Melissa and waved three fingers in Owen's direction.

"I thought you'd be long gone, Dan…I've taken up too much of your time," Owen said sluggishly.

"Not at all, sir. This has been quite an adventure for me. For all of us, I suppose," he said with a wink. "And what a pleasure getting to know more about your family."

"I've been blessed, Dan. Wonderful family. I look at them… and I see the movement of time." He stopped abruptly and coughed heavily once. Dan wasn't sure if the dampness in his eyes was from the cough or his sense of pride. "My beautiful wife, she made all this…" He scanned them—three generations. "Sorry, I'm not quite awake, I think. What I mean is…what I mean is…I still miss her."

—⋘— Chapter 49 —⋙—

I was confused. "Everything is so different, sweetie. It's got to be close."

"So much traffic," Shirley observed. "I can't believe I ever called this place home."

I still hadn't gotten the hang of the GPS and some woman's voice kept reminding me I had screwed up again. A big red flag with "The Pike" printed near it was supposed to reassure me we were on the right path.

"Destination in five hundred yards," she clamored.

It was surreal. It had been seventy years since I had proposed to this lovely woman on this very spot. The Pike Outlet Mall? This couldn't be it. It felt so far inland, so far away from the beach. Had they filled all of this in since 1951? Rainbow Pier, gone?

"Where are we, Owen?"

"The magazine said there was still a carousel somewhere around here, honey. I just need to figure out where and how to park. There doesn't seem to be a parking lot anywhere." We passed perfect rows of palm trees and finally a sign that said "Pike parking, $16 for 24 hrs." We didn't need twenty-four hours to go around the carousel a few times. My GPS kept insisting I get onto another highway, Pine Avenue. I finally relented. As we passed by something called the Laugh Factory, I saw on my right, the image of that Ferris wheel. It was weird, nothing like the way I remembered it, now a shouting blue and white pinwheel near the only patch of grass anywhere around. Huge buildings stood like cliffsides behind it—a cinema, restaurants, and so many storefronts with equally stunning lights. Ahead of us, like the silhouette of a mountain range, a whirling steel frame that had to be the rollercoaster wound up and across the roadway. As I squinted, I realized it was a bizarre bridge of some kind. In fact it looked like the entire midway now consisted of only the Ferris wheel. Gone were the low white buildings that bordered the area like military barracks and with them the bustle of the outdoor concessions and food galleries. The spider web frame that stitched together the colossal superstructure for the Cyclone, towering above everything else, was nowhere to be seen. Just this single, lonely wheel between a little patch of grass and a shopping center.

I turned right and drove toward it and was surprised to see a row of angled parking on this multilane roadway. A wheelchair spot was just opening up, and I maneuvered into it and hung up our tag.

"Well, I guess we're here," I said, letting out a deep breath.

"Where are we, Owen?" Shirley sounded concerned.

I was about to answer, but did a double take as I happened to glance back to the Ferris wheel. "Look sweetie! There it is! The carousel."

CHAPTER 49

"I see it! Oh, Owen, you found it."

I hoped it wouldn't be too much for her. We had a little walk ahead of us. It wasn't like I took any distance lightly but I still liked to walk. Shirley had grown increasingly unstable on her feet. She seldom went shopping, except for a few kitchen needs. We kept a walker in the car. "Let me see how this all works before we go over there, honey. I'll just be a minute." At ninety-five, nothing took me a minute, but I didn't want to leave her for very long. I fiddled with the radio screen. "Here. Our favorite station. Be right back."

This carousel was different. Wasn't it? It was under a more sophisticated enclosure, and I couldn't make out if it was even the same one. It had been so long. It seemed more polished and the entrance certainly didn't have that carnival feel anymore. A polite young woman asked if she could help me.

"My wife and I haven't been here since 1951. It's our seventieth anniversary, and I proposed to her on the carousel."

She smiled warmly. "How beautiful! Congratulations! 1951? Well, that carousel was dismantled a long time ago when the area was first redeveloped. I can remember the roof of the building sitting in the parking lot when I was a girl. However, this is a very old carousel. They brought it here from back east."

"How much?"

"Two dollars each. But for you, how about half price for your anniversary?"

"Thank you. You're very kind."

I returned to the car as quickly as I could. "A nice young lady offered us an anniversary present. Would you like to take a ride?" Shirley looked at me. Her beautiful face could still light up a room, but the twinkling that I saw in her eye was reflecting from a tear.

"Can we go home, Owen? I don't know this place. I...I don't know where we are."

I had hoped it was just the music. Maybe a sad song. It wasn't. It was time to go home.

THE LAST WORD

Chapter 50

As afternoon became evening, the nurse slid the third floor window aside so a little fresh air could circulate and blow out some of that hospital air, as Owen referred to it. She then adjusted the flower container and a couple of "Get Well Soon" cards on the utility table. A call tone sounded on her wrist-screen, and she groaned and shook her head as she hurried away.

"Thank you, Lillian," Owen said to her back. He turned his head and smiled at Dan. "The orange juice is good in here," he said, releasing the straw after a sip. "The cobwebs are finally starting to clear, I think."

Dan was grateful for that. He'd not been sure earlier in the day how this was shaking out. But for the moment, Owen was sitting up higher in the bed and seemed reasonably lucid.

"You know, I'd thought about returning to Long Beach with Shirley for some time…but I was concerned with the traveling. Shirley hadn't seen her younger sister in years." He drew another uncertain sip of juice through the straw. "It was our seventieth. I didn't know if she could…if either of us would hold out five more years." He took a labored breath. "She lived another two."

"She had health issues at that point?" Dan asked, suspecting it was a question he already knew the answer to.

"She struggled with a number of things…the onset of dementia or something was a part of it." He swirled the cup in a mixing motion but with no purpose. "In the end, of course, it was her strongest asset, her heart that failed." There was a short, awkward silence. "It really cleared out around here, huh?" Owen said, noticing that the crowd of friends and family members had dwindled to just Dan.

"Heh, yeah, I guess it's dinner time for the young'uns," Dan said. "I expect they'll be back before long."

Lillian returned to the room at a brisk nurse-march with a dour expression. "I'm afraid we're going to need to move these get well cards somewhere else," she began.

"Don't tell me there's rules against cards these days," Owen muttered.

As he spoke, another nurse walked in from behind Lillian holding a box and set it down on Owen's bed. The box was overflowing with envelopes. "What's this?" he said, confused.

"They're for you! So far, we have about three hundred."

Dan gave a whoop! "Son of a gun, Owen. Very cool! I didn't think people sent cards anymore."

Lillian gave a wry smile. "Most of these were hand delivered to the front desk. They've been coming in all day. And just so you know, some folks aren't going with cards. Our e-messaging site is overflowing with mail. It's so bad we had to set up a referral site just for you. There's thousands in there from all over the world."

"Well, I'll be darned. I…don't know what to say…" Owen stammered.

"Well, that's a first," Dan joked. "Kind of gives you hope, doesn't it?"

Owen slowly shook his head. "You just can't ever guess what's going to happen, can you?" With that, he eased his head back against the pillow and gazed up at the ceiling. He briefly shut his eyes to gather his thoughts…"

Tinian, August 5, 1945

~~ Chapter 51 ~~

It was hard to fathom. I looked out from the operations window toward skies of near endless blue dotted with billowing clouds that stretched out above the acres of runway packed with aircraft. Today…well, this was the final time for us, and it's the flight every crewman looks forward to and dreads at the same time. Tomorrow, we ship out.

I had that dream again last night. The one where I'm rushing around gathering up my stuff and I can't find anything. I'm late and I can hear the plane warming, but can't find my flight jacket. I run out the Quonset door and I'm suddenly on the runway. The guys are waving, yelling "C'mon! We've got to go!" I rush up to the rear hatch, dropping gear all along the way, and as I set a foot on the first step, I suddenly realize, I have no shoes! The plane's not heated and we're going to be at 20,000 feet! "Don't worry," they say. "We're late! You can wear this." They hand me a parachute.

Then I woke up. Not the way I wanted to feel heading out in the dark on my last flight before going home. *Please. Be uneventful.*

For an hour or two, it was just that. Boring patrol. And we weren't carrying bombs anyway. It seemed almost fitting that for our final flight, we were back in one of the older PB4Y-1s like the one that first brought us to Tinian. Without blister turrets, I swung the gun back and forth in the window a few times as I looked out over the water, remembering what it felt like to do it for the first time with Paul back on Ford Island.

This flight, like so many before it, would take us through the early morning darkness and into the sunrise to a turnaround point some seven or eight hours away. A lot can happen in sixteen hours. Or nothing. The plane began to chatter, then the chatter became that now familiar dance of twenty foot swings in elevation that meant we were entering a sizable storm. Rain began dripping off the gun barrel, so there was not much to do but sit down and ride it out. Four hours later, it began to subside.

We broke through the west side of the front and into open seas where cottony piles of clouds reflected brilliant morning sun. A rainbow filled much of my square window, and below us, a white capped cobalt ocean was streaked with radiant orange and green. I thought to myself, *I will miss this side of things*. So much of what you see is impossible to describe to someone who hasn't observed it, who doesn't share the experience.

"Owen!" Across from me, Andy, our starboard gunner shouted to get my attention. "Hey, I have something down here."

About the same time, our copilot said the same thing over the intercom. A small ship was drawing nearer. A target. But once again, we had no bombs. Only the extra fuel to extend our patrol range. The option now was a strafing run, then a steep pullout to regroup.

The Skipper circled and swung us around to an attack line, but before we could make our move, the ship began firing. It was equipped with a large caliber cannon that rotated and followed us everywhere we went. Shells were bursting all around us as we tried to find a weak spot to make our run. If we only had our bombs!

I could hear them talking. "If we make a run, we'll likely get hit, probably lose an engine or worse. They've got a good bead on us with that gun," came the copilot's voice. The damn thing just kept popping away and following us as we circled. "We have four hours of a storm to get back through. On two or three engines? Not today. I'm going to call it off." So we did.

The storm bounced us around with a stiff headwind, and although he second guessed himself all the way in, it was a good call by the Skipper. We broke out into the open, and I could see the hills of Guam to the south and Rota up ahead. We swung wide to the north and headed for home.

CHAPTER 51

Tinian's North Field was something to see from the air. In the relatively short time we had been here, it had gone from a modest Japanese airstrip to what was now referred to as the largest airport in the world. It was packed with gleaming B-29 Superfortresses and had Seabees and crewmen buzzing around everywhere. To the south and a little beyond the island's midpoint was our Navy airstrip, West Field, somewhat smaller and home to our PB4Ys and an assortment of other aircraft. Together they looked to be nearly a third of the island. Like a permanent pair of aircraft carriers strapped together.

We were beginning our approach when Andy waved at me. "Sounds like we're moving into a holding pattern," he said. "Mayday or something." It happened a lot around Tinian with all the aircraft in and out of here that frequently came back on empty or beat up or both. We banked and entered the pattern, then cut across near a section at the very top of the North Field taxiway where the island's east and west shorelines converged, almost forming a tip that pointed directly at a solitary B-29. With my trusty field glasses, I could make out a group of brass in officer's caps conferring at one end and a lonely figure working on the other, apparently painting the nose. I couldn't make it all out, but he had completed some lettering and I suspected he was setting up to add a pinup girl next. It was another thing I'd miss about this place. I found it an amusing contradiction, these profound instruments of violence adorned with such clever artwork that only a U.S. military guy would dream up.

We circled once and came in, rolling down the mat and then taxiing through the network of runways and intersections and past scores of Navy aircraft, each impressive and parked with support personnel scurrying between them. My throat tingled, from pride I guess, and we cornered and gingerly taxied onto the parking apron—one last time.

The walk across the tarmac took me past a swarm of Seabees, and somewhere in the middle, a voice rang out. "Owen, is that you?" It was Erwin!

"I figured they sent you home by now. Nothing left to build," I kidded.

He grinned. "Nope, still here. I was just about to get a picture of your plane. You know me. Won't be happy till I get 'em all. Boy, I'll tell ya', we've been working night and day up at North Field and putting together some strange stuff. Hey, you doing anything right now?"

"We ship out tomorrow. Just packing up my gear and saying some goodbyes. I'm really glad I ran into you. What's up?"

"Well, I was just heading over for my shift. Hop in and I'll show you something." We squeezed in a jeep with two other Seabees and drove to a parking area at the south end of North Field. Erwin told the other two he'd catch up with them later and we cut across the apron and between several groups of hangars. He told me they'd just finished working on a new building and every part of it needed to be grounded and protected from lightning strikes. After a considerable walk, Erwin had me pretty much lost. "Alright, stay next to me and follow my lead."

We crossed a patch of grassy coral toward a single B-29 parked near one edge. I suddenly realized that it must be the same one I saw from the air. A couple of guys were working on the far side of it and hadn't noticed us and we cautiously walked up to the paving and stopped.

"I saw a fellow painting this as we came in. Is that the name of the girl? The one he's going to paint?" I asked.

"No girl on this one. It's the pilot's mother. *Enola Gay*. I wanted to be sure and get a picture of it. That building I told you about, there's something big going on in there." He stopped and squinted through the camera sight. "We all figure this is a special plane." He took a couple of shots, then adjusted his lens. I pulled my little Argus out of my side pack to try one. "You want me to take it for you?" He reached out for my camera. "Stand over there. A little to the side. A little more. That's good. Perfect." He snapped it, then looked at my camera. "I rigged up a little darkroom over at the paint shop. I can develop them for you."

"I still have a couple shots in there I'm saving for the ride home. Thanks anyway." As he handed it back, I could see those men around the plane had spotted us. We decided to skedaddle.

CHAPTER 51

We walked back part of the way and Erwin turned toward me. "So tomorrow's the big day. You ship out. Lucky dog."

"I'll leave it to you to hold down the fort. See if you can win this thing, OK? I don't want to have to come back out here."

"Naw, we got it. Don't you worry. Want a lift back?"

"You know, I think I feel like walking." He smiled warmly and we shook hands—and then went our separate ways.

THE LAST WORD

Chapter 52

"Jonas! Well this is turning into quite a reunion," Owen beamed, a little surprised by all of the attention.

Jonas walked across the room holding a balloon. On its side, printed in old style italic, were the words *Vintage Dude - 112 and Counting*.

"You know me better than I realized. Thanks, Jonas."

"Whew, I was hoping." He breathed a sigh of relief.

Dinner time had come and gone and the room was again becoming crowded. The day nurse whispered to Sandy that the shift was about to change, and the evening staff should have more room to circulate should Owen have any issue or adjustment to his IVs.

"That's OK, Mom," Melissa chimed in. "I should get Amy home. It's about time for a bedtime story, isn't it, sweetie? Say 'bye to Poppa." She had hold of little Amy's wrist and the two of them waved in tandem. Melissa gave Owen a kiss on the forehead. "See you tomorrow, Poppa. Rest easy, OK?"

Owen thanked her and blew a kiss to his great-great-granddaughter. Dan could see a wave of emotion rinse across his face.

"I'm a lucky man," Owen confided.

"That you are, sir."

Sandy thought it was a good time to present Owen with his chest, and she lifted it into view. "Guess what I found," she said in a change-the-subject way.

Sandy filled Owen in about locating the box with Dan's help. But she hesitated to say anything more, judging that her dad would elaborate if he chose to.

"Smells like my box," he said and quickly turned his head away, overcome by several deep coughs. He then swept it with his eyes like an old war buddy. "Tells you what ninety years of humidity can do."

Jonas looked over at the others and sensed the time was right. "We found this canister of undeveloped film down in there, Owen. Inside a little tin. Hope you don't mind, but I had a friend work with it and he made some prints." He handed a packet to Owen. "He told me how fussy an old film roll can be—dampness, possible light contamination. The roll can even stick to itself. He has a lab and experience in taking special precautions with the film."

"I'll be darned. It's been down in there all this time?" He motioned with a finger. "Wonder where I took these? I had a little bitty Argus I carried around with me."

Owen tipped the folder and the photos fanned out into a loose stack on his bedsheet. Everyone crowded in as he lifted the first one. "This is the Skipper's dog! What was his name? Can't remember. Everyone loved that dog. He loved to drink beer!"

Jonas said, "I really want to ask you about this next one." He looked at Owen and waited for a reaction.

Dan was the first to respond. "You were on a runway with the *Enola Gay*?" he said in amazement.

"A lot of us were. Like I said, Tinian was a busy place." He laughed. "Actually, it was parked."

Jonas shook his head. "How were you able to take this picture? You couldn't have known."

"No, I had no idea. A buddy of mine was a Seabee working at North Field and took me up there. He had a feeling something was happening from the work they were doing. I always wondered what happened to that picture."

Dan thought it irresistible that the crew of the Enola Gay and Owen shared a moment on a remote Pacific island on this particular day.

Each was about to depart in opposite directions, and within twenty-four hours each would see the unprecedented end to the war from a very different perspective.

CHAPTER 52

He asked, "Do you remember where you were when the *Enola* dropped the bomb? What you thought?"

"I was on my way to Hawaii. Probably somewhere out of sight of land and most communication. There were rumors, then a special announcement, but I'm sure none of us realized the significance. We cheered and probably ate ice cream. Sounds so distasteful now."

"And you were still on your way when the word of the Japanese surrender reached you?" Dan asked.

"Our V-J Day was on deck. I didn't kiss anybody but there was plenty of it going on. Some of the guys weren't too fussy, I guess."

Jonas was curious about his arrival back in Hawaii and the U.S. mainland. He asked if there was fanfare or celebrations.

"At Pearl, I was surprised to see, after all this time, that there were *still* battleships in the harbor—underwater. It looked like the hangars and airstrip had been refurbished, maybe even by the time I went through in '44." He studied the photo again. "I remember it being pretty emotional. We moved on and under the Golden Gate from there. Stayed in town for a while." He grinned, "Yeah, I'd have to say we did a little celebrating in Frisco. It had been quite a while since we'd seen food like that. We hung out and explored—maybe a couple of days. Then we moved south to San Diego again."

"Here's a picture of an island from the air," Jonas said. "Would you recognize it?" He pointed at a photo.

"Let's see. Hmm. We're pretty low, but I think that's Japan."

This caught everyone by surprise.

"We were out on a mission looking for a picket ship that was loaded to the gills with anti-aircraft guns. They used them as sentries along the coast."

Owen launched into the tale and Dan thought to himself that he would savor this one. This voice, this storytelling took him places he never wanted to forget. He whispered to Samantha to record it, and then settled in as Owen's crew approached the enemy ship at fifty feet or so off the water. Dan could picture the big plane, laden with bombs, when suddenly a fighter appears, but it never sees them. Their skipper pours on the power, climbing, giving chase after the unsuspecting Zero, cruising serenely down the coast.

"That's when I took this. See him there? Just a speck," Owen said, regaining some of the vitality that had been missing since yesterday.

The Japanese plane cut inland near Nagoya Bay. The Skipper caught him there and everyone started firing. Owen wasn't sure but guessed the bow gunner scored a hit, and the fighter went into a spin. "I followed him down with my eyes, and I suddenly realized, we're over an airport!" There were hundreds of warplanes and anti-aircraft emplacement below them. Owen said the area immediately erupted in gunfire and there were explosions all around them. The pilots powered up and away from the airfield as quickly as they could. "Later, the Skipper admitted, 'I was hustling to get us out of there, but I'm kicking myself for not dropping our bombs first!' I hadn't noticed either."

Dan was thoroughly absorbed in the story and photograph. "Wow, so here is that doomed fighter right above the coast of Japan."

"Or," began Owen, "could be the coast of Australia and that's just a seagull."

The four of them laughed as Owen selected another photo and gazed at it for a long time.

"My crew," he began. "That's our plane and all the guys."

Sandy pointed to his image. "I recognize that fellow," she said. "Who is that with his hand on your shoulder?"

Owen lingered before answering, savoring the snapshot. "That's Johnny."

"Handsome guy," Jonas observed.

"You all were!" Sandy said. "It seems like every picture I see is of a movie star! You World War II guys were a handsome lot!"

"Speaking of Johnny," Dan said, "we found some letters in there, too. Sorry if we were prying. It was unintentional."

CHAPTER 52

Sandy handed the letters to her father. He shoved against his glasses and focused on the pages of blue paper, filled with a woman's graceful handwriting and her familiar reflections about a time he'd prefer to forget. He looked up and removed his glasses, then sat back and massaged the red imprints remaining on the bridge of his nose. "Sandy, Jonas? Could you excuse us for a few minutes?" Owen said.

Dan watched as the two of them left and wondered what was happening. "Everything all right, Owen?"

"Dan, I feel like I've known you for a lot longer than three days. Perhaps, in a way, I have," he said, looking uneasy. "I wanted to show you these letters, but since you've probably read them... well, what do you make of it?"

Dan was feeling unsure of how he should answer this. *Does he want my opinion? Is he angry that Johnny wasn't straight with him?*

"I'm not sure what you mean, Owen."

"I had Sandy call your paper, Dan. It was important to me." He pussyfooted and took a breath. "You've probably wondered why." Dan nodded. "I know you told me your dad passed away. What did you say his name was?"

"Adam. Adam Callahan. Why?"

"And your grandfather's name?"

"Gerald Callahan. I'm not sure I'm..."

"Take a look. In both of these letters...there is a friend."

Dan was bewildered. "A friend? Oh, Jerry?" He felt a twinge of apprehension. "You don't mean...it isn't like Jerry and Gerald have anything to do with each other, right? What do you mean?"

"Dan, Jerry's last name was...Callahan. But he wasn't your grandfather. Your grandfather...was killed in a plane on a runway at Tinian."

"I don't understand," Dan said. "You mean I'm related to...I'm Johnny's grandson? How? Dad was his son?"

Owen's eyes were the tip-off, the bellwether of just how tired he was. Yet a sense of relief swelled inside him. "I've been trying to find a way to tell you. I didn't know you yet...but I promised myself I'd find someone in his family before I died. It has taken almost ninety years."

Dan sat down in a chair a few feet from Owen's bed. He stared ahead dumbstruck for a few seconds. Owen slumped a little, then felt the need to say something. "I'm sorry, Dan. Are you… feeling up to talking about it?"

Dan looked across at the old gentleman who had carried this deep sense of obligation around for a lifetime. He gently moved his head side to side. "There's not too much to talk about, I guess. I mean, in reality, my father never knew. And I certainly never knew…I don't think I'm feeling much of anything." He stood. "It was a grandparent ninety years ago, you know? Both of them passed away when I was really young and I scarcely knew them. It's like finding out from ancestry testing or something."

Owen looked a little flabbergasted. For days, even years, he had dreaded this moment. He felt he had crushing news that could change somebody's life forever, and…*it didn't*.

"Well…" He gave a long sigh. "Well, shit, that's a relief!" Their laughter echoed in the room until Owen began coughing again.

Once he'd settled down, Dan's expression still showed concern. "Need anything? A sip of your drink? I could ring the nurse."

"No, it's better now." After a break, "Much better, in fact. Listen…there is one other thing."

Dan held his breath. "You're not going to tell me that my mother wasn't my mother now are you?"

"Shucks that would have been a good one. But no, nothing like that. Since I was on kind of a roll here…the wooden chest… in it were two very special items. A flag and a ceremonial belt."

"Yes," Dan said. "I recall them both."

"They belonged to my friend, Taiki, and he had hoped I might find a relative of his to return them to. I never could."

"And you would like me to help look for one?" Dan anticipated.

"With your connections, familiarity with modern technology, I just thought…"

CHAPTER 52

"I'd be honored to help with the search, Owen. In fact, I'm slightly familiar with an organization that might be able to assist us."

"Then my most pressing business is finished. Thank you."

A new night nurse interrupted when she slid aside the curtain. Peering over her shoulder was a pair of red and white checkerboard glasses. "Surprise!"

"LaTeesha!" Owen said, smiling widely. Then he reconsidered a moment. "This doesn't mean...not rehab..." he said, scrunching down against the bed's back and pillow.

LaTeesha exchanged a hand slap with the nurse. "What did I tell you, girl? I knew he'd say that!" she said with a horse laugh, momentarily drowning out the monitor's beep. "Don't you worry, Mr. Owen. I'm leavin' you alone *today*. This is my friend, Mo'Nique. We worked together back in the old days." She wrinkled her nose, pressed a hand next to her mouth and whispered to him, "Don't know what she might have up her sleeve, though. Aw, I'm foolin' with you! She's the best, so you got nothin' to worry about." She took his hand and let out a slow breath, then smiled at him tenderly. "How you feeling, hon?"

"A little better now that you've told me that." The group of them laughed and LaTeesha held Owen's hand in hers and blinked. Then blinked again.

"Damn cold weather keeps foggin' up my glasses," she said. "Well, listen. This nurse here has got work to do and I'm afraid I do, too. Gotta run. I'll check in on you tomorrow, OK?"

"That would be wonderful," Owen replied. As the ladies left together, still chattering like parrots, Owen grinned warmly. "Don't know what I ever did to deserve her. But whatever it was, I'm glad I did it." He watched as Dan stood and unconsciously stretched his arms in front of him, then added, "I guess you should tell the others that we're...done."

Dan walked around the bed toward the door, casting aside the curtain, and lingered there. He stared back at Owen and felt a sudden sense of kinship. Warmth that you might feel for a favorite uncle, or even—a grandfather. "Owen, when you're up to it…" He hesitated. "I *would* like to know more about him. More about Johnny."

    The old man smiled.

San Diego, September of 1945

— Chapter 53 —

San Diego. It was good to be back on the U.S. mainland, home again, even though my home was still a long train ride and longer thumb away. But San Diego also meant unfinished business. Awkwardness. Nervousness. Maybe cowardice. No, I had to see this through. I had to find Helen.

I still had his bag and knew word of Johnny's death was delivered in person to his parents. Surely Helen was informed. If she hadn't already moved on by then. I wondered what she was like?

I'd tracked down her address, a little town maybe an hour and a half hour north of Los Angeles near a small naval base on the coast. I was working up my courage on the train ride. The bar across the street from the depot looked mighty inviting, but I thought better of it, not having a clue how any of this would go down. I started walking.

Jenkins Street. Her house was cute, with a neat lawn and flower boxes under the windows. I walked up the sidewalk rehearsing what I was going to say first. As I reached up to grab hold of the brass door knocker, the door swung open. It was a man.

"Uh, hi. I…uh, I came to speak to Helen?"

"And who might you be?" he inquired suspiciously.

"My name is Owen. I knew…Johnny was my friend."

He wasn't expecting that and had a change of heart. "Of course. Won't you come in." He left the room briefly, then came back holding her hand. She was a delicate and attractive brunette, hair combs holding her hair back, and she wore a blue ruffled skirt with a loose white top that suggested she was expecting again.

"I guess I always knew you'd come. It's really nice to meet you, Owen." Her eyes welled up and the words stuck in her throat. "Would you like to sit?"

"I'm sorry I didn't introduce myself. I'm Jerry. I'm Helen's husband. I imagine there are some things you two should talk over, so I'll excuse myself. Honey, call if you need anything." He left us alone, two uneasy strangers.

We talked about how soon the new baby was due, what life was like with doctor's visits and getting a room fixed up, just so—for two babies.

"What's his name?" I had to ask.

Helen smiled. "Adam. He's down for his nap. I suppose it was crazy of us to have another one so soon, but…it was important to Jerry. And to me." She looked at me for a long minute, then asked, "Did he…suffer?"

"I don't think so. It happened so fast. There was nothing we could do."

The relief of months of worry, stress, and uncertainty overwhelmed her and she collapsed into my arms, uncontrollably sobbing. She tried to speak, but I couldn't make out what she was saying. I could tell that she still loved him and had not forgiven herself. It was as if she felt, in some small way, responsible for his death.

As she regained her composure, she told me that Jerry was a kind and gentle man who had always been there for her. She had assumed she would be breaking up with Johnny when she saw him that last time. Then she was pregnant, and soon he was gone.

She finally worked up the courage to tell her parents after trying to conceal the fact for nearly five months and, of course, she also wrote to Johnny to give him the news. News that she had wondered for months how to share with him. She had hoped in bringing them all in, that she would have the support she needed to get through this difficult and delicate time. Except for Jerry, she was going down this road alone.

CHAPTER 53

Her parents didn't take it well. "Helen, what were you thinking? What will the neighbors say?" She was ashamed, upset. She wrote to Johnny again.

After the news of Johnny's death reached her, she was lost for a time but had to think of the baby. Jerry didn't try to hide his affection for her. As she healed, the two of them became closer. In the end, they had a quiet wedding a few weeks before the baby was born—just close friends and family—and began to build a new life.

I wondered if I could stay in touch with her. I wanted to see Johnny's son. Maybe, at some point, tell him a little bit about his father. I guess it was corny, but I felt like I owed him that. She agreed to let me stop by some day. Someday…in the future.

When I left her house on Jenkins, I felt like I needed some air. Since I didn't have a car, I started walking—and I didn't have the foggiest notion about where I was going or why. To the beach? I hadn't been in warm water in some time. Maybe a swim would help. A street sign ahead said "Ventura Road." I liked the sound of the name. I decided that a hike up to Ventura to see what it was all about might do me some good. I slung my duffle bag over a shoulder, confident the walk couldn't be any worse than Basic. Within a mile, I hit an intersection with the Old Highway 1. This held a fascination for some reason and I followed it north.

How different it was to walk rather than drive along the roadway. Neighborhoods were filled with tidy little yards, robust blossoming shrubs, curious pets. Forlorn palm trees stood tall, here and there, far removed from the coconut plantations and dense jungles I had become accustomed to. The highway leading north at the outskirts of Helen's town came with a change in traffic, and was more of a highway than I had expected. One or two autos slowed and offered me a lift. My duffle bag was an ID badge, as clear to them as the uniform I had packed away in it. I kindly thanked them and continued walking.

Scraps of paper bounced and leaves rustled with each passing car along this thoroughfare as it wound more to the west. Whiffs of auto exhaust and salt air blended in the breeze, not unlike so many island locations with their busy runways. I walked along small woodlands and a patchwork of orchards, enjoying glimpses of the mighty Pacific, my old friend. To the east, the hills rose, sheer and angular, and a sea of gray rooftops ahead hinted at the population of a town between the ridge and the shoreline.

By the end of the afternoon, my stomach began to growl, and I wondered if I'd made a bit of a miscalculation about the distance to Ventura. A cafe sign up ahead offered hope. I stopped in and took up a stool at the counter.

"What can I get you?" an attentive and cordial lady asked while she wiped and cleared the counter.

"Coffee. And maybe a sandwich."

She brought me a cup and gave me a smile. "Just get back?" she asked.

"How'd you know?" I smiled.

"We get a lot of the guys up here from L.A. and San Diego. Not sure where they're going, what they're gonna do now. Feeling a little lost."

"Wow, you're good. Yep, that would be me. I thought I was heading to the beach, but now it seems north feels better. Don't have a clue what's up there though."

"Listen, I don't know what you're after, but whenever I feel the need to get centered, relaxed, or whatever, I like to go up to Big Sur. Open spaces. Get in those big trees."

Huh. Big Sur. I'd heard of it, but had no idea what it was about. Or how to get there.

"It's a half day drive. There's a Boy Scout camp in there, and I'll bet they'd put you up right in the middle of some of the most beautiful country you ever saw."

"You make it sound very tempting."

"Hey Ralph, you're heading up to Carmel tonight, aren't you?" her question directed to a nearby table.

And within thirty minutes, I found myself in a flatbed truck full of orange crates heading to a place called Big Sur. It was dark when we arrived.

CHAPTER 53

The waitress was right. The scout facilities were vacant, and I tiptoed around and found an open, empty cabin. It beat sleeping in a PBY and, truth be told, I could have slept almost anywhere. I was beat.

Sunlight poured in through a window at dawn and the air was alive with the sound of birds. I peered out and looked right into the side of a massive, rugged red tree trunk. There was absolutely no sign of anything like a top to this thing. Once outside, scores of similar trees dominated the forest, each a giant red column disappearing into a cloud of green foliage. It was a cathedral and unlike anything I'd ever seen before.

The next I knew, I had been wandering around for a solid hour and had gotten myself thoroughly lost. But I didn't care. For the first time since I'd been home, I'd had some clarity. I was going to go to work. In the woods!

THE LAST WORD

Chapter 54

"Oooh! Watch out, it's too hot!" Sandy said, trying to warn Jonas about the coffee. Vending machines in this hospital hawked the usual foods and an array of knickknacks that made them seem like robotic convenience stores. Socks, eye drops, nail clippers, book and movie downloads, espresso. But they weren't any better at figuring out coffee temperatures than they had been in the 1970s.

Jonas, heeding her words, blew across the open container and then set it down. "What do you think was going on with those two?" he asked. "I felt like we got kicked out."

"Curious, wasn't it. I have a hunch."

"Oh?"

"I think it might have something to do with those letters Dan and I found. They were letters from home and written from a crewman's girlfriend. Or wife, depending on how you look at it." Sandy filled Jonas in on the particulars of what she and Dan had stumbled upon, but something still puzzled her.

Some years ago, she had gone to quite a bit of trouble looking around online for an investigator for Owen. He wouldn't elaborate and she just did as he asked. Over the course of the next several months, he had received several calls and some correspondence—all in letter form delivered by U.S. mail. No e-messaging. She had been curious but didn't want to seem snoopy. Then it was over, and she hadn't given it any more thought. Until now.

Earlier this week, she was watching the evening news when the anchor made a somber announcement: *A story tonight coming from Japan. The last surviving veteran from World War II has passed away today at one hundred and twelve. The last* American *veteran, Sergeant Warren Johnson, died in July of this year.* She scarcely heard anything else in the broadcast and wandered in to talk to Owen. He was dozing and startled awake as she approached. "I told him that the last war veteran died today. He said, 'What war?' I told him, 'Yours!' He just said, 'Huh, imagine that. Maybe we should make a call.'"

Sandy wanted to call that news anchor and straighten him out. Owen insisted he wanted to get in touch with a certain newspaper in Winona. He had decided if they wanted an interview or something, he preferred more of a small town kind of deal. No fancy, big city reporter. "It sounded like baloney to me," she said.

She and Jonas continued to shuffle through conspiracies of one kind or another, until they saw Dan striding quickly up the hallway. He looked alarmed.

"Sandy, you need to come in here. Owen's having some kind of a problem."

The three of them hurried back to a room filled with warning tones and lights and Mo'Nique standing over Owen's bed. He was flushed and seemed to be breathing heavily, and she looked up at Sandy. "I've given him something to relax him. The coughing is painful, and the doctor may add a suppressant for that."

"He just started coughing as I was coming out to get you," Dan told Sandy. "He couldn't stop, so I called the nurse in."

Sandy drew closer to Owen's bed. "Dad?"

He smiled up at her with a wink. Mo'Nique said a doctor would be in shortly to do a closer exam, and she suggested they give Owen a few moments to rest up first. The three of them reluctantly left, Sandy visibly rattled.

A pulmonary contusion is a possible outcome from the fall," the doctor began. "A lung can bruise and fluid can make breathing more difficult. You may have noticed a difference in the pace of his speech. Stopping to breathe. We have him on oxygen and he seems reasonably comfortable."

"Is this...will it heal or is there something more that he will need?" Sandy asked, her eyes welling up.

CHAPTER 54

"Normally, cases like this heal with time, but at his extreme age, well, we have to be prepared for complications." The doctor sat down beside her. He carefully adjusted his tone to be gentle and reassuring. "I have to be honest with you. I've never worked on anyone your father's age before. This is highly unusual, as I'm sure you know. Here's my sense of his situation." He touched her hand as he continued. "His oxygen level will be affected and a ventilator may come into play. I prefer he not stay horizontal any longer than necessary—pneumonia is a serious concern for anyone of advanced years and, of course, he's a centenarian. But to get him upright...I'm sure he has significant pain." He smiled at her. "Although your father is one tough cookie, and so far, he hasn't admitted to any."

Sandy, puffy eyed, shared an elongated chair in the waiting lounge with Dan and Jonas. Dan was wildly fishing for something to say when she broke the silence.

"You know, this has been *so* good for him," she began, her voice quivering. "I think he seemed more energized in the last few days than he has been in probably ten years," she added. "And I've learned so much. I want to thank you both for that."

"Sandy, I..."

"No, it's true," she continued over his reply. She wrapped her arms around herself in a hug. "His days came and went without much for him to look forward to anymore. Nothing to excite him. After that first session with you, it was all he would talk about. His memories, it's like he was reliving them. He was traveling back in time, back at a reunion with his buddies, on the farm, or in the air with Johnny," she said, as she removed a handkerchief from her bag. "Closure was important to him, too. He's always been like that." She dabbed at her nose and then looked Dan in the eye. "This has been a special gift, Dan. To the both of us. However this turns out, for a few precious days—he was a young man again."

THE LAST WORD

Long Beach, Summer of 1950

Chapter 55

How weird it was to be in Long Beach, sitting at this large, round table with a beer in my hand and staring across at the faces that made up my world for a few months in and around a Shangri-La called New Guinea. All of the faces, except one.

My Black Cat Squadron mates loved swapping stories, and we had lots of them. We spent more time laughing about the silliness of our lives in a war zone than we did recounting any of the dramatics. Ed nearly falling into the latrine trumped any night bombing run we could think of.

Eventually, they asked me about the rest of my tour, the part after Johnny and I had moved on from the Black Cats. "What was the Liberator like? What did you guys do up there?" There was no way around it. I'd have to relive one of the worst days of my life.

My mind was filled with two occurrences that had so moved me that I was brought nearly to tears. It had only been six months or so earlier, that I had attended another reunion in Chicago. Our entire Privateer crew from our final mission was there. Even the Skipper. The drinks loosened our tongues and before long, we were on Tinian's runway again. At night, waiting to taxi and overloaded. Then I could see it written on his face—the pain the Skipper carried around with him for so many years. He agonized over the decision not to take off, the precious seconds of braking that had been lost because he believed the gear was up. Could he have made it into the air? Would Johnny still be alive? Tears swept across his cheeks and we tried to console him. It was impossible to know if the crash that killed Johnny had actually saved the rest of us. The burden of making that split second call lived within him. And surely would for the rest of his days.

Then this morning, a half dozen hours before today's Black Cat reunion, I had another visit to make. I had called Helen at her home an hour and a half north of Long Beach. She hesitated, but agreed to let me stop by. I had come a long way, after all, and this was part of the reason.

The house on Jenkins Street still looked adorable. This time, it was Helen, herself, who greeted me. "Hi. Oh, your face. Is everything all right?"

"Yeah, sorry. Believe it or not, I had chicken pox last month. It's gone now, except for a few spots. Embarrassing, really."

"So, you're not contagious…" she asked, cautiously. I shook my head and emphasized I wasn't. "OK, well I won't hug you, just the same," she said with a nervous laugh.

We walked through the house toward the back door and rear yard. "Your place is quite lovely, Helen," I told her.

"Thanks," she said as she opened the door and stepped outside.

A short distance away, Jerry was gently pushing a gleeful toddler seated on a swing.

"Nice to see you, Owen. This is Adam. Say 'Hi' to the man, Adam.'"

It was the chubby-cheeked face of my best friend. There was no mistaking the twinkle in his blue eyes. I felt my throat tighten as I tried to speak. "Hi, Adam. Wow! That is quite a swing you have there." The four of us made small talk for another half hour, and I discovered that in addition to being a top-notch swing rider, that Adam also had the chicken pox last month. Soon, Helen announced it was time for his nap.

"Could you put him down, honey, and check on Allison?" she asked Jerry.

We walked over to a small patio area to talk. "Allison. Is that your daughter?" I asked.

She smiled proudly. "She's a princess. That's what Jerry calls her."

CHAPTER 55

She told me that she had thought about this day since the last time we'd met. Little Adam had a father and that was Jerry. The only one he'd ever known. They felt it was better to leave it that way and not create any unnecessary stress for their young children. Maybe someday, they would feel differently. But that time was not now or in the near future. She stammered a little as she told me that she was sorry but it was for the best.

I drove to the reunion feeling exhausted, hollow. She was probably right. And maybe she would feel differently in five years. Or ten. I tried to convince myself that you never knew what the future might hold.

"Owen, remember in New Guinea when that tracker brought in the wild pig?" one of the guys asked, breaking me out of my trance. I did remember. This was the side of my brain I preferred to be in, for now. Thanks, guys, for the diversion.

The reunion was beginning to wind down, and Alex had a crazy idea. "Anyone feel like going to the Pike later? Ride the famous 'Cyclone Racer?'"

THE LAST WORD

Chapter 56

From the pages of the **Winona Bulletin**, Sunday, October 24, 2038:
*Excerpt: The Owen Trimbel Interview Exclusive to the **Bulletin***
by <u>Dan Callahan</u>

Day Four

  This was a difficult time for Sandy Atkins. Yet through it all, she was a gracious host and doting daughter, tending to her father's every need and giving me support and access to both him and his life story. She is a remarkable woman, a product of a unique and charmed gene pool. And there was no mistaking the heredity responsible for it.
  He had been resting for several hours when she called me to his room. She said he was alert and asked if I could join them again for a few minutes before leaving town. She met me in the hallway and we walked the few steps to his bedside. The room was dimly lit, but he opened his eyes and offered me the familiar smile I had come to know so well.
  I slid a chair over beside him. An oxygen tube sagged beneath his nose, his voice as quiet as a breath. In a pastel string of broken sentences, he asked me, "Did you get what you needed? Any other questions? About anything?"
  It was pure Owen. Sandy had told me he was a man who needed closure. Someone who didn't believe in leaving things undone, who was concerned more about others than himself—a trait that characterized so many members of the *Greatest Generation.*

I stared at him for what seemed like several minutes, but I knew from his gaze that he was waiting for me to ask him something else. What an extraordinary man.

Only a day ago, he had revealed to me an astonishing secret about my own ancestry. It was then that I discovered his closest friend and confidant—a fellow gunner and crewman for two tours in the South Pacific, a man whose last moments unfolded inside a burning airplane on a darkened airstrip while Owen watched helplessly—was my own grandfather. Yes, Owen was indeed a man who sought closure.

His face was chalky, his eyes tinged and melon-pink, with tired vessels and swollen lids. The few white hairs left on his head and face were backlit by the nearby window's diffuse light. He was a handsome man, still. Soft-spoken, with reasoning skills I'd never anticipated. Weary eyes seemed to examine mine. They were filled with kindness and comfort. They encouraged me. I needed to ask something, but I fumbled for the words. What would I say to this icon—the last rhino, snow leopard, warrior? Uncertain, my voice crackled. With one last question.

"If you could say just one thing to the world before your time on this earth is over…what would it be?"

Owen stared straight ahead into my eyes and, as I looked into his, they welled up, a silvery tear forming and rolling down his cheek. He gathered one more breath, and whispered, his voice almost holy:

"Remember."

Epilogue

It was with some degree of satisfaction that Dan would recall the scores of reporters hovering around the hospital the day he asked Owen that last question. Owen continued resting for an additional two days, then was spirited away to an assisted living home on the outskirts of Bemidji. The word from the doctor? "I'm afraid he's gone." That sent them scurrying to their cars to dictate their stories, accurate or not.

Sandy felt her dad's privacy was the single best thing the doctors could do for him, and he was comfortable and lucid for over a month at the home. It was a month that included an outpouring of kindness and samaritanism exceeding anything Sandy or her father could have ever imagined. Statements of support and donations on Owen's behalf to veterans' organizations and World War II memorials nationwide persisted beyond Owen's *own* ability to do so. He never regained his strength, but finished his time on earth under his own terms.

And he indeed beat his Japanese counterpart by eight days.

A small family ceremony was held at the old farm, and Dan and Jenna attended it. Half of Owen's ashes were placed at the base of a magnificent spreading box elder tree in the center circle of the driveway. It spanned nearly one hundred and fifty feet from one side to the other, and had been extensively cabled and propped with support posts. Sandy believed her dad planted it around 1950.

The Department of the Navy sent out three honor guard representatives and several spokesmen, and a flag folding ceremony was an emotional cyclone for all in attendance including the commander-in-chief, himself. Twenty-one guns rang out in three waves from seven uniformed marksmen.

The remainder of his ashes were placed in a tin and several members of the family participated in an honor flight in one of the only PBY-5s in the world still airworthy. His ashes were scattered by seaplane over a lake in the Mississippi Headwaters Park.

Dan spent the balance of the year working intermittently with Sandy, developing more of the details of Owen's life from her memory of them. She was an active journal writer and preferred the approach of fashioning a personal memoir to simply writing his life story. She accumulated a collection of his photographs, everything from a grade school picture to the powerful photos found in the film canister. Dan suggested using one of Owen's maps from the chest to begin some of the chapters, and together with his library of books filled with highlighted passages and almost twenty hours of taping, there was no shortage of raw material. For the cover, the two of them settled on a stunning photo of the old tree, the box elder, its branches encircling the book from the right edge of the front cover, across the spine, and finally stretching its fingertips to the opposite edge of the rear. A circle of life. With some additional research on Samantha's part, *Remember* was ready for publication.

It was an immediate New York Times bestseller. A movie appeared to be on the horizon. Owen's dream of providing an endowment for his loved ones would be fulfilled, and like one of his named roses, his heritage was secure. More importantly, *Remember* would also do its part to spark renewed interest in a time long past and instill a better understanding of the sacrifices routinely made by our military men and women and their families. And at Owen's insistence, Dan spent a portion of his time during presentations and book events encouraging his audience to save the history of their own family members who may have served in Korea, Vietnam, or any of the other countless conflicts that asked so much of them. As Dan and Sandy had learned, it is rare that we are given this opportunity twice.

Meanwhile, Taiki's wish to restore his sister's keepsakes to another relative posed some challenges. Dan knew of a group with roots in northern Oregon, about as far away from Tule Lake as is possible within the state. The Obon Society had a history of reuniting flags and other items with families in Japan.

They had a considerable interest in this one due to the unusual set of circumstances and connection to Owen. They were able to determine the family name, *Miyata,* easily enough, but it is a Japanese surname much like *Jones* is in the United States. Other clues appeared among the handsomely brushed strokes encircling the flag's red center. A neighborhood and another name were deciphered, and eventually, a meeting in Japan with Shintu Priests and a Minister of Foreign Affairs was arranged. The granddaughter of a cousin had been located in a community in a suburb of Hiroshima. After ninety-three years, the missing spirit of Taiki's relative was restored to the family in Japan.

In April 2040, Dan received a call from a female author who was writing a memoir for a Women's Army Corps member or WAC. After a few minutes on the phone with her, he found that the title character of her book lived to be one hundred and fourteen and was one of two women who had indeed survived Owen. The other was a resistance fighter in the Netherlands, not truly a member of the military, but someone who often put her own life on the line.

The WAC insisted the author not do anything that would diminish Owen's accomplishments. Despite the life threatening risks many women in the war endured—everything from the female test pilots that shuttled newly built aircraft around the United States to the nurses caring for the injured at Corregidor when it fell—she was in tune with many of the women of her generation, feeling indebted to and appreciative of all that these men had sacrificed. She "soldiered on" as the expression goes and stepped up for men in combat, then and now. Perhaps she was too modest, as she was a woman who gave navigational training to male crewmen at a flight school in the states, and also spent time rigging parachutes—two jobs that should be considered essential to the conduct of a world war. Both women had passed away by the time *Remember* was published. Yet it was hard for Dan not to wonder, *Was there anyone else still out there?*

It appeared that Owen would go down in history as the last U.S. combat soldier, and perhaps the last individual worldwide that had formally served in an armed forces unit. Whether another participant would surface, man or woman, remained to be seen. Dan, for one, was satisfied that the legacy of the man he had come to know had served the *Greatest Generation* well—as its last survivor.

Enjoy the book?

Please let other readers know and help share the book's message of saving our war veterans' legacies. A simple sentence or two as a customer review on Amazon is hugely helpful.

If you'd like to know more about the Black Cats, please try **Sketches of a Black Cat**, the true story of the author's father, a two-tour veteran in VP-54 and VPB-54. Details and contact information are available at:

sketchesofablackcat.com

Made in United States
Troutdale, OR
03/19/2024